THE TRIP

ALSO BY AUDREY J. COLE

Stand-Alones

Missing in Flight

The One

Only One Lie

The Pilot's Daughter

The Final Hunt Series

The First Hunt

The Final Hunt

The Last Hunt

Emerald City Thrillers

The Recipient

Inspired by Murder

The Summer Nanny: A Novella

Viable Hostage

Fatal Deception

THE TRIP

AUDREY J. COLE

Published by Thomas & Mercer, Seattle
www.apub.com

EU product safety contact:
Amazon Media EU S. à r.l.
38, avenue John F. Kennedy, L-1855 Luxembourg
amazonpublishing-gpsr@amazon.com

ISBN-13: 9781662520730 (paperback)
ISBN-13: 9781662520723 (digital)

Cover design by Ploy Siripant
Cover image: © Wirestock / Getty; © A-Star / Shutterstock

Printed in the United States of America

THE TRIP

PROLOGUE

Memorial Day Weekend, 2005

"This is it!" Beth broke the foreboding silence, quickening her pace on the trail at the front of the group.

The four of us had hiked without a word for the last several hours, the weight of leaving Courtney behind hanging over us like a death cloud, leaving no room for conversation.

Beth pointed ahead. "I remember that log with the mushrooms on it being on the path at the start of our hike."

"That's what you said yesterday," Emma said, her curly blond ponytail swaying from the breeze as she took an athletic stride over the log a few feet in front of me. Despite her knee injury, I was having trouble keeping up with her.

Beth's steps shifted from a walk to a near run.

"What if you're wrong?" Emma called after her.

We all knew the answer, even though none of us spoke it. *Then we'll stay lost out here. Without food. And no way to call for help.*

My stomach growled. It had been twenty-four hours since I finished my last protein bar. I was so hungry it hurt. That morning, I'd woken to the sound of Emma puking beside my tent after she ate what she thought were salmonberries but were apparently something else. This morning, Emma had hiked the first few miles hunched over, stopping to throw up two more times, leaving the rest of us too scared to try any of the berries we saw along the path. But if we were stuck out here much longer, we were going to have to risk it until we figured out which ones were edible.

I spotted a squirrel scampering up a moss-covered tree and envisioned myself throwing a rock at its head before it disappeared around the other side of the trunk. I then imagined roasting its tiny body over a fire and immediately pushed the thought away, surprising myself as much by my urge to kill as my desire to eat meat when I had prided myself on being a vegetarian for the last two years.

The only plus side to my hunger pangs was the distraction they provided from the painful blister on my heel that had burst a few miles back.

I stepped over the log Beth had sped past but had no memory of seeing it at the start of our trip. However, it felt like a lifetime ago with everything that had happened since then, so I kept the thought to myself.

I thought of Courtney, the only one of us not making it out of the woods. How could I be so selfish, worrying about my next meal? I imagined Courtney's body, lying dead on the damp forest floor, her cold, decaying carcass ravaged by wolves before being picked apart by scavengers. Vomit rose to the back of my throat.

I started at a grunt behind me. I spun around, heart racing as I envisioned the massive cougar I'd encountered yesterday when all I'd had to defend myself was the engraved pocketknife Courtney had given me at the start of the trip—thankfully, the wild beast moved on to something else.

I spotted Gigi on her hands and knees on the dirt path, her long dirty-blond bangs half covering the painful grimace on her face. "I can't go any farther! What the hell were we thinking? We're going to be lost out here forever." She broke into a sob as she lowered her head toward the path. "My blisters are killing me."

For as long as I'd known her, Gigi had never done well with pain. Looking at her, I was filled with frustration. My heels were raw, too, but her growing panic wasn't doing anything to help us.

"Here, let me help you." Begrudgingly, I dropped beside Gigi and draped her lanky arm over my shoulder before pulling her to her feet.

"Need more help?" Emma asked.

I shook my head, practically dragging Gigi along the path as she winced in pain with each step.

"Just a little farther," I told her, hoping it was the truth.

"It better be," Emma said. "If Beth led us the wrong way *again*, I'm going to lose my shit."

"I see the van!" Beth cried.

"Thank God," Gigi muttered.

I let go of Gigi and hurried after Emma, slowing when I emerged from the tree-lined path onto the gravel parking lot. Straight ahead was Beth's minivan, parked in the same spot we'd left it and still the only car in the remote trailhead parking area. My lungs deflated with relief. I hunched forward, keeping my eyes fixed on the white vehicle while resting my palms on my knees.

I straightened, my relief muddled with guilt when it struck me that we would be driving out of here with one less person.

Emma turned to me as Gigi hobbled out of the woods. "Check your signal."

I slid my backpack strap off my aching shoulder, unzipped the front pocket, and turned on my phone as we continued toward the van. It seemed like an eternity as I waited for the screen to light up.

"No service," I said, lifting my phone in the air.

"Let's go." Beth opened the driver's door. "We'll drive until we get one."

I climbed into the passenger seat as Emma and Gigi piled into the back.

"What about yours?" I asked, motioning to Beth's Nokia flip phone in the center console as she sped down the narrow gravel road.

Beth pushed her glasses up the bridge of her nose before opening the phone. A bead of sweat dripped down the side of her round cheek beneath the bright-red gash on her temple. The screen remained black as she held down the button on the side. "It's dead."

Of course it is, I thought. None of us were prepared for what had happened on this trip. Gigi's phone had gone into the river yesterday when Courtney had fallen in, along with both their backpacks containing most of our food. By then, Emma had completely drained her phone battery by leaving it on to continuously search for a signal when we were out of cell-service range. None of us had brought a charger, knowing we wouldn't have any reception for most of our three-day trip.

I kept my phone lifted toward the windshield, hoping it would help find a signal while Beth accelerated down the windy path. As she plowed over a pothole, the top of my head hit the ceiling, but my eyes stayed glued to the screen as the van's tires created a cloud of dust out my side window.

"Stop!" I yelled.

Gigi was thrown forward when Beth laid on the brakes. Gigi's thin arms stretched beside me, her palms pressing against the dash as we came to a stop, and I dialed 911.

"911 operator, what's your emergency?" a staticky voice asked.

"My friend," I spurted. "She's . . . missing. We were camping—rafting—on the Sol Duc River, and she . . . um . . ." I glanced at Beth, who stared back at me. "Fell from the raft." The splash when Courtney hit the water filled my mind. "That was yesterday. And we can't find her. We got lost on our way back and—"

"Miss, I need you to slow down. Can I have your name? And tell me where you are."

"Palmer. Palmer Montague. I already did—we were on the Sol Duc River. She's gone. We need help *now*!"

"Ma'am, just stay calm. I need you to be more specific. *Where* on the Sol Duc River? Can you give me another landmark near you, like a trailhead?"

I turned to Beth, kicking myself for not paying better attention when we got here. Instead of parking at the Sol Duc Trailhead, we'd taken a windy backroad to a secluded trailhead Courtney had heard about from her brother. *What the hell were we all thinking, gallivanting into the woods like that without at least taking note of where we were?* "What was the trailhead called?"

"I don't know." Beth shrugged, her eyes wide.

I twisted toward the others in the back seat. Emma shook her head while Gigi cast her a blank look as if trying to recall the name.

"I can't remember." Gigi bit her lip. "I thought Beth wrote it down."

Beth shook her head and threw the van into reverse. "I wanted to, but you and Emma were making fun of me for taking too many safety precautions."

I pressed my hand against my forehead, willing myself to remember as the van rolled backward. It had been Courtney's plan to come here, but how had none of us paid better attention to our location?

"Wait!" I reached across Beth's lap. "Stop or we'll lose my signal."

The emergency operator's voice returned. "Miss? I need you to tell me where you are. Can you find the name of the trailhead?"

"Lost Creek Trail!" Gigi yelled, swiping a long strand of blond hair from her face. "No wait, I remember—Grave Creek Trail!"

"Grave Creek Trail," I said into the phone.

"Okay, that's good. And your friend, when did you last see her?"

"Yesterday, around noon. She fell into the water when we were rafting the Sol Duc River. It was about ten miles northeast of where we are now." I shifted in my seat, conscious of the pocketknife that was no longer in my shorts pocket.

"And that was the last time you saw her?"

She's dead, I wanted to scream. Instead, I swallowed hard, three pairs of eyes on me as raindrops began to beat against the windshield.

"Yes," I lied.

Chapter One

Present

"Have fun, but don't stay up too late." I bend over and pull both of my girls into a tight hug.

"We won't!" Abagail and Emily chime in unison.

"I love you." After planting a kiss on each of their heads, I let go.

"Love you too," Emily calls as they run from our front porch and hurry across the street.

A heaviness fills my chest at the thought of what I have to tell them as I watch them bound up our neighbor's drive without a care in the world.

When my neighbor Morgan opens her front door and lets the girls inside, I wave.

"Thank you!" I call.

"No problem." She returns my wave.

I wait until she closes her door to go back inside. As the door clicks shut, I sink against the entryway wall and check to see if Matt replied to my last text. *Of course he hasn't,* I think after unlocking my screen. I thrust the phone into my jeans pocket, chiding myself for getting my hopes up. *The girls and I are the last thing on his mind right now.*

I move into my living room and contemplate opening a bottle of wine as I sag onto the couch. A knock sounds on the door. One of the girls must've forgotten something.

The knock sounds again after I stand. When I open the front door, Beth envelops me in a hug. Her heels make us nearly the same height.

"You okay?" she asks, pulling away.

My throat constricts as the events from the last seventy-two hours ricochet through my mind. Thank God Beth is here.

"Sorry—stupid question." The top half of Beth's dark hair is pinned back, revealing the razor-thin scar on her right temple. "Of course you're not."

She shuts the door behind her, then lifts a red wine bottle by the neck. "When I saw your text, I thought we might need this."

As she moves past me, I see my makeup smeared on the shoulder of her trench coat. When we get to the living room that looks out to a street lined with homes that appear almost exactly like mine, only different colors, she gestures to the couch.

"You sit," she says. "I'll get the glasses."

Her heels clack against the hardwood as I slump onto the suede sofa. When Beth returns holding two generously poured glasses of wine, I'm staring at the professionally taken family photograph on the wall, knowing I'll need to take it down and replace it with one of just me and the girls.

"Thanks," I say, tearing my eyes from the five-year-old photo taken when I was ten pounds lighter and Matt and I were still in love. Or at least I thought so. The girls were only four, standing between us wearing matching white dresses.

Bitterness rises to the back of my throat when I take a sip of wine, thinking how Matt left without telling them, leaving me to do the explaining.

Beth sinks into the cushions beside me. "Where are the twins?"

"Having a sleepover at the neighbor's. I haven't told them yet."

Beth extends her arm over the back of the couch, tucking her ankle under her knee as she turns to face me. "So, he *moved in* with her?"

I nod. "He's going to. Matt got an apartment in Renton, and she's moving from Colorado so they can live together."

Beth wrinkles her nose. "Wow. And she's what? Twenty-six?"

I drop my gaze to my glass, annoyed that Beth is making me repeat the detail she already knows. "Twenty-three."

"Yikes." Beth winces, bringing her glass to her lips. "And this is the same woman Matt posted a photo with at his conference in Denver? The one you were worried he might've slept with?"

She's hardly a woman, I think. *She's barely an adult.* "Yep."

"I thought you asked him about her, and he admitted they'd had a few drinks at the bar. But that he'd apologized and said it was nothing," Beth says after taking a drink.

"Yeah, that's what he said." I run my finger around the rim of my glass, remembering that sickening moment when I found out. A moment I know I'll never forget. "I found an Instagram DM from her on Matt's phone about a month ago—along with a topless selfie—and confronted him about it. Once I got over the shock, I was livid." I point to the doorway at the start of the hall. "I made him sleep in the guest room ever since. He insisted he was telling the truth that they'd only had drinks together in Denver but that she'd reached out to him online after he got home." Matt also told me that they shared a connection he hasn't felt with me in years, but it hurts too much to say it. "He promised to stop messaging her." I frown, meeting Beth's eyes. A warm flush of shame rises to my cheeks for being so stupid to think he was telling the truth. "But apparently, he didn't."

"You didn't even tell me," Beth says.

"I know. I wanted so badly to believe him and forget about it. Then last week Matt came home late, and we got in a huge fight. I accused him of being with her, but he denied it and told me she lives in Colorado." I glance at the guest room. "Last night he never came home at all. Then, this morning I noticed he'd taken half his clothes out of our closet, and I called his office. He told me he was done—over the phone—and that he'd gotten an apartment, saying that *Sydney* is moving from Colorado to live with him." Saying her name makes my stomach curl. "And . . ." I frown and pick a piece of lint off my black sweatpants. "He said that he'll be back next week to get the rest of his things." I exhale, resting the stem of my glass on my knee. "Guess I should've trusted my gut."

"I'm so sorry, Palmer."

My gaze locks with Beth's. The somber look in her eyes reminds me of how she looked at me that day on our rafting trip twenty years ago, when we rejoined the others without Courtney. I force the memory from my mind. "Let's talk about something else. I need to stop obsessing about it." For the first time, I envy Beth's having never gotten married. Matt's leaving is so painful, it feels like I'm being ripped in two. Thinking about how I'm going to tell the girls makes me queasy. "How was your first graduation as university president?"

Beth slips off her heels and rests her bare feet against the edge of the coffee table, the shine of her pink-polished toes reflecting the light from the ceiling fan.

"Oof. Well, the graduation itself was good, but so far managing college *professors* is a lot more work than managing college students. Now that the spring semester is finished, I spent all day schmoozing with a group of wealthy alumni at a fundraiser downtown." Beth presses her glasses up the bridge of her nose. "Feels like I spent the day dancing for tips."

A half smile reaches my lips as I envision Beth, always the bookworm and rule follower, on a stripper pole.

Beth frowns, her gaze moving to our family portrait. "I never liked Matt, you know."

I twist in my seat. "What? Yes, you did. You're just saying that to make me feel better." Beth had made quips about Matt over the years, but I never thought she'd meant anything by them. She's always been a girl's girl. And protective of me.

Beth shakes her head. "I've known he was an asshole for years. Remember that time we went on a double date when I was seeing that English professor?"

I rack my brain. "At the Italian restaurant?"

"Yes. You and I went to the bathroom, and I came back to the table first as the waitress brought the check. Matt was totally ogling her, not realizing I was standing right behind him, then made this crude comment to my date about her ass. How if he weren't a married man, he'd get a piece of that."

I recoil. "No. *Matt?*"

Beth presses her lips together and nods slowly. "Yes. *Matt.*"

"You never told me."

Beth lays a hand on my knee. "I should have, and I'm sorry. I knew he'd deny it, and I didn't want to cause problems between you two. Or you and me, for that matter. Look, I know his leaving is a shock, and it's hard right now, but I honestly think you'll be better off without him."

I take a large gulp of wine, hoping she's right.

"You should come," Beth says. "On the sailing trip," she adds when I don't respond.

She didn't need to clarify. I knew what she meant.

"I don't know . . ." I'd been quick to say no when Gigi invited me last month to sail from Seattle to San Diego. Gigi played up the trip like it was a tribute to Courtney, to memorialize her on the weekend that will mark twenty years since we came home without her. But all Gigi cares about is growing her already huge TikTok following, and her sponsor who's paying top dollar for the trip. Gigi hasn't called me in years, so I was surprised when she called last month with the invite.

Beth is the only one out of the group that I've stayed in close touch with. The thought of seeing the others, and the memories it would dredge up, was more than I could stomach. So, I used my parental responsibilities and work as an excuse not to go. I swallow over the lump that forms in my throat at the thought of my job at the hospital, wondering how I'll ever go back.

I turn to Beth. "I'm surprised *you're* going. Plus, you hate boats. And you know Gigi only wants us to go to fuel her publicity of the trip. She knows the four of us all back together again will get a lot of coverage. How'd you even get the time off?"

"The board insisted I go."

I nearly choke on my wine. I sit forward, clearing my throat. "*What?* Why?"

"Remember that article in the *Times* that came out last year right after the university announced me as their new president?"

I nod, lifting the glass to my lips. It highlighted the vast number of people who went missing in the Pacific Northwest's national parks, particularly in Olympic National Park, where Courtney vanished. The article raised several conspiracy theories that could explain a portion of the disappearances, but when it came to Courtney's, the *Times* article cited foul play. It named Beth as one of "the four" who returned without Courtney on that now infamous trip. The piece made sure to cast the four of us in a bad light, as countless articles had done before, highlighting the suspicion we all fell under for coming home without Courtney and how we were scrutinized for not looking harder for our volleyball captain, who was never found—especially after Courtney's reputation came to light.

The article failed to mention the heavy rainstorm that pummeled the area right after I called 911 and how it hindered initial rescue efforts by limiting visibility not only for the search and rescue helicopters but for those on foot. The storm was also to blame for washing away any evidence of Courtney's footsteps in the remote forest.

Instead, the reporter closed the part about Courtney with a quote from a retired detective: "If you want to murder someone and get away with it, do it in Olympic National Park."

It doesn't matter how many years go by, we'll always be marred by that horrible trip.

I take another large drink, recalling the *Sequim Gazette*'s front-page headline splayed across my parents' kitchen table after we returned—without Courtney—from our rafting trip. ACCIDENT OR MEAN GIRLS MURDER PLOT?

News vans were parked outside my home for weeks afterward. At first, I'd been naive enough to speak to them—until that mistake brought a torrent of allegations, publicly marring my reputation so badly I was afraid to leave the house for months. Last year, when Courtney's parents died tragically in a plane accident, the news coverage started up all over again.

Beth sets her half-full stemmed glass onto the coffee table with a clink. "After the *Times* article ran, Julie Stevens—who cofounded Auspex with Courtney's father—publicly withdrew her financial support to the university. Apparently, she was one of their most generous alumni supporters." Beth flicks her hand through the air. "Anyway, one of the board members saw Gigi's TikTok bragging about her luxury sailing trip to honor Courtney twenty years after her disappearance. They called an emergency meeting and insisted I go, afraid the university would lose more donors if I didn't." Beth purses her lips. "You can't leave me alone on a boat with Emma and Gigi. Two weeks trapped with those divas? I'll never survive. Besides, it would be good for you to get away."

I'm not sure I can handle seeing them again. I take a long sip of my wine and set the glass on the coffee table beside Beth's bare feet. I've spent the last twenty years trying to block out that horrible weekend and everything that happened after we came back without Courtney. What the media, Courtney's parents, and the police accused us of. I rub a hand over my face and reach for my wineglass. It hits me again that Courtney's parents died without knowing what happened to her, without really being able to say goodbye.

Beth twists on the couch to face me. "Look, I know Courtney was no saint, but she's not here. I'm sure none of us like to think about what happened, but I think it might be . . . nice that we can at least remember her by all getting together again. Courtney would've wanted that."

I stare out the window at the swing set in my side yard that my girls no longer use. An image of Courtney at seventeen flashes in my mind. Her flaming red hair, big green eyes, and magnetic smile. She was so beautiful, so popular, and could make you feel on top of the world with her vivacious laugh. She was also the cruelest human being I'd ever met.

"I don't know . . ."

"Didn't you say your sister's flying up from LA tomorrow? She can watch the girls. And you're only part time, can't you trade your next few shifts? Or call in sick. Tell them you have a family emergency, which you do."

I shoot Beth a sideways glance, surprised at her suggestion. She's always been a rule follower. Sometimes annoyingly so.

"I'm actually on leave at the moment."

"*What?* Since when?"

My chest tightens as it strikes me that now that Matt has left, I'll have to either start looking for a new job or go back to my current one. But after what happened, how will I even go back to nursing?

"Since I found the messages from Sydney on Matt's phone." It was also right after Gigi called about the trip. Even now, I'm not sure which event rattled me more. "I made a mistake at the hospital, a medication error. It could've been fatal if the night shift nurse hadn't caught it." I rest my palm on the top of my head, unable to meet Beth's eyes as shame rises to the back of my throat. "I've never messed up like that before." I close my eyes, painfully recalling the moment when I arrived for my next shift and walked past my patient's empty room. When I asked if he'd been discharged early, I learned that I'd hung the wrong IV fluid, which lowered his sodium to a critically low level. He'd had a seizure and been moved to ICU—because of me.

I haven't been that shaken since the day I was grilled by that detective about what happened to Courtney.

"I called out sick for my next two shifts, then was called in for a meeting with my manager. I told her about Matt's affair, and she suggested I go on leave while I sorted out my personal life—and the hospital investigated my near-fatal error. After they determined it was my fault, I met with my manager again to review my mistake, and she cleared me to work again.

"Last night was supposed to be my first shift back, but when Matt never came home, I had no one to watch the girls, so I called in sick. Today I asked my manager to extend my leave, even though my sister agreed to come stay for a few weeks." I blink away the tears that blur my vision. "I'm terrified of making another mistake. I feel like I can't trust myself." An image of Courtney getting dragged down the Sol Duc River's fast current floods my mind.

I don't tell Beth that ever since Gigi's phone call, my thoughts have been consumed with Courtney. Deep down, I know it wasn't Matt's affair that caused me to screw up at work.

Beth squeezes my hand. "You're human. We all make mistakes sometimes. That doesn't make you a bad nurse."

"I could've *killed* a patient, Beth."

"But you didn't."

I skirt my gaze away from Beth to the family photo on the wall, which jabs at my heart every time I look at it. At the sight of the twins' sweet smiling faces, I inwardly curse Matt. *How could he do this to me? To our girls?*

Beth reaches out to take my hand. "Maybe this trip is what you need to put the past behind you. Your sister can stay with the girls. You *need* this."

I swallow the large lump that forms in my throat at my next thought. *How the hell am I going to provide for them if I'm no longer capable of being a nurse?*

She's right. I need to get away. Clear my head and get myself together. Not just for me, but for the girls.

"All right, fine. I'll go."

Chapter Two

Present

Three days later, my Uber brakes to a stop at the entrance to Elliott Bay Marina.

Biting my lip, I glance at the gleaming Puget Sound beyond the village of yachts and sailboats moored at the marina. I pull out my phone and text my sister, grasping for an excuse not to go.

> Are you sure you'll be okay with the girls? Two weeks is a long time.

When I don't get out, the driver glances over his shoulder. "We're here."

My phone chimes. I look down at Kate's reply. I'm sure! You need this. Have a great trip. We will be FINE. Xo

I exhale, watching a family make their way down the pier, the father with his kindergarten-aged daughter on his shoulders. The girls think Matt is on a business trip. He agreed we should tell them the bad news together when I get back. Dread fills my stomach like a bag of cement as I imagine their shattered faces when we tell them he's moving out.

Aside from Kate and Beth, I haven't told anyone about Matt's leaving me, not even my mom. I'm dreading telling her nearly as much as the girls. She's always loved Matt; thought he could do no wrong.

Will she blame me for his cheating? Wonder what I did to make my "perfect" husband stray?

"This is your stop," the driver says louder than before, as if I didn't hear him the first time.

"Thanks," I mutter, grabbing my duffel bag as I slide out of the back seat.

I saunter toward the water, scanning the rows of boats while trying to remember where Gigi's assistant said the sailboat would be docked.

I sling my duffel bag over my shoulder. After reading the email from Gigi's assistant last night, I'd swapped my suitcase for the bag. Yesterday morning Beth, Emma, and I were copied on the formal email specifying what to bring and telling us to pack light and make sure we bring soft luggage that could be easily tucked away in the boat's limited storage. The idea of the four of us, plus the two crew, stuffed into a boat too small for regular bags is about to give me a panic attack. I shake my head, thinking about how Gigi herself couldn't be bothered to give us the trip details and how little she's changed from high school.

I shade my eyes with my hand from the sun reflecting off the water and take a left after stepping onto the dock, then head past a line of large yachts toward a row of sailboats. A seagull squawks overhead. When I checked the weather forecast last night on my phone, it showed that Seattle will be getting rain later in the week. But today the sky is clear, and the Sound is smooth as glass. Hopefully, we'll avoid the rain as we sail south on the Pacific. With nearly two dozen rows of boats, the marina is bigger than I expected. Now, I wish I'd paid better attention to where Gigi's assistant said the boat would be.

I scan the dock for a sign of Emma, dreading what it will be like to see her again after all these years. The four of us stay in loose contact through a group text thread, which stays silent most of the time aside from the occasional happy birthday or funny meme. The last time we were all together was ten years ago when Beth graduated with her doctoral degree from Elliott Bay University. It was before Emma's home-renovation career took off and when Gigi was still an aspiring lifestyle and travel vlogger. There had been so much going on at graduation that the four of us never had a quiet moment to outwardly reflect on Courtney not being there. But I could feel it, and I'm sure the others did too.

I start down a row filled with more sailboats than power cruisers. Three slips down, I stop in my tracks at a young woman untying a sailboat from the dock. Her long red hair cascades down to the middle of her back just like Courtney's did. A middle-aged woman appears on the vessel's deck. Her short hair is the same shade of red, only mixed with some gray.

"Do you want your hat, Mel?"

"No, thanks," the younger woman calls, jumping onto the boat.

I let out the breath I'd been holding. It's been years since I thought I'd seen Courtney. After she disappeared, I used to see her everywhere: at the store, on the beach, driving a car. But it was never her.

I study the size of the vessel as they pull away from the dock. A tremor runs through my veins as I imagine taking a boat of that size all the way to San Diego. What was I thinking, letting Beth talk me into this? What if I never come back? A shudder runs down my spine as I envision my twin girls being raised by Matt and his twenty-three-year-old girlfriend.

I should go home.

I start to turn around when I hear a giggle—more like a *cackle*—from the next row over and recognize it immediately. Gigi.

I am so *not ready for this.*

Gigi is propped up on the sailboat's railing, scantily clad in a checkered bikini even though it's barely over sixty degrees. I glance at my cutoff jeans and faded T-shirt, imagining how I'll look in the modest one-piece I packed. I'd picked black, hoping it would have a slimming effect on the ten pounds I'd put on over the last few years. *There's no way I'm getting a photo next to Gigi in my swimsuit,* I think as I continue down the floating walkway.

I watch Gigi's long blond waves lift into the air from the wind coming off the water while a younger woman takes her photo from the deck. I head toward them, but Gigi doesn't seem to notice me as I move up the dock and turn down the adjacent row.

When I get closer, I'm relieved to see the sailboat is much bigger than I expected. The white vessel with navy blue trim is twice as long as the one I was just looking at. *Thank God.* Its polished, brand-new exterior gleams in the sun. Above one of the four diamond-shaped windows that adorn the hull's side, *Nautical Nirvana* is painted in blue cursive. I can see why the San Diego yacht-rental company is paying Gigi top dollar to document the boat's maiden voyage from Seattle. Even at first glance, it's stunning.

I scan the boat deck but don't see any of the other women despite yesterday's email stressing the importance of being on time. On the rear deck, a man with salt-and-pepper hair stands behind one of the two large steering wheels, his blue polo tucked neatly into his khaki shorts. Not seeming to notice me, he taps the screen of an instrument pod mounted above the wheel. According to Gigi's assistant, the boat came equipped with a captain and first officer who doubles as a chef.

Gigi tucks a strand of long hair behind her ear. "Wait!" she yells at the woman taking her photo. "Take that one again." She cocks her head. "My hair was in my eyes."

The young woman holding the phone, whom I assume must be Gigi's assistant, points in my direction. "There's someone behind you."

Gigi turns. "Oh. Hi, Palmer. Come on board, but do you mind staying on that end of the boat for a minute? I'm just having my assistant get some content before we depart."

"No problem," I say, stunned by how little Gigi has changed.

Gigi wastes no time rattling off more instructions to her assistant as I search the side of the vessel for somewhere to climb on.

"As soon as Palmer's out of the way, get a video with the other boats behind me. Start on my left side and then pan to the right."

A muscular man with a full head of wavy brown hair and a short-trimmed beard emerges from the boat's belowdeck interior, wearing the same shirt and shorts as the older man behind the wheel, only he looks about twenty years younger. Seeing me, he strides to the middle edge of the boat where there's a gap in the outer railing.

"You can come aboard right here." He gestures to the plastic steps on the dock. "I'll take your bag while you climb on."

I meet his gaze as he extends his hand toward me. He's close to my age, maybe a little older—probably early to mid-forties.

I slide my duffel bag off my shoulder and allow him to take it before I climb the steps. "Thanks."

His biceps bulge out of the fitted polo that slides up his arm as he takes the bag from me, revealing part of a tattoo. I don't have to see the full letters to recognize the Marine Corps acronym: *USMC*. I've cared for several patients with a similar marking.

"Grab this stanchion." He points to a vertical silver pole attached to the deck. "You can use it to pull yourself up."

I grab onto it and accept his hand with my other, then step through the opening in the cable railing on the side.

Once I get both feet on board, he lets go. "I'm Adam, the first officer slash chef." He offers a handshake, and his grip is firm and warm.

A dimple appears on his cheek when he grins, exposing perfectly straight white teeth as I return his handshake. Something about him strikes me as familiar. I study him for a moment before my gaze falls to his other hand, bare of a wedding ring, and I'm suddenly conscious of my own. A jab of pain stabs at my heart.

"Welcome aboard," he says.

"Thank you," I say, distracted, wondering if Gigi specifically requested to have such an attractive first officer for her "content."

"Hey, Adam?" Gigi's voice is coated with sweetness as she calls from the other end of the boat. "Would you mind getting a quick photo with me before my assistant leaves?"

"Cabins are below deck through the companionway," Adam says, gesturing toward the open doorway from where he'd emerged. "Please help yourself to champagne in the galley when you get below." He hands me my bag and flashes me a final smile before spinning around toward Gigi. "Sure."

Before going below deck, I glance up at the mast, which is taller than the flagpole at my twins' school. About two-thirds of the way up, a rectangular white plate is affixed to it.

"Palmer!" Beth appears in the doorway from below deck.

I've never been happier to see her. Her shoulder-length dark hair is in a ponytail, and I'm glad to see she's dressed as casual as me, in a long-sleeved shirt and shorts. I close the distance between us, glancing at the captain behind the wheel who barely looks up from the navigation screen.

"We're sharing a stateroom," Beth says, holding a half-drunk champagne flute. "Come check it out."

The older man looks up from his screen and nods at me before I follow Beth down the narrow half flight of stairs. "Welcome aboard," he calls. "I'm Captain Nojan."

"I'm Palmer. Nice to meet you."

He looks to be around sixty, and I hope that means he's been sailing for decades. Matt and I went on an Alaska cruise for our fifth anniversary, and even that made me nervous. But that had to have been much safer than what we're about to do. As I descend the wooden steps, I think about the rain I saw on the forecast, suddenly imagining what it will be like to be stuck in the cabin with all of them, with no escape to the decks. I remind myself that it's nearly June, which means we should have calm seas. I'm sure we wouldn't be going if there were any forecasted storms, but I make a mental note to ask the captain before we embark.

"Wow," I say when I reach the bottom of the steps.

Beth turns. "I know, right? The boat looks like it's brand new."

The interior isn't huge, but it's bigger than it looks from the outside, and it's pristine. The gleaming countertops and light wood-paneled walls give it a modern yet warm feel. The hatches above our heads and rectangular windows at eye level fill the space with natural light.

To my left is a kitchen fitted with a microwave, stove, dishwasher, and fridge. A bottle of champagne rests in a bucket of ice on the speckled countertop beside prefilled plastic flutes and a fruit tray. Beside the tray, napkins are folded like origami, but I can't tell what they're supposed to be. I grab a glass and follow Beth through the living area where a large white-leather booth wraps around a wood table mounted to the floor. Across from it is a matching couch.

"I was just about to change into my thong bikini," Beth says. "After I change, maybe you can take some shots of me for my Snapchat." Beth tosses a smile over her shoulder as I laugh.

"Gigi hasn't changed since high school, has she?"

Beth shakes her head. "Not an ounce."

"I'm surprised you even know what Snapchat is."

"I don't really." Beth points to one of the two doors ahead. "We're in here."

I follow her inside, seeing now why Gigi's assistant told us to pack light. The room is just large enough for the double bed, which butts against the wall on either side, narrowing to fit within the curve of the bow. There's less than three feet from the head of the bed to the door—enough room for a small, padded bench on one side and a single cabinet on the other.

"Cozy, huh?" Beth asks as I set my duffel bag next to hers on the bench.

My gaze lands on a framed photograph hanging on the wall—my twin girls at an Oregon beach. I took it last summer, but I'd never sent it to Gigi.

"Did you bring that?"

Beth follows my gaze. "Oh, no. Gigi asked me to send her one of your girls for a surprise. I knew that was one of your favorites. The photo was already up when I got here."

My breath catches at Gigi's sweet gesture as I take in my girls' beaming smiles. "That was so . . ."

"Thoughtful? I know." Beth holds up a hardcover book, its cover streaked with crimson splatters that mimic dripping blood. Artfully fake, but also disturbingly lifelike. "Gigi got this signed edition for me even though it doesn't release until next month."

Seeing the author's name, I recognize her as one Beth loves.

"Gigi contacted the author and promised to share the book on social media if she sent her a prerelease copy." Beth opens the book to the title page. "And Gigi had her sign it to me."

"That's so cool," I say. Maybe Gigi *has* grown up since high school. I peer through the open doorway, my pulse quickening. "Is Emma here yet?"

"Nope. I was the first one here."

I plop onto the edge of the bed and feel some tension release from my shoulders, thankful to have a moment alone with Beth before I face the others. "Is Gigi's husband here?"

Beth shakes her head. "Haven't seen him. I'm surprised he didn't come to see her off. I expected him to be taking the photos of her send-off, not her assistant."

"Me too." I've seen Gigi's doting European hotel-heir husband in several of her posts online, where they appear joined at the hip. After meeting in Milan, Gigi and Alex were married in Venice two years ago, an exclusive event to which none of us were invited. According to one of her posts, Alex took most of her photos and did all the behind-the-scenes work for her vlog. But Gigi's following has grown so big, she must've had to hire more help.

"Can you do me a favor?" I ask. "Don't say anything to the others yet about Matt leaving me."

"Of course not." Beth crosses her arms, glancing up as the sound of Gigi's laugh carries through the windowed hatch above the bed. She meets my gaze. "Look, I know you don't want to go on this trip. I didn't, either, but now that I'm here, I really think it will be good for all of us to remember Courtney—together. And to let go."

A look passes between us, an unspoken understanding of what she's referring to.

Beth's expression darkens. "We can't change the past. We were kids. It's not like you meant to—"

"Knock, knock!"

Gigi appears behind Beth in the doorway. I'm surprised I didn't hear her come down. She's tied a see-through mesh cover-up over her bikini bottom. She slides past Beth and holds her arms out to me.

"You disappeared so fast I didn't get to give you a hug."

I stand as she squeezes me between her long skinny arms.

I bulge my eyes out, pulling a face at Beth, who stifles a laugh. Gigi releases me and takes a step back, then leans her thin frame against the cabinet. I sense curiosity in Gigi's gaze, along with a dash of judgment, as she takes in my appearance.

I point to the framed photo of my twins. "Thank you for putting up the picture of my girls. That was a nice surprise."

Gigi smiles. "You're welcome. I wanted you to feel at home." She puts her hands on her hips. "Emma is late, as usual. Even though I made sure to have my assistant tell her to be on time." She rolls her eyes. "Once she gets here, we'll set sail." She presses her palms together in front of her chest. "I'm so glad we can all get together to honor Courtney. She would've wanted this. I'm just sad she can't be here with us. But she'll be here in spirit. Sometimes, I still can't believe she's gone, after all this time. We never got that closure, because, well . . ."

Gigi trails off, and I can see we're all thinking the same thing. *Because we never found her body.*

"Anyway," Gigi adds. "I miss her every day."

No, you don't, I think. She's acting like Courtney was a saint. While we all felt indebted to Courtney in some way, like the time she paid for Gigi's prom dress when she couldn't afford it, we were also no strangers to Courtney's cruelty. I study Gigi batting her eyes as if she were blinking back tears, and I wonder if her obsession to be constantly seen by the world in her best light stems from what Courtney did to her in our senior year.

Gigi twists to check her teeth in the small mounted mirror, and it hits me that her thirst to be seen as perfect is probably more due to us being labeled as murderers after returning from the rafting trip.

"I guess sisterly bonds never really dissolve," Gigi says.

When I catch Gigi's insipid face in her reflection, I see her as she was that day twenty years ago when her face was twisted in anger at Courtney, the rapids roaring behind them as they pushed off from the rocky riverbank. Rage can do funny things to people, make them do things on impulse that they can't take back. Of course, I knew that better than anyone.

Chapter Three

September 2004

"A *D minus*? Are you serious?" Courtney lifted her Spanish test off her desk as Mrs. Herrera continued passing them out to the rest of the class.

Courtney turned to me, her lip-glossed mouth half open in shock. "But we studied."

Beth twisted in her seat in front of mine and pointed to me. "No, *we* studied." She looked back at Courtney. "You were texting all night, remember? Then you left early to go to that party on Bell Hill."

"Oh yeah." Courtney sank back in her seat, letting her test fall onto her desk. "But still, I sat there with you guys for like an hour." Her eyes widened. "I won't be able to keep playing volleyball this fall if I don't raise my grade."

Beth shrugged. "Do the extra credit."

"The short story?" Courtney looked at Beth as if she'd just asked her to kiss Kid Rock. She lifted her test in the air. "How could I do that? I don't even know what half these words mean."

Eyeing the red markings all over her test, I raised my brows.

Courtney lifted her gaze to mine. "Okay, more than half. Practically none of them." Her attention darted to Beth. "But you can." She lowered her voice when Mrs. Herrera moved to the front of the class and turned her back to write on the whiteboard. "Write it for me. *Please.*"

Beth shook her head. "I'm working this weekend."

"So?" Courtney leaned forward. "You'll still have time. I have like three parties that I already said yes to. Come on," she whispered. "It's not like you have a social life."

The bell rang as Beth shot Courtney a look of annoyance. "No," Beth said, grabbing her backpack and heading for the door.

Courtney reached into her backpack and spritzed herself with her blue bottle of Ocean Dream perfume, which she liked to refer to as her "signature scent." I coughed as the mist hit my throat, all strong flowers and fake sandalwood, like I'd just swallowed a department store.

"You don't need any more of that," I told her. "I could already smell it all through class."

Courtney let out a dramatic sigh as she tucked the perfume back into her bag, tilting her head as she gave me that look—the one that screamed *You just don't get it, do you?* "It's not for you, Palmer. I read in *Seventeen* that guys are drawn to a girl with a consistent, alluring scent." She elbowed me playfully in the ribs. "You should try it sometime."

"No, thanks." I slung my JanSport over one shoulder and followed Beth, with Courtney trailing close behind.

"Hey, Beth."

I spotted Ryan Mendoza, one of the most popular guys at school, slowing to give Beth a fist bump.

"Hi, Ryan."

He nodded to me. "Hey, ladies."

Even though he acknowledged Courtney, he avoided her gaze as we continued down the hall. I smiled at her once Ryan was out of earshot.

"I think he's still scared of you from that time you pushed him off the monkey bars in second grade after he stole Beth's glasses." I nearly cringe recalling the audible snap of his bone when he hit the pavement.

A look of amusement crossed over Courtney's face. "Oh yeah. That little turd deserved it after making fun of Beth like that." She grinned. "And he never stole Beth's glasses again."

It was true. *No one* dared make fun of her after that.

When we reached the hallway, Courtney draped a long slender arm over Beth's shoulders, which lifted her tight black T-shirt a few inches above her low-rise jeans. "Anyway, back to my extra credit, you need me on the volleyball team. How are you going to get scouted for that scholarship you can't shut up about if we don't make it to the finals?"

Jake and Tyler, two other seniors on the track team, strode down the hallway in our direction. I watched their gaze travel to Courtney before falling to her exposed midriff. I fell in line beside Courtney, who acted like she didn't notice their stares. But I saw the flicker of satisfaction in her green eyes from the attention.

"Maybe you should study harder next time," Beth said.

"Come on," Courtney pleaded. "Just this once. You'll be doing the whole team a favor. Plus, you owe me one."

"For what?" I asked.

"Ugh." Beth lifted her head toward the fluorescent lights. "Fine, I'll do it."

"Yay!" Courtney wrapped her arm tighter around Beth. "You're the best."

I shook my head at Beth for how easily she allowed Courtney to manipulate her.

Courtney threw a glance over her shoulder as Jake and Tyler went into a classroom. When she turned back, her eyes were sparkling. She leaned in close and lowered her voice. "Jake and Tyler told Emma this morning that Bryson brought a dozen roses to school to ask out his homecoming date"—she fluttered her eyelashes dramatically—"a.k.a., *me*. Don't say anything, okay? I want to look surprised when he asks."

I'm shocked the senior quarterback hadn't asked Courtney already. She'd been laying it on him *hard*, falling over him every chance she got. I was sure they'd be together before now. Last weekend, Gigi had thrown a party while her parents were working, and Courtney planted herself on Bryson's lap until she'd gotten so drunk Emma had driven her home. Once Courtney set her sights on something, she didn't let up until she got it.

After Courtney had left, I stumbled onto Bryson and Gigi on the front porch. He had his arm around Gigi, who was wearing his jacket. Knowing how Courtney felt about him, I'd been surprised to see Gigi cozy up to Bryson. At first, I thought Gigi and Bryson were joking around. But by the end of the night, Gigi's head was on Bryson's shoulder, and they looked undeniably like a couple. Gigi had to have known Courtney had gone home drunk—she wouldn't have dared to do that in Courtney's presence.

The bell rang for third period, but Courtney was still rattling on about homecoming. The three of us headed for chemistry, and we came around a corner to see Bryson moving toward Gigi at the other end of the hallway. With one arm tucked behind his back, he tapped Gigi on the shoulder.

"Walk faster," Courtney barked under her breath. "He must be asking where I am."

Beth and I picked up our pace to keep up with Courtney while Gigi whirled around from her open locker to face Bryson.

Bryson whipped the roses out from behind his back and extended them toward Gigi. He said something that I was too far away to hear.

Gigi covered her mouth with her hand. "Yes! Of course I will!" She threw her arms around Bryson's neck as Courtney stopped in her tracks.

Mark and Chase, two of Bryson's friends, appeared at the other end of the hall. Chase whistled.

"Bryson's got a homecoming date!"

Mark slapped Bryson on the shoulder as they moved past. I glanced at Courtney, whose smile had gone wooden.

"Hey, Court," Bryson called when he saw us.

At the sound of Courtney's name, Gigi released Bryson and took a step back. She cast Courtney a sheepish look as Courtney resumed her stride, heading straight toward them. Beth and I looked on as Gigi tucked a long strand of blond hair behind her ear.

"Oh, hey, Court." Gigi's voice was calm, but I could tell she was bracing for Courtney's reaction.

We all were. I recognized the look on Gigi's face, desperately seeking Courtney's approval—a look I'd worn many times since meeting Courtney in kindergarten.

Courtney squealed. "That's great!" A wide smile spread across her face as she bounded toward them with a bounce in her step. "So happy for you two."

Gigi's shoulders sagged with relief as Courtney embraced her.

A look passed between Beth and me. Gigi seemed to accept Courtney's reaction as genuine. But I knew better and could see that Beth did too. I saw the look in Courtney's green eyes. For a flicker of a moment, they went cold, emitting one emotion: hatred.

And it scared the shit out of me.

Mrs. Herrera stopped in front of Courtney's desk to lay a sheet of paper on it. "This is your work?"

The sun from the window reflected off Courtney's carrot-red hair as she looked up from doodling a knife in her notebook. "Of course."

Courtney didn't even hesitate. She lied so well that even I almost believed her. It gave me chills.

Mrs. Herrera crossed her arms. "I've never seen you use these types of words before."

Courtney shrugged. "I've been studying a lot."

Mrs. Herrera pursed her lips. She tapped the short story that Beth had typed up over the weekend. "If that's the case, I want to see a better score on our next exam."

Beth waited until Mrs. Herrera moved to the back row, then whispered to Courtney. "I dumbed it down so it could pass off as yours."

I laughed. Courtney frowned.

"You're welcome," Beth added.

"Thanks," Courtney muttered.

The bell rang as Courtney unzipped her backpack and folded the paper inside. A gasp erupted from behind me. I turned to see Tiffany showing Megan a text on her phone.

"No phones in class," Mrs. Herrera shouted.

"But the bell rang," Tiffany said.

"I don't care."

Tiffany turned to Megan, tucking her phone into her pocket. "They're in the hall."

Wondering what Tiffany was referring to, I followed Beth and Courtney out of the classroom. When I stepped into the hallway, everyone I passed was holding a sheet of paper, whispering among themselves.

I spotted Emma walking toward us, clenching a paper in her hand. Unlike the others who looked entertained by them, Emma looked pale. Her hair was pulled into a high ponytail, and she wore the Juicy Couture sweat suit Courtney had gifted the five of us for Christmas last year, each in a different color. Nearly all of Emma's clothes came from Courtney, who knew Emma's mom couldn't afford to buy her the same labels the rest of us wore. Emma didn't like handouts, so Courtney would cut the tags off new clothes, then give them to Emma, pretending she didn't want them and acting as though Emma were doing her a favor for taking them off her hands. For as mean as she could be, Courtney was also incredibly compassionate.

I moved toward Emma. "What is it?"

She extended it toward me. Beth and Courtney leaned over my shoulder.

I drew in a breath. It was a photo of Gigi straddling Luke Cross, her boyfriend for most of last year. They were shirtless and looking up seductively at the camera. *SLUT* was printed in bold hot-pink letters above the enlarged photo.

"These were taped to everyone's lockers," Emma said. "They're even up on the walls around the school."

Beth swiped it from Emma's grip. "Oh no. This is bad."

I met Emma's gaze. "Has Gigi seen it?"

Emma nodded. "That's why I was coming to get you. She's freaking out. She won't come out of the bathroom. Come on."

Courtney, Beth, and I followed Emma through the maze of students holding copies of Gigi's photo. Some were laughing, some were murmuring, and others were just staring at the printed photo in silence. I bumped into two freshmen ogling the photo as they walked.

"Oh my gosh," one of them said. "Is that Gigi *Harris*?"

The other one nodded after apologizing for bumping into me. "And Luke Cross."

"Skank," the other girl said.

Ahead, Selena, the new girl on our volleyball team who'd moved to Sequim over the summer, stood outside the girls' bathroom with her arms crossed, a worried expression across her face.

"Is she okay?" Beth asked Selena.

Gigi sobbed from inside the bathroom. Selena shook her head. "Of course she's not okay."

Emma led the way into the bathroom, holding the door open for the four of us to enter.

Gigi was hunched over one of the sinks, her palms pressing against the counter. Her body heaved with each sob. She looked up when we all stepped inside.

She snarled upon seeing Courtney. "You did this." Gigi lunged at the redhead, black streaks of mascara streaming down her face as she shoved a finger in Courtney's face.

Courtney's back slammed against the tiled wall. I stepped closer to the door. I'd never seen Gigi like this, so clearly ravaged by her anger.

Courtney shook her head. "No."

Liar, I thought, remembering Courtney get up to use the bathroom with her backpack during Spanish period. That must've been when she did it.

Gigi narrowed her eyes. "Yes, you did. You wanted Bryson. When he asked me out and not you, you couldn't handle it."

Two sophomores entered the bathroom, stopping dead in their tracks when they saw what was happening.

Emma stuck out her long arm. "Use another bathroom."

The girls retreated without a word.

"You're the only one I sent that picture to. And you promised me you'd delete the email after I sent it. That was over a year ago, but no one cares now. Now that I've been labeled the school slut, Bryson already called off homecoming with me." Gigi sniffed. "I told him that photo was taken last year, but he didn't want to hear it." Gigi lowered her face to Courtney's, baring her teeth. "You win. It's over. Happy?" Her last word came out a hiss.

Gigi stepped back, and the four of us watched in intense silence as Courtney moved toward Gigi. "I swear I didn't do this. Didn't Luke take the photo? Maybe he—"

"He wouldn't."

"Someone else then. Believe me, I would never do this to you. I'm so sorry, Gigi."

Gigi held still as Courtney wrapped her arms around her while she sobbed, too broken, apparently, to put up any more of a fight.

While the other three looked on, I turned away. Gigi may have *wanted* to believe Courtney, but I doubted she really could.

I couldn't.

Chapter Four

Present

While Gigi uses the stateroom mirror to reapply her lipstick and Beth checks her phone, I dig my own phone out of my bag to make sure my sister hasn't texted about the girls.

"We'll probably lose cell service when we get out to the Strait of Juan de Fuca," Gigi says. "But we'll have internet through Starlink the whole way so I can post live feeds of our trip."

That must be the flat white plate I saw secured near the top of the mast. Seeing I have no new texts, I drop my phone back into my bag.

Gigi lifts her head to the sound of the female voice on the dock. She clasps her hands together. "Finally. Emma's here."

Beth returns her phone to her bag and leads the way upstairs. I follow Gigi. Seeing how perfectly toned her thighs are, I wish I had gone on a diet before the trip.

When we reach the cockpit, Captain Nojan is on the radio. I trail Gigi and step onto the deck, seeing Emma on the dock. Adam extends his hand to Emma, but the home renovator shakes her head. Instead, she grabs the shroud.

"I'm good," she says, using her tanned, muscular arm to pull herself onto the boat.

The last time I saw Emma was in the news last year after a video surfaced online of her at a house she was renovating in Capitol Hill, screaming profanities at one of her contractors before throwing a screwdriver at him. She was sentenced to community service after pleading guilty to assault. Not long before the incident, Emma had shared a link in our group text thread to an *Architectural Digest* article that featured one of her projects—a Seahawks player's Lake Washington home that Emma had fully renovated and designed. But after the incident, when I saw the word *bitch* spray-painted across her face on a billboard on the 405, I wondered about the effect Emma's volatile outburst has had on her business.

She's always had a temper, but I was surprised to see that it's gotten worse as she's gotten older, not better. Recently a few home-DIY articles featuring Emma popped up on my news feed, so I guess her out-of-control temper hasn't ruined her career after all.

She looks good, I think. In her cargo pants and ribbed tank top, she's still the tomboy, and even fitter than she was in high school. With that sweet smile, one would never guess she was capable of such explosive rage.

Emma and I never meshed, but that's not what causes my unease at seeing the house flipper. I swallow back the guilt that rises in my throat, thinking about the "accident" our senior year that left Emma with a broken ankle.

Emma manages to make Beth look petite next to her. At five foot seven, Beth is the shortest of all of us. Beth's glossy dark waves are a sharp contrast to Emma's short blond curls. Emma's once-thin lips are now unnaturally plump with filler.

I'm suddenly self-conscious of every line on my Botox-free face.

"*So* good to see you!" Gigi gushes, pushing past Beth to get to Emma first.

Emma scans the deck after Gigi embraces them both. "Where's Alex? Didn't he come to see you off?"

"He wanted to, but he had business in Spain."

"He's in the restaurant business, right?" Beth asks.

Gigi's smile fades, and I wonder if Beth guessed the wrong profession on purpose to annoy her.

"Hotels."

"Oh, right." Beth nods. "I knew that."

"Gigi," the captain calls from behind the wheel at the back of the boat. "I need to speak with you."

"Okay," Gigi says over her shoulder. She turns back to Emma. "Sorry, I'll be right back." Gigi heads toward the helm, leaving Beth and me with Emma beside the boat's towering mast.

Emma offers me a warm smile, having seemingly accepted my long-standing lie that Bryson and Jake were responsible for her ankle injury, which only makes me feel worse.

"You look well," Beth says after the three of us exchange awkward hugs.

And well off, I think.

Emma runs a hand through her curls without returning the compliment. "Thanks. I'm so glad I could make it. I wasn't sure when Gigi first asked me since I just bought a prewar home in Upper Queen Anne that needs to be fully gutted, and I'm in the middle of two other huge renos."

I slide my hands into the back pockets of my shorts, surprised to hear that Emma is still in high demand after her assault.

"But the couple whose home I am redoing in Magnolia is so high maintenance that I figured a break would be good. Otherwise, I might strangle them."

Beth lets out a short laugh as I study Emma, wondering if she's partly serious. I try not to think about the close quarters we'll all be sharing over the next two weeks.

"And Gigi promised we'd have internet, so I left my site superintendent in charge."

Emma's gaze drifts to mine, and I force myself to return her tight smile, remembering how she and Gigi distastefully approached a documentary producer in college, hoping to talk about our notorious rafting trip—saying they wanted to set the record straight on our innocence. They wanted Beth and me to be a part of it, too, but we refused. We'd been burned by the media before, and after the trauma we'd endured, we had no desire to insert ourselves back in the limelight.

Courtney's parents were equally sickened when they were contacted by the film producer and declined to be interviewed. Fortunately, without more willing participants, no film was made.

Emma gestures to Beth. "Congrats on becoming the Elliott Bay University President. The youngest in history, right?"

"That's right."

Emma's gaze travels to mine. "What are you up to these days, Palmer?"

Adam's deep voice comes from behind me. "Emma, your stateroom is down below. I can show you where."

I turn, grateful for the interruption.

"Thanks," Emma says.

She allows Adam to take her bag before she follows him toward the narrow set of stairs.

I turn to Beth after watching Adam disappear below deck. "Does he seem familiar to you?"

"Yep." Beth finishes what's left of her champagne. "He looks like Chris Pratt."

Now that Beth says it, I see the resemblance to the A-list actor in Adam's muscular build and the hint of auburn in his closely trimmed beard.

"And he's hot, that's for sure." Beth elbows me as a grin spreads across her face. "And there's no wedding band."

Before I can answer, Gigi's voice comes from across the deck. "I don't *care*!"

I whip around to find her with arms crossed, glaring at Captain Nojan. Whatever she and the captain are discussing, she does not look happy about it.

The captain glances at Beth and me before returning his attention to Gigi. "I really feel that we should tell the—"

"No." Gigi shakes her head. "I already told you. It's fine. End of discussion. We're all here now, and I want to leave on time."

"Fine, but don't say I didn't warn you," the captain calls as Gigi strides away, her thin cover-up fluttering in the wind.

"Warn you about what?" I ask when Gigi gets closer.

Gigi smiles, the irritation now wiped clean from her face. I glance behind her at the captain, who regards her with a scowl before starting for the bow.

"It's nothing." Gigi swipes a manicured hand through the air. "He was afraid he hadn't brought enough vegetarian meal options. I told him it's fine since Palmer and I are the only two vegetarians on board, and I plan to be eating light on the trip anyway." She turns to her assistant sitting on the bow. "Hey, Carissa? Can you come here for a sec?"

I follow Gigi's gaze to the twentysomething girl with a wiry frame who gets to her feet. She'd been so quiet, I hadn't noticed her there.

"Sure," Carissa says.

"We need to refold the napkins in the galley before we leave," Gigi tells her assistant when she reaches us. "They are supposed to look like swans, not sad paper airplanes."

Carissa's expression falters, and Gigi lightly touches her arm.

"It's okay." Gigi smiles. "I'll show you the trick to refolding them. It took me awhile to figure it out too."

"Since when did you turn into Martha Stewart?" Beth asks as Carissa heads below.

Gigi shrugs. "Just want to be a good host."

Beth lifts her empty champagne flute. "Believe me, you are."

Gigi starts to follow Carissa, then turns to Beth and me. "If you guys don't mind, I'll need some help taking videos since there isn't room for my assistant to come along. I'm going to need *a lot* of content for this trip. My sponsor is paying top dollar for me to promote them."

I lean into Beth as Gigi continues toward the companionway. "You didn't tell me we'd be filming Gigi the whole time," I whisper.

"We'll get Emma to do it." Beth cracks a smile. "I'm sure she takes a lot of selfies."

I turn so that my back is to Gigi. "It looked like the captain was telling Gigi something serious. Do you think she was telling the truth about the vegetarian thing?"

Beth squints from the sun as she eyes Gigi before she disappears below deck.

"Nope."

Chapter Five

Present: Day One at Sea

"On your life vest, or PFD, you'll also find a whistle that you can use to signal for help and notify others of where you are." Captain Nojan lifts the whistle attached to the life vest he's donned for the safety demonstration. "If for some reason your vest doesn't inflate if you fall overboard, pull on this toggle." He lifts the lime-green plastic handle attached to the base.

Still docked at the marina, I stand against the railing on the foredeck between Gigi and Beth, where all four of us are lined up wearing life preservers across from the captain and Adam. I feel beneath the black life vest slung around my neck, making sure it has the toggle Nojan is referring to.

"Safety is my number one concern on this journey." Nojan scans our faces. "There are four things I want you to remember. First, when you're moving about the boat, use one hand to hold on at all times. I want you to use the old proverb: One hand for yourself, and one for the ship." Nojan holds a hand in the air while grasping the shroud beside him with the other. "Second, always ask my permission to go forward of the cockpit." He gestures toward the bow. "Third, always wear your life vest when you're on deck."

I glance at Gigi, who's adjusting her thin life vest to make sure her cleavage is visible through the middle. Beside me, Beth grips her straps and casts a nervous glance at the water.

"I'm going to need to take mine off while filming my content, though," Gigi says.

The captain shakes his head. "Not when you're on deck, you won't. Even on a *good* day, the open ocean will be ten times rougher than these protected waters of the Sound."

Gigi cocks her head, and even behind her oversize sunglasses, she looks unconvinced. I follow Beth's wary gaze to the water lapping gently against the hull. The back of my leg brushes against the thin, low cable railing I heard Nojan refer to earlier as the "lifeline," although there doesn't seem to be anything "lifesaving" about the flimsy cable that comes just above the top of my knee.

Nojan grabs a loop attached to the base of his life vest. "After we pass through the Strait of Juan de Fuca and get out to open ocean, you will also need to tether yourself to the ship with a line before moving about the deck. Our charted course will take us over two hundred miles offshore. The first day at sea can be rough for everyone as you get used to the rhythm of the ocean. It usually takes only a day or two to get over the initial seasickness you may feel while your body adjusts to being on the ocean." He turns to Gigi. "I wouldn't expect you to be feeling good enough to be filming much content during that initial period."

A day or two? I gaze out at the calm waters of Puget Sound. I'm normally not prone to seasickness, but the only time I've been out on the open ocean was on a cruise. *How rough is Nojan expecting it to be?*

"Why so far out?" Beth asks. "I thought we'd hug the coast more on our way to San Diego."

"Good question, Beth. The sea state is better, and there are fewer ships, crab pots, et cetera. It's the most 'comfortable' route, if you will. This boat, the Emerald 55, is the first of its kind to be completed, and there are currently three more in production at the Emerald Wave shipyard on Lake Union. This ship was designed as a blue-water boat, which makes it optimal for ocean sailing. I believe you'll find it quite comfortable once you get used to being out on the open waters."

As he continues with the safety instructions, I try not to dwell on all the worst-case scenarios that flood my mind. My gaze moves up the towering mast and lingers on the weather vane at the top. I had no idea the mast would be so tall; it looks higher than the boat is long. I watched a reality show once in which a sailor had to climb to the top of their mast to repair something at sea. The thought of climbing to the top, even while docked, sends a shiver down my spine.

"Lastly, always be mindful of the boom." He swivels to rest his hand on the thick gray beam that's secured perpendicularly from the tall mast beside him at his shoulder. "Many people have died getting hit by these, either thrown onto the deck or into the water. The boom can swing out ninety degrees across the cockpit on each side of the boat, one hundred and eighty degrees in total. We have something on board called a boom preventer that will keep the boom from swinging too far in the event of an accidental gybe or tack. But—"

Gigi lowers her sunglasses to the tip of her nose. "An accidental what?"

Nojan stands tall as if making a conscious effort to be patient. "A change of direction. But even with a boom preventer, accidents still happen. So, when you leave the cockpit, keep your weight low by bending at the knees and make sure your head and body are not in the way of the boom when moving about the ship. Understood?"

"Understood," Emma, Beth, and I chime in unison.

Gigi shrugs.

"Good. In the event we capsize—"

"*Capsize*?" Beth says, her soft voice rising in alarm.

Thinking of my girls, I nearly grab my bag and leave.

Captain Nojan raises his palm. "Not to worry. I've sailed this route over three dozen times and have never had a vessel capsize." His gaze flicks to Gigi. "And I don't plan on starting with this trip." He lowers his hand. "But in the rare event that we do, it is important for you to stay with the boat and hold on. It is much easier for rescuers to spot a boat than people floating in the water. We also have a life raft mounted to the foredeck in front of the dinghy, which contains emergency communication equipment."

I scan the deck near the bow, not seeing any kind of raft.

"It's kept inside what looks like a large white suitcase," the captain adds.

Then I see it, but it doesn't make me feel any safer. If we encounter swells big enough to knock down this large vessel that's been engineered to stay afloat, how would we all survive in an inflatable raft?

"And like I said"—Nojan's attention travels to Beth—"when we get out of these protected waters to the open ocean, it will get rough. And I don't want anyone panicking on my boat. So, if any of you—"

"We'll be fine!" Gigi swipes her arm through the air for emphasis and sways against Emma, nearly losing her balance even though we're still docked.

The captain narrows his eyes. "There will also be no falling overboard from having too much to drink."

"Aye, aye, Captain." Gigi offers him a sloppy salute before breaking into a giggle.

Captain Nojan frowns, looking at the rest of us. "Any questions?"

"Do these life vests come in any other colors?" Gigi asks.

The captain huffs a sigh and looks to the rest of us. "Any *real* questions?"

The three of us shake our heads.

Nojan nods. "All right, then we'll be on our way."

Ten minutes later, we pull away from the marina.

"Look!" Beth nudges my arm when we near the break wall and motions toward a sea lion's head protruding above the surface.

"Bon voyage," Gigi calls over the boat's other side, blowing a kiss to her assistant filming our departure from the dock.

After we leave the marina, Gigi peels off her mesh cover-up and lies out on the foredeck. *Brr,* I think, seeing goose bumps form on her thighs. Emma excuses herself below deck to call her site superintendent before we lose cell service.

I settle in beside Beth on the padded bench at the top of the companionway as we turn away from the city skyline and sail north through Puget Sound. Captain Nojan stands behind us at the stern, steering the boat with one of the two large leather-wrapped wheels while Adam moves between the two risen sails, following Nojan's orders to trim and ease their tension. A lump forms in my throat when I spot the roofline of Elliott Bay Hospital downtown, where I nearly killed my last patient. I look away, twisting to take in the shoreline of Bainbridge Island. A ferry blasts its horn as it pulls away from the terminal, heading downtown.

"That's Kristin Hannah's house." Beth points over my shoulder.

My gaze follows the direction of Beth's finger, and I smooth back the hair that blows loose from my ponytail.

"The two-story one with the boat docked in front of it?"

"That's the one."

I place my palm on my head to hold back my hair and take in the large, shingle-sided home with forest-green trim settled on a secluded lot on the corner of the island. "Pretty," I mumble, wondering what it would be like to be a famous author, waking up to the ocean every morning, probably with a doting husband bringing you coffee.

"I downloaded the first season of *Firefly Lane* for us to watch on the trip," Beth says, her dark waves blowing wildly around her round face.

"Oh." I feign a smile. "Great."

Beth frowns. "You watched it already, didn't you?"

I wince. "I'm sorry. I know I promised to wait until you finished the book, but with everything that's happened lately with Matt and my job . . . I needed an escape."

Beth's expression softens. "Well, I guess you'll just have to rewatch the first season until we get to season two, which I also downloaded."

I bite my lip. Beth gapes at me.

"Oh my—" She scoffs, swiping a strand of hair off her cheek. "You watched *both* seasons?" Her jaw drops open in horror. "You did!"

I wrinkle my nose. "I'm sorry."

She swats me playfully on the arm. "That's okay. I get it." She sighs, glancing toward the bow. "I'll just become best friends with Gigi instead."

She cracks a smile as I turn to watch Gigi now standing near the bow, holding onto a shroud and staring out at the water. Gigi lifts the back of her hand to her cheek. *Was she wiping away a tear?*

No, I think, as Gigi's lips form a wide smile and she angles her phone toward the sky to get her full body into the camera. We hit a wave from a speedboat cruising by, and I gasp as Gigi stumbles to the side of the boat, dropping her phone on the deck before doubling over on the lifeline's wire cable.

Adam rushes toward Gigi from the other side of the boat, and I cover my mouth with my hand as Gigi manages to pull herself upright before he reaches her. Beth gasps as Gigi falls to her knees to rescue her phone before it slides overboard.

I keep my fingers pressed to my lips as Adam helps Gigi to her feet. He looks on in amazement as Gigi returns to the bow and resumes recording as if nothing happened. I shake my head, turning around to watch downtown Seattle shrinking in the distance.

"It's so beautiful out here on the water." Beth shades her eyes with her hand, eyeing another sailboat going by as my thoughts drift to my girls at home with my sister. I feel a pang in my heart at how much I'm going to miss them these next two weeks.

"You okay?" Beth asks as if reading my thoughts.

"I've never been away from the girls this long."

"They'll be fine." Beth pats my knee. "Plus, you can video call them through Starlink every day if you want. And I'm sure they're having fun with their auntie."

She's right. I recall the excitement on their faces when I told them they'd be spending the next two weeks with Aunt Kate. She's always spoiled them, since she has only boys. My girls were so ecstatic, they jumped up and down when Kate promised to take them back-to-school shopping at Bellevue Square later today. They're probably there now.

My thoughts shift to Matt. Before I can stop myself, I imagine him enjoying a lazy, naked Saturday in bed with his college-aged girlfriend in her crappy one-bedroom apartment. My chest constricts, and I thrust the thought from my mind.

From the corner of my eye, I clock Gigi moving toward Adam who's standing beneath the sail at the middle of the boat.

"I'll take another drink," she yells over the wind. "Hey, Adam? Could you open another bottle of champagne?"

Captain Nojan's voice booms from the stern. "Not until we maneuver through the Sound. This is a busy channel."

I turn to see him gesture at the small sailboat sliding through the water on our starboard side before pointing to a cargo ship ahead.

"I need Adam on deck while we navigate the Sound," the captain says. "If you want a drink before then, you'll have to get it yourself."

"Fine." Gigi huffs and unsteadily makes her way toward the companionway past Beth and me. She pauses when she reaches the steps, casting a look at the two of us over her shoulder. "Anyone else want more champagne?"

I shake my head. "I'm good."

"I'll take one," Beth says, following Gigi below and leaving me alone on the deck with my thoughts and the two-man crew.

I study the snowcapped Olympic Mountains to my left beyond Sequim, then Whidbey Island on my right. We're flanked by evergreen-covered land on each side.

A pop erupts below deck, followed by a playful shriek from Gigi. I look down the stairs toward the noise. Gigi's mom is a recovering alcoholic, very active in AA for all the time I've known her. Because of that, Gigi hardly touched alcohol in high school. She offered to be our designated driver on more than one occasion.

I spy the southern tip of Whidbey Island before the boat turns northwest. I think of Gigi's husband, absent from our send-off. Is Gigi just letting loose or numbing herself from something in her seemingly perfect new life?

I stare straight ahead in the direction of my hometown, dreading the thought of sharing the boat's close quarters with a drunk Gigi for the next two weeks. If something *is* eating away at Gigi, I doubt it's from the new life she's created, but rather our old one.

The one we've never quite managed to escape.

Chapter Six

Present: Day One at Sea

"Did you notice Gigi ogling the chef on our way down?" Beth asks in a lowered voice, closing the cabin door behind her.

I stiffen at hearing her say *ogling*, the same word she used the other night to describe Matt's inappropriate behavior toward the waitress.

"How could I not?" I unzip my bag and search for my sweatshirt, trying to force away the mental image of my soon-to-be ex-husband *ogling* a beautiful young woman's ass.

"You would never know she's married from the way she's throwing herself at him," Beth adds.

There's an extra edge to Beth's voice. Sometimes I wonder if Beth is lonely, living with just her cat. No husband, no kids. Beth stays busy with her career, but I know my best friend would like to be married, have a family. Even though she acts like it doesn't bother her to be single. That it's her choice.

I used to wonder if Beth's coolness to Matt over the years was due to jealousy, but now that I've seen Matt's true asshole self, I feel bad for thinking that. I look at Beth, the scowl on her face about Gigi's flirtations nearly making me laugh.

"Did you see her in the kitchen? I thought she was a vegetarian," Beth says.

Earlier, on our way to our stateroom, we spotted Gigi in the galley, her hand on Adam's shoulder as she leaned over him, asking to have a bite of the meatballs he was sautéing.

"And *what* was she wearing?" Beth shakes her head.

I picture what Gigi had changed into when I last saw her—a long-sleeved skintight black-spandex onesie with cutouts across the chest and midriff. I shrug. "I think it's called a catsuit."

I check my phone. Seeing that I've lost service, I make a mental note to get the Starlink password from Gigi so I can WhatsApp my sister. Beth slips a sweater over her T-shirt as a knock sounds on our door. Beth opens it while I pull my sweatshirt over my head.

I expect to see Gigi, but it's Emma.

"You guys coming to watch the sunset?" She adjusts a monogrammed shawl around her shoulders.

"Yep," Beth says. "We were just throwing on something warm."

Adam is alone in the kitchen when we follow Emma up the stairs to the deck. I regard his profile as he chops mushrooms. He catches my stare and smiles. A dimple appears on one side of his face. I look away, feeling a flush of warmth on my cheeks.

Gigi is seated on the padded cockpit bench, in the same spot that Beth and I sat in earlier. She's already opened the wine. At the stern, Nojan is stationed at one of the wheels. The wind died down when we reached Port Townsend, forcing Nojan to lower the sails and start the motor.

"Being on this boat reminds me of my grandparents' sailboat." The wind catches one of Emma's blond curls, and she tucks it behind her ear. "Except it was way older. I practically lived on that thing in the summers as a kid while my mom worked."

"I remember that," Gigi says. "The *Fancy Free*, right?"

"Yep." Emma smiles, nodding.

When she hands Emma a glass, Gigi's gaze is unfocused, as if she's had too much to drink already. Emma sinks next to her and throws a tanned leg over Gigi's lap, giving her a close-lipped smile. In return, Gigi taps her champagne glass against Emma's.

"Oh, look. It's Sequim," Beth says as she and I take a seat on the bench across from Gigi and Emma.

I recognize the Dungeness Spit in the distance and the lighthouse perched on the end of it. The sea around it is smooth as glass.

"Remember when Courtney convinced us all to take the trek out there to stay fit in the offseason?" Emma says.

Gigi smiles. "I showed up in flip-flops, not realizing how long of a hike it is. My feet were killing me."

"Wasn't it something like eleven miles?" Emma peers over her shoulder at the lighthouse in the distance.

Beth grimaces behind her glasses. "It was brutal, I remember that."

Emma extends a toned arm toward Gigi. "And I gave you a piggyback ride part of the way back just so we wouldn't have to hear you complain about your feet hurting."

Gigi's mouth drops open. "I didn't complain."

"Yes, you *did*," Beth and I exclaim in unison.

Gigi grins. We all share a laugh before a silence falls over us as we regard our hometown from the water. Gigi empties the bottle, filling two more plastic wineglasses with a surprisingly steady pour given all the champagne she's consumed since getting on the boat. She extends drinks to Beth and me, raising her own after we take them.

"To Courtney," she says.

"To Courtney," the three of us echo, clinking our glasses together.

On the beach, I spot Gigi's three-story childhood home, where she threw countless parties while her mom worked nights as an ER doctor and her dad was away on business trips. Her father, born in Armenia, did a lot of business overseas. Gigi's beauty, a striking blend of her father's wide hazel eyes and her mother's blond hair and full lips, gives her a unique, almost exotic appearance.

"Do your parents still live on the beach?" Emma asks Gigi.

She nods. "Yep. They're retired now, so they spend a lot of the winter in Arizona."

I think of my childhood home a few miles inland and closer to Sequim's quaint downtown, much smaller than the expansive waterfront home Gigi grew up in. My mom still lives there, too, but I haven't been back in years. I've spent too much of my life there already.

I remember those first few weeks after our rafting trip, coming home from school, the sickening feeling I'd get in the pit of my stomach when I turned on the road that wound along the Dungeness River to my house. Knowing the news vans would already be lined up at my driveway, I'd hunker down in my seat and pull on the baseball hat and sunglasses I'd started keeping in my car.

We only had a carport, no garage, so there was no getting around the photographs and accusatory questioning from reporters for the few moments it took me to get inside the house. My mom would stay up until midnight to run out and get the mail, after they'd all left for the day. But sometimes a news van would camp out all night.

That summer after graduation, I hardly left the house, unable to face the scrutiny from reporters—and strangers—everywhere I went. My sister, Kate, decided to stay in Pullman for the summer, where she was going to college seven hours away, so it was just my mom and me.

I gaze in the direction of my childhood home and think of my mom and how hard that summer was for her too. My lungs stiffen with dread at still having to tell her about Matt's leaving. I still recall the look of shock on my mom's face the last time I told her something she didn't want to hear—that I wasn't going to college.

"What do you mean you're not going?*" Mom looked up from the kitchen table, surrounded by a stack of bills.*

"I can't." I lowered my gaze to the table, unable to bear the look of bewilderment on her face. "Not after everything that's happened. I can't even go to Safeway without strangers glaring at me—or asking what really happened to Courtney." I gestured to the closed living room blinds, shielding us from the news vans parked in our front lawn. "I can't even get the mail!"

Mom pushed her checkbook aside. "You have to, honey. Between your academic and volleyball scholarships, you got a full ride. You can't stay here." Her eyes darted toward the windows we kept covered at the front of our small house. "You're not guilty of anything. It's a tragedy what happened to Courtney, but it was no one's fault. You can't let those vultures keep you from living your life."

Tears blurred my vision as I stared back at her. If only she knew the truth.

I shook my head. "I've already decided. I'm not going."

"Sweetheart." She pursed her lips and set down her pen. "You've wanted to be a doctor since you were little. You were so passionate about becoming an oncologist after your Aunt Karen's diagnosis. You can't give up your dream. Throwing your life away won't bring Courtney back."

It crushed me to see the disappointment on my mom's face. I could tell she was devastated by my decision. She'd worked so hard to provide for me and my sister after our dad had left. She'd implored us both to go to college, not wanting us to ever have to struggle like she did.

"I'm sorry, Mom. But I can't go." My voice broke. "Not when everyone thinks I'm a murderer."

But that wasn't the real reason, I think as my gaze shifts to a kayaker paddling along the shore of the spit. The truth was that I didn't deserve to go, not while Courtney's unfound body lay decomposing somewhere in the Olympic National Park. Not after what I'd done.

Chapter Seven

October 2004

"You do it." Courtney thrust the bottle of Dawn dish soap at me in the corner of the locker room.

In the background, the hiss of showers rose, drowning out our whispers.

"I don't know . . ." I glanced at the door to the gym where Beth and Gigi were still running laps after we'd beaten them in a scrimmage during volleyball practice.

Beth's words to me in the hallway before first period replayed in my mind.

"I'd be careful, Courtney's probably using you for something."

"Using me?" I snapped at Beth.

The bell rang, and the morning crowd began to empty into various classrooms down the long hall. When I got out of Courtney's car in the school's parking lot, Beth had given me a death stare. And now she was talking to me like Courtney and I couldn't be growing closer because she actually liked me?

Ever since Courtney had suggested I stay with her while my mom was with her sister in California, Beth had seemed weird about our friendship. My aunt was literally dying of cancer, and apparently all Beth could see was how Courtney was stealing me away.

"Buttering you up," Beth added. "You know Courtney. Don't you think it's weird that she insisted you live with her while your mom is with your aunt?"

"No, we're friends.*" I followed Beth inside Mr. Guthrey's classroom, trying not to take offense at what Beth was implying.*

"Yeah, but not like that," Beth said over her shoulder. "I'm guessing she wants something from you."

Now I was irritated. Beth already shared a room with her younger sister, so I couldn't impose on her like that.

"Would you rather my mom pull me out of school and homeschool me in California? That'd be awesome, spend half my senior year in a completely different state."

Beth didn't say anything, her gaze on the whiteboard at the front of the class.

"I think it was generous," I said, "Courtney offering to have me stay." Was it really so hard to believe that Courtney and I could be close? "You're just jealous. And mad that I never called you back last night." I slid into the desk beside Beth.

"Whatever." Beth flashed me a dirty look that I hadn't seen since elementary school. "Just don't say I didn't warn you."

"Come on." Courtney squeezed my arm, lowering her voice. "It will be so funny. Every volleyball captain deserves a little initiation."

I shook my head, glancing at the outline of Emma washing her hair behind the shower curtain on the other side of the locker room. Two other girls from our team occupied the shower stalls on either side of her. "I feel bad. What if she gets hurt?" I thought of the division championship game we had coming up this weekend. Emma was our best player, and if we won, we moved on to regionals.

Courtney rolled her eyes. "It's just a joke. Don't be a pussy." She pressed the dish soap against the towel wrapped around my chest.

I started to shake my head again when a twinkle appeared in Courtney's eyes. "Does Jake know you have that photo of the two of you from our sophomore yearbook in your locker?" She smiled. "I'll tell him if you don't do it."

My mouth fell open in horror. "You wouldn't!" I'd had a thing for Jake since freshman year, even though he was way out of my league. And he was now dating Emma. I don't know how Courtney had seen the photo—I'd kept it tucked away. And the only person who knew about my secret crush was Beth.

"What would Emma think of you burning a candle for her new boyfriend?"

I glanced at the door of the gym. Still closed.

"Come on!"

Reluctantly, I allowed Courtney to pull me toward the three occupied showers. Emma was singing Alicia Keys's "If I Ain't Got You."

Courtney slid the rubber mat out of the way with her foot and pointed to the concrete floor. *Do it,* she mouthed.

I leaned over, then paused. Hearing a click, I looked to Courtney, who held up her phone.

"What are you doing?" I whispered.

"Just capturing the moment so we can laugh about this later."

I straightened, letting the dish soap fall to my side. *What if Emma breaks something?* "I can't."

Emma turned off the water. Courtney's eyes rolled upward in exaggerated annoyance. She swiped the soap bottle from my hand and squirted the clear-blue liquid over the floor in front of Emma's shower. My mouth fell open at the soap glistening on the concrete floor as Courtney pushed me back behind a row of lockers.

The door to the gym swung open while Courtney and I crouched. Courtney pressed her finger to her lips when we recognized Gigi's voice as she entered the locker room.

"Those laps were brutal! Next time—"

An ear-piercing scream erupted from the showers seconds before a thud—and a crack—sounded against the cement floor.

"Emma!" Gigi shrieked.

Courtney's eyes doubled in size, and she buried the soap bottle beneath the clothes in her locker.

"Aah," Emma moaned in agony as Coach Kelly came flying through the door.

"What the—" Our coach raced across the room while Courtney and I emerged from behind the lockers.

The two other girls had come out of their showers, dripping wet and clutching their towels. They gaped in horror at Emma, writhing in torment between their feet.

Gigi and Beth were crouched around Emma on the floor. In the eleven years I'd known Emma, I'd never seen her cry—until now. Her face was beet red, twisted in pain. Tears streamed down both of her cheeks. She cried out, forcing her eyes shut as she reached for her ankle.

That's when I saw it. I gasped while Coach Kelly got to her knees, inserting herself between Gigi and Emma.

"Don't touch it!" Emma screamed.

The side of Emma's ankle jutted out at a horrifyingly unnatural angle, and her foot lay limp on its side.

"There's soap on the floor," Gigi exclaimed, lifting her hand off the concrete.

Beside me, Courtney drew in a sharp breath.

Coach Kelly's head whipped in our direction. "You were the only other two in here. Did you do this?"

"No." Courtney shook her head. "But we saw who did. Two guys. They had hoodies on, so it was hard to see their faces. But they were tall, like Bryson and Jake. I'm almost positive it was them." Courtney gestured to me. "We heard them snickering before they ran out the fire door. I thought they were just being pervs."

Emma gritted her teeth. The color had drained from her face, which was now nearly as white as her towel. "I didn't hear anyone."

Coach Kelly frowned. Her eyes shifted to mine. "Is that true, Palmer?"

Emma's tear-filled eyes locked with mine. I looked away, afraid she would read the guilt on my face. I knew I should tell the truth, but I sensed Courtney's ice-cold stare in my periphery.

I swallowed, hating myself. "Yeah, I saw them too."

◆ ◆ ◆

"Come on in, girls." Emma's mom swung the door wide to Emma's private hospital room in Port Angeles when Beth and I arrived. "Thanks for coming," she said, leading the way to Emma's bed by the window. "You know, Gigi's mom was the one who treated Emma in the ER. She was wonderful," she said over her shoulder. "Sweetheart, your friends are here."

Emma opened her eyes, looking groggy. She wore a blue-and-white hospital gown, and her right ankle was elevated, concealed in a protective splint.

"She just got out of surgery," her mom told us. "So she's a little drowsy."

Beth went to Emma's side. "Hey, how are you feeling?"

"Like shit," Emma said.

"Emma Grace . . ." Her mom frowned. "Watch your language."

Emma's gaze traveled to her ankle. "I'll be out for the rest of the season. So much for playing in our division championship this weekend."

Emma's eyes narrowed when she spotted me standing behind Beth. I swallowed.

"Hey, Emma." I felt horrible, knowing Emma was hoping to get scouted by the Elliott Bay University coach who was rumored to be coming to the division tournament.

Emma was hands down the best player on our team. While the rest of us had aspirations of other careers, Emma's dream was to play in the Pro Volleyball Federation after college. Playing for Elliott Bay University would help her chances a lot.

Emma opened her mouth to speak, but her mom's phone rang. She dug through her purse as the ringing grew louder, then checked the caller ID on the flip phone.

"It's my boss. I'll be right back." She exhaled, lifting the phone to her ear as she left the room. "Hi, Dr. Campbell," she said as she stepped into the hall.

"Where's Courtney?" Emma asked.

Hearing her name made me feel sick to my stomach.

"And Gigi?"

Beth bit her lip, looking at me to answer.

"Courtney insisted they still go to the football game."

Emma rolled her eyes. "Of course she did."

"But they're coming here afterward," I quickly added. "And Courtney asked me to bring you these clothes she didn't want."

I set the Nordstrom bag that reeked of Courtney's perfume on a chair, and my face flushed with shame, knowing Courtney's shallow peace offering in no way made up for what we did.

Emma glared at the bag. "I'm not her charity case anymore." She leaned back against her pillow and met my gaze, her eyes brimming with tears. "Courtney did this on purpose. And she can't buy her way out of it."

I wanted to admit it. Tell her she was right. But then I replayed the threats Courtney had made to me after I'd pulled her aside and insisted we tell the truth while Emma was being hauled away in the ambulance.

"We could get expelled!" Courtney hissed.

I gaped at her. "But we didn't mean for Emma to break her ankle. And I didn't do it—you did."

Courtney narrowed her eyes. "That's not what the photo shows on my phone," Courtney said, as if I were the stupidest person she'd ever met.

I went quiet, taken aback by her threat.

"Plus, the school won't care that it was meant to be a joke. They'll just destroy our lives. We could even be facing criminal charges. Didn't you see the news about what happened to those two sophomores last week in California who were charged with harassment after prank calling?"

"It was an accident," I said to Emma.

"You're covering up for her. Stop lying." Emma sat up in bed.

I shook my head. I was planning to go to medical school. I couldn't face expulsion or have something like this on my record.

Emma's eyes narrowed at the silver Nordstrom bag. She gripped her hospital water jug until her knuckles turned white, then threw it at the shopping bag.

"Emma!" Beth said, her eyes wide. "Calm down."

"I'll kill her."

"*Emma*," Beth pursed her lips as if she were scolding a child. "Don't say that."

"Oh, stop!" Emma said. "Courtney did this on purpose. Now she's going to replace me as the team captain, and with me on the bench, she'll have less competition to get scouted this weekend. I know you had nothing to do with it, Palm."

Beth looked at me, and my face flushed with guilt. I hadn't even told her the truth.

"Whatever Courtney's threatening you with, it isn't worth it," Emma continued. "She's reckless. *Dangerous.* She needs to face the consequences this time. Palmer, come on. You saw her, I know you did. Tell the truth."

Emma's intense blue eyes drilled into mine as Beth waited expectantly beside me.

I slowly shook my head. "It was two guys, like we said."

Emma tore her gaze from mine and silently watched the rain beat against the window.

I hated myself for lying, knowing my friendship with Emma would likely never be the same. Emma didn't deserve this. But if I told the truth, Courtney would make sure I took the blame for what she did. A shiver ran down my spine as I recalled searching Courtney's eyes for even a flicker of regret after Emma had been taken away in the ambulance.

Instead of remorse, Courtney's eyes had held a cold, hollow indifference that could only belong to someone who enjoyed watching others break.

Chapter Eight

Present: Day One at Sea

Gigi and Emma turn around in their seats to look at Sequim, all of us seemingly lost in our thoughts as our hometown drifts by in the backdrop. It's undeniably beautiful with the snowcapped Olympic Mountains behind it. But there's a heaviness in my chest, no matter how long I look at it. Despite how much I sometimes hated Courtney, it feels selfish, somehow, to enjoy the moment without her.

"I just read this true crime book," Beth says, breaking the silence. "*And the Sea Will Tell* by Vincent Bugliosi, the district attorney who prosecuted Charles Manson."

I turn toward her, wondering what this has to do with Sequim.

"It's about this couple, Buck and Jennifer, who sailed a rickety old sailboat to Palmyra Island, a deserted atoll smack in the middle of the Pacific, in the seventies. They meet a wealthy American couple on the island, and Buck murders them so that he and Jennifer can steal their sailboat and take it back to Hawaii."

Gigi and Emma exchange confused glances, apparently wondering the same thing as me.

"In the book," Beth says, "Bugliosi explains the difference between nautical twilight and civil twilight. *Nautical* twilight is an hour before sunrise when the fifty-three stars used for navigation at sea are no longer visible. *Civil* twilight is a half hour before sunrise, when you no longer need artificial lights, like headlights, when outdoors."

Clearly bored, Emma looks down and picks a piece of fuzz off her shawl.

"And *dawn*," Beth continues, "actually describes a time somewhere in between these two."

Gigi scrunches her nose as much as her Botox allows. "And you're telling us this because . . . ?"

Beth shrugs. "I just thought it was interesting."

Gigi flicks Emma a look of annoyance, taking me back to the start of our hike twenty years ago, when Beth rattled off facts about cougars: how they hunt, stalk, and kill. Freaking us all out until Courtney ordered Beth to shut up.

Gigi extends her wineglass toward Emma. "Emma was just telling me about her new boyfriend. *And* her housewares line that she's launching next month."

Gigi shifts to face Emma. "What's it called again?"

"Poppy."

"Congratulations," Beth says.

"Yes, that's incredible," I add.

"Thank you," Emma beams, tucking a short blond curl behind her ear. "It's going to be a lot of bright colors, very eclectic. I'm really excited about it. I'm technically not supposed to say anything yet, but I'm very close to signing an exclusive distribution contract with Target."

"Wow," Beth says.

"That's wonderful." Gigi clinks her plastic wineglass against Emma's.

"Yes," I add. "Congratulations."

"But enough about me." Emma lifts her glass toward Beth. "Did I read that you're the first female university president in the history of Elliott Bay University?"

Beth clears her throat. "Yep. And the youngest. By over twelve years." She grins. "But who's counting?"

I laugh along with the others.

"But, seriously," Beth adds. "I'm really grateful for the appointment. You guys know it's always been my dream to become a university president, but I didn't know if it would ever actually happen—especially not this soon. Some days I still have to pinch myself. I've even already been approached about a Senate run in the next election."

We all know Beth is politically connected, which helped her get the appointment in the first place. But I'm surprised that she's sharing this news of her potential Senate run with the others after she swore me to secrecy about it. Although maybe she feels a need to impress, for which I can't blame her.

"Wow, that's awesome," Emma says.

I smile at Beth, proud of how successful she's become after the trauma of returning home without Courtney our senior year. *They all have,* I think, as my gaze drifts to Emma and Gigi. *Except for me.*

"Yes, it is." Gigi sits tall. "Well, not to brag, you guys."

"*But* . . ." Beth drawls.

I chuckle.

Gigi rolls her eyes. "*But* I just got a message from Alex who told me that, as of today, I now have *three million* followers on Instagram." She runs a hand through her long blond waves that still manage to look perfect despite the wind. "He said he has a surprise for me when I get home to celebrate. He's *so* sweet."

At the mention of Gigi's husband, Emma looks down for a moment, and I recall Emma's divorce, right after my twins were born, following her short-lived marriage to her college boyfriend. I've always wondered if it was the result of Emma's temper. Thinking of my own failed marriage, I'm struck with a pang of guilt for judging her. What will people say about me when they learn of Matt's leaving?

Gigi pauses to take a drink, holding her finger in the air to signal she's not done talking. "And I think it's an Aston Martin."

Emma squeals, reminding me of the girl she was in high school.

"So, Palmer." Gigi raises her glass to me. "Tell us what's new with you. What great and exciting things are happening in your life?"

I cast a sideways glance at Beth as the devastating events of the last month play through my mind like a depressing movie.

"You're a nurse now, right?" Emma asks.

Yes, and I nearly killed someone. I study the fading Dungeness Spit, thinking of my girls and how I'm going to move forward with no husband and no job. Fear stabs my chest.

I nod, afraid if I open my mouth I might start to cry.

Gigi leans forward. "How are things with . . . Matt, right?"

All of them, including Beth, watch me, their gazes lingering as they wait for my answer. After taking a drink from my wine, I paste a wide smile on my lips. "They're fantastic. We're really happy."

"That's great," Emma says.

"So good," Gigi adds.

Beth studies me. I break eye contact to finish my wine because I know what she's thinking: Gigi isn't the only one on board who can lie through her teeth.

Chapter Nine

Present: Day Three at Sea

Giving up on sleep, I climb out of bed at the first spark of daylight, careful not to wake Beth. I hardly slept, waking to my legs shifting from side to side with every swell. Just as Nojan had warned, the four of us were mostly bedbound yesterday after we'd reached the open ocean. My stomach feels more settled this morning than yesterday even though the Pacific's waters are much rougher than I imagined.

When I step out of my stateroom, the smell of coffee fills the quiet galley. I pour myself a steaming cup from the half-filled French press before going to the upper deck.

Finding Adam at the helm, I sit on the cockpit bench and take in the gorgeous reddish sunrise peaking over the horizon. There's no longer any land in sight. Instead, a seemingly endless ocean surrounds us in every direction.

"Morning." He smiles.

"Morning." I scan the deck, thinking Nojan must be below. It's just the two of us.

"Did you find the coffee?" he asks. "I just made some before taking watch."

I lift my insulated mug. "I did, thanks."

I take a sip, the first I'd been able to stomach since we left the protected waters of the Strait of Juan de Fuca. It's almost eerily quiet as we continue to sail away from the mainland, our only power coming from the wind. After taking another drink, I send a text to my sister asking how things are going, even though she probably won't be up for another hour to get the girls ready for school. A few conversations down, I see the last text I sent Matt nearly a week ago asking why he wasn't home, to which he never responded.

"Bastard."

"Excuse me?"

Startled, I turn to the attractive first officer still at the helm. I'd forgotten I wasn't alone. "Oh, not you. My husband." I lift my phone. "Ex-husband," I correct myself. "Well, almost. He just left me for someone he works with, who's also fifteen years younger than me." I cringe at my oversharing to this handsome stranger. *Just stop talking. You don't even know him.* "Sorry," I fumble. "I don't know why I said that last part."

His expression softens. "Don't be sorry. That's awful." He flips a switch on the control panel next to the wheel and steps out from behind the helm. "He sounds like an idiot."

My cheeks flush when he takes a seat beside me. I glance beyond him toward the wheel as the bow pitches over a swell. "Don't you need to be steering?"

He shakes his head. "It's on autopilot."

"Oh, right," I say, feeling stupid. "Of course."

Adam gazes out at gently rolling waves. "I've never been married, but I know what it's like to feel betrayed by someone." He turns to me, close enough for me to see the flecks of gold in his green eyes.

My pulse flutters. Damn, he's hot. He's even more attractive up close.

"I can't imagine that person being your spouse," he adds.

"It sucks," I say.

He gestures toward the lower deck. "At least you've got some great friends here to help you through it. Seems like you've all known each other a long time."

I follow his gaze. "Since we were kids."

"You're lucky. I've lost touch with all my friends from high school. You and Beth seem really close. Not everyone has that."

I nod. "Yeah, we are. Can't imagine going through this without her." I turn toward him, not sure how we fell into such deep conversation. I'm suddenly self-conscious of saying too much, expecting him to be looking for an excuse to return to the helm. But he looks completely relaxed as his kind eyes seem to search mine.

"That must be nice to have a group of friends that you can confide in."

"Well," I think of Gigi and Emma, asleep in their separate cabins. "It's just Beth actually. The others don't know yet about my split from my husband. It just happened, and honestly, their lives just seem so perfect, I couldn't—"

"Don't worry," he places his hand on my forearm before getting up. "You're secret's safe with me. We're all guilty of not being exactly who we present ourselves to be at some point or another. And if I had to guess, their lives aren't as perfect as they're letting on either."

I shift in my seat. "Why do you say that?"

The companionway door flies open, revealing Gigi's top half. Her blond hair is a mess of waves. Eye patches are stuck beneath her eyes, and she's wearing tiny satin pajamas that could double as lingerie.

She looks past me without so much as a greeting. "Hey, Adam. Could you make me an almond milk latte and a veggie omelet? And can you put more veggies in the omelet today? I'm not one to complain, but yesterday's was a little heavy on the egg whites."

"Sure," he says.

"And maybe less mushrooms, more spinach," she adds.

After Gigi disappears below, he gives me a playful wink. "Just a hunch."

Half an hour later, I go below. My coffee mug is empty, and I'd been sitting in mostly silence with Nojan ever since he got up to replace

Adam at the helm. My stomach grumbles as I descend the steps. I felt too seasick to eat much yesterday, and I find myself suddenly hungry.

Adam looks up from the dinette table where he's cleaning off Gigi's dirty breakfast dishes. I cringe inwardly, seeing Gigi on the couch transfixed with her phone screen. Even my nine-year-old twins know to take their dishes to the kitchen when they're done eating.

"Can I make you something?" he asks.

I separate a banana from the bunch on the counter. "No, thanks. I'll start with this."

I sit beside Gigi, but she doesn't look up. I glance at her screen as I peel my banana, surprised to see she's not on social media.

"Since when have you played chess?"

"Oh." She glances at me for the first time since I came below deck. Her cheeks flush. "Most of my life, I guess. My dad taught me when I was six."

I sit back. "I never knew that."

"Well, it's not exactly something I'm proud of. It's kind of nerdy."

I take a bite of my banana. "I don't think it's nerdy. I'm impressed."

"Well, thanks." Gigi pushes a pawn deep into enemy territory in what looks to be a sacrifice, then turns to me. "But don't tell anyone, okay? It doesn't exactly fit with my brand."

She returns her attention to her game as I watch over her shoulder and take another bite. "What's that?" I point to the number in the corner of the screen.

"My winning streak."

I nearly choke. "You're on a streak of forty-one?"

"Yeah." Gigi bites her nail, looking nervously at her screen. Then I see why. I know the rules of the game, although I've never been very good.

YOUR MOVE flashes on her screen in bold white letters. It's over. Her king was one move away from being exposed to a double attack.

Gigi opted against defending her king. Leaving it exposed, she promoted her pawn. I hold my breath, knowing her winning streak is about to be over. Then I see it. Her newly anointed queen trapped her rival's king in checkmate. My mouth falls open as confetti explodes on her screen.

YOU WIN! appears in the same white letters as before. I watch Gigi calmly close out the gaming app.

"How did you see that?"

She shrugs.

"That was . . . impressive."

"It's just a game," she says as my stateroom door opens.

Beth emerges in flannel pajamas with a yawn. On her way to the bathroom, her gaze travels to Gigi. "Getting an early start on your content?"

Gigi flashes me a look before giving Beth a smile. "Sure am."

As the boat rocks beneath us, I roll into Beth on our double bed and open my eyes to the afternoon sun shining through our small cabin window.

"I don't know how you can read and not feel seasick," I say, seeing the tattered paperback of *The Handmaid's Tale* in her hand.

I binge-watched all five seasons of the show last summer, telling Beth she should watch it too. But of course, she starts with the book.

Beth shrugs. "I feel fine." She turns the page. "Guess I should've been a sailor," she adds without looking up.

I shift back toward my side of the bed, this time smacking into the wall as the boat dips to the side. After lunch, Beth and I retreated to our stateroom for a short respite from Gigi's animated live stream videos. I reach for the *Condé Nast* magazine I found in the galley and read until my eyes grow heavy, which doesn't take long. I'm drifting when an angry voice in the stateroom next door jolts me fully awake.

"You've got to be shitting me. They can't do that!"

I sit up, recognizing Emma's husky, angry voice carrying through the thin wall that divides our staterooms.

"I don't care! They can't pull my line," Emma yells. "You can't let them do this, Ryan. It's too late for them to back out. You promised me this wouldn't happen. We have to fight this."

A thump rattles the wall, likely from Emma beating her fist against it. Beth and I exchange a look.

"I am calm," Emma shouts. She huffs a sigh. "All right, fine. I'll call you later."

Emma goes quiet, and I lean closer to Beth.

"I thought her fist was going to come through the wall," I whisper.

"What do you think that's about?" Beth asks in a muted tone.

"I don't know."

Beth glances at the wall. "Maybe we should go see if she's okay."

I lie back down, recalling the black eye Emma gave Luke Branson for making a snide remark after Gigi's topless photo was spread around school. "I think we better let her cool off first."

Emma's stateroom door slams.

Beth leans back on her elbow. "You're probably right." She opens her book.

I wonder what Emma was referring to. It sounded serious, likely an issue with one of her current remodels. Emma's temper probably makes it sound worse than it really is. I close my eyes again, wanting a nap before Gigi summons us to her group photo shoot on the upper deck. "I hope it's not rough like this the whole way."

A knock sounds, and Emma's voice bleeds through the door. "Hey, Beth?"

Her calm voice is a stark contrast to the one we just heard inside her stateroom. Beth tosses her book on the bed and scoots to the edge. I sit up as she stands to open the door.

"Hey," Emma steps inside, her face slightly flushed. Otherwise, she displays no trace of the anger we overheard. "Oh." She stops, seeing me on the bed. "I thought you were on the deck."

I fight not to scrunch up my face. Despite Emma's pleasantries yesterday, I wonder if she still carries a grudge for thinking I covered up for Courtney. I swallow the guilt that rises to the back of my throat. After all this time, I've never told Emma the truth.

Emma glances behind her before motioning to Beth. "Close the door," she says in a lowered tone.

Beth obliges. "What is it?"

Emma casts me a wary gaze before perching on the end of the bed. She bends one knee onto the mattress, twisting to face both of us.

"It's Adam." Her tone is hushed, barely above a whisper. "Didn't the captain say he had years of sailing experience?"

"Yeah. Why?" Beth folds her arms and sits beside Emma.

"Because"—Emma glances at me—"just now, on the deck, the captain told him to ease out the jib."

Beth's eyebrows crease together. "What's a jib?"

"The headsail." Emma points toward the bow. "Anyway, after Adam let the sail out, he wrapped the jib sheet *counterclockwise* around the winch."

Beth and I exchange a look of confusion.

"So?" Beth asks.

Emma's eyes widen. "You *never* wrap a line counterclockwise on a sailboat!" She runs a hand through her short curls. "It's like the first thing they teach you."

"Maybe he just made a mistake," Beth says. "It's pretty rough out there."

Emma lifts her gaze to the windowed hatch over our heads. "Fortunately, Captain Nojan caught him doing it and made him redo it the right way. At least the captain seems to know what he's doing."

Beth laughs. "Gigi told me yesterday that she requested a hot deckhand. I thought she was joking, but maybe she really did. It wouldn't surprise me, knowing Gigi and the way she's been drooling over him.

"I agree that the captain is obviously competent," Beth adds. "So, Adam just needs to be able to take instructions, right? Maybe he has more experience as an onboard chef."

Emma chews her lip. "I suppose so. The meatballs he made last night were amazing."

I picture the angles of Adam's jaw, and again I feel the sense of déjà vu that spread through me two nights ago when he smiled. "Do you think there's something familiar about him?" I ask Emma.

She shakes her head. "No, why?"

"I feel like I've seen him before, but I can't place where."

"I told her it's because he looks like Chris Pratt," Beth says.

"He does," I say. "But I still feel like I know him from somewhere."

Emma gestures toward me. "Don't you work at a hospital? Maybe he was a patient."

I stare at the wooden cabin door. "Maybe." But he doesn't seem to know me.

"Hey, guys," Gigi's soft voice sounds on the other side of our cabin door.

Emma stands and opens it, pressing one hand against the wall as the boat shifts.

Gigi looks pale, her skin nearly the same shade as the oatmeal-colored Lululemon hoodie she has her hands jammed into.

Gigi lifts her aviators to the top of her sun hat, revealing cheeks heavily caked with blush—a failed attempt to hide her seasick pallor. In fact, I think she's made it worse.

"I want to get a group photo on the deck."

"Can we do it later?" Beth lifts her book. "I'm reading, and Palmer's trying to take a nap."

Gigi shakes her head. "Sorry, I have to post it when my followers are most active."

Beth groans.

"It won't take long," Gigi adds.

Emma follows her out of our cabin. "My producer is on me to get a post out anyway."

"Come on." I tug Beth's arm, lowering my voice. "It's just a photo. Plus, her sponsor's paying for this whole trip."

"Okay, fine." Beth stands, and we pull on our life vests.

As I climb the stairs, the boat dips, and I reach for the handle mounted to the wall to keep from falling backward onto Beth. The wind whips my ponytail in front of my eyes when we reach the deck. After pushing my hair back, I spot Captain Nojan at the helm. Adam, wearing a matching navy polo, is stationed a few feet in front of the captain, letting slack out on a line.

"Hey, Adam," Nojan says. "I need you to take the helm."

My gaze lingers on Adam as he wraps the line around a winch three times—clockwise, I note—before turning for the large steering wheel near the stern.

"Passing the helm," Nojan says when Adam reaches him.

Nojan steps aside for Adam to take his place behind the wheel.

"Taking the helm," Adam says.

I study Adam's long tanned fingers gripping the steering wheel. Before I can stop myself, I start imagining how his hands would feel running over my body. I lift my gaze to Adam's face as he catches me looking at him. He maintains eye contact for an uncomfortable moment until I look away. My heart flutters as my eyes fall to my wedding ring, glittering in the sun. Why was he staring at me like that? Did he like me looking at him? It's hard to imagine he'd be attracted to me with Gigi parading around her perfect body. Maybe he was trying to make me feel uncomfortable after catching me staring at him.

I follow Emma toward Gigi, who is seated in the covered cockpit taking a series of photos with her selfie stick. Beth stumbles forward, bumping into my back as the boat sways from a large swell.

"Sorry, Palm," she says, sliding onto the nearest bench beside Emma.

"I need you to keep us on a broad reach while I use the head," Nojan says to Adam, pointing at the weather vane at the top of the towering mast. "The wind's starting to shift to the northeast, so make sure you head up if we start sailing by the lee."

"Got it."

I study Adam, who looks confidently at the navigation screens mounted above the wheel as Nojan moves past me to the companionway. Emma's concerns over Adam's inexperience play at my mind, making me wonder if we're all a little paranoid after our rafting trip.

Whitecaps have formed on the growing swells beyond the boat. I shade my eyes with my hand to gaze at the horizon, pivoting to take in the water all around us. My arms prickle with goose bumps. The coast has disappeared. We're surrounded by choppy seas as far as the eye can see.

The floor shifts beneath my feet. I reach for the table to steady myself.

"Palmer." I turn to the sound of Gigi's voice.

"You sit here," Gigi points to the open spot beside Beth and climbs onto the deck behind the bench. "Emma and I will sit up here." Gigi sinks to her knees as I sit.

"Ready?" Gigi asks once Emma is on the deck beside her.

Gigi extends her arm, lifting her phone above our heads with the aid of her selfie stick. "Smile!"

I lean into Beth and beam at the camera, filled with a strange sense of familiarity of when we reached the trailhead the morning of our fateful hike and Courtney took a photo of all of us for the last time.

A second later, Gigi lowers her phone. "Oh, Palmer! You got cut off. Hang on guys, let me take another."

After we do another take, I lift my eyes to the mainsail flapping in the wind.

"The mainsail is luffing," Emma says.

I crane my neck to see Emma frowning as she looks up at the weather vane. I follow her gaze, seeing the arrow pointing straight behind us.

Emma turns toward the helm as Gigi gets to her feet.

"Everyone stay where they are," Gigi says. "I'm going to grab a quick video pan of all of us."

"Hey, Adam?" Emma calls, pointing toward the large sail. "We're heading straight downwind, and the mainsail's luffing."

Gigi shrieks as a gust of wind comes over the side of the boat. I spin to see her sun hat fly off. She twists and lurches forward, reaching for her hat blowing toward the bow.

"Gigi, watch out!" Emma screams as Gigi steps onto the elevated roof of the saloon while her hat lifts higher into the air.

And that's when I see it. The boom swings over our heads from the force of the wind, straight toward Gigi. Gigi turns to the sound of Emma's scream as the boom smacks her in the temple.

I gasp as Gigi stumbles backward, falling off the raised platform onto the deck. Her selfie stick clamors to the deck beside her.

"Gigi, don't!" Emma cries.

I grip Beth's arm as we watch Gigi roll to grab her phone before it slips over the edge.

The boat turns violently, heeling toward the ocean on our side. Keeping hold of the lifeline, Emma reaches for Gigi with her other hand.

"Gigi!" Adam yells, rushing toward her in my periphery.

But he's too late. Gigi rolls under the lifeline—into the water—as the bow lifts over a large swell.

Chapter Ten

October 2004

The night of Emma's "accident," Beth drove me home to Courtney's house. I'd planned on telling the truth after Beth and I had visited Emma in the hospital. But after seeing the pain Emma was in and the strained look on her mom's face, which mirrored the look my own mom so often wore, I hadn't been able to bring myself to do it. Her mom had raised Emma on her own, just like my mom had raised my older sister and me. Emma probably knew as well as I did how much harder this injury would make life at home, what with her mom juggling a job and raising Emma alone. And even if I did convince Emma that Courtney was to blame, it wouldn't be for long. Courtney would use that photo she took to ensure I went down for what she'd done. Unless I could convince Courtney to do the right thing.

After hearing Courtney come home from the football game, I went to her room. She was reclining against her cushioned headboard, writing in her diary when I reached her half-open doorway.

"Hey," I said. "I need to talk to you."

"Oh. Hey, Palmer." She set down the leather-bound diary open on the bed beside her. "Sure, what's up?" Her sweet, innocent smile made my stomach twist. She had to know what I needed to talk to her about. Did she really have no remorse over Emma lying in a hospital bed because of what we'd done?

"Emma had to have surgery on her broken ankle. It's bad, Courtney. She's still in the hospital." I sighed, collapsing on the end of Courtney's four-poster bed. "I feel horrible." My gaze dropped to my hands in my lap. "We have to come clean about the dish soap. We can't let Bryson and Jake get blamed for that."

"Nothing is going to happen to them."

I turned to face her. "How can you say that?"

Courtney flicked her eyes toward the ceiling as if I were the dumbest person in the world. "Because they're *guys*." She tossed her pen onto her diary that lay open on the bed between us.

I looked down at the lined pages and gasped. I slid the diary closer to me. *"Courtney."*

She had drawn a picture of me pouring dish soap on the locker room floor. Courtney stood beside me, covering her mouth. Emma was on the floor, her face contorted in pain with her ankle bent in a way that wasn't right. Courtney had always been a good artist, but if it weren't already clear enough who the people were, she'd written our names above our heads.

I looked up and gaped at her. "Why would you draw this?"

"That's private." Courtney snatched the diary off the bed and snapped it shut before setting it inside her nightstand drawer.

"What if someone finds it?"

She shrugged. "Relax. They won't."

I felt my eyes narrow. "You drew *me* squirting the soap. You were the one who did it."

"Only because you chickened out." She folded her arms. "I drew it the way it was supposed to go."

I stared at her in disbelief. "Did you *want* that to happen to Emma?"

She scoffed, casting me a wounded gaze. "Of course not. I feel horrible, Palmer. It's awful." Then she stood, flicking her long red hair behind her shoulder before pulling off her sweater.

I trailed Courtney toward her walk-in closet, gritting my teeth. Through the French door windows leading to Courtney's second-story balcony, Sequim's city lights twinkled at the bottom of Bell Hill. On a clear day, you could see Mount Baker in the distance. The smell of the Ocean Dream perfume inside her closet was so potent it made my eyes burn.

"You saw how bad Emma's ankle was," I continued. "She'll be out for the rest of the season. She could even have permanent damage. We have to tell the truth. What if Bryson and Jake get expelled?"

Watching Courtney change into her Victoria's Secret PINK pajamas, I thought of the two California sophomores she had said were facing criminal charges for prank calling.

"They won't. Their reputation doesn't matter like ours. No one's going to care if they think Bryson and Jake squirted the dish soap on the floor. But if we say *we* did it"—Courtney moved away from her walk-in closet, pointing a finger at her chest—"we'll get kicked off the volleyball team! Plus, we didn't say we saw them squirt the dish soap, just that they were in the girls' locker room being stupid. So, they'll hate us. Who cares? Trust me, nothing's going to come of it."

Later that night, when I laid in the guest room on the other side of Courtney's wall, I prayed she was right. But as I stared at the ceiling in the dark, all I could think about was that picture Courtney had drawn. Why had she done that?

Courtney's reassurance that no one would see it didn't make me feel any better. She had shown me pieces of her diary before, including an entry about how she'd discovered that Gigi had cheated on her boyfriend our sophomore year. Although, after seeing Courtney's drawing, I wondered if Gigi hadn't cheated after all. Courtney even took her diary to school in her backpack sometimes. What if she showed someone that drawing?

I rolled onto my side, knowing I couldn't leave that drawing in Courtney's diary. Especially if I played along with Courtney's lie about Bryson and Jake. I'd have to sneak into her room when she wasn't home and destroy it.

◆ ◆ ◆

Courtney's bedroom door opened with a creak. I cringed at the sound, pausing in the darkened doorway to see if I'd woken her. But the only sound coming from inside her room was Courtney's soft snores.

I crept toward her bed. It had been a week since I'd seen that disgustingly twisted drawing in Courtney's diary, and I'd given up on thinking I could sneak into her room when she wasn't home. Today in Spanish class when Courtney unzipped her backpack, I'd spotted her diary tucked between two notebooks. For the rest of the day, I imagined her showing it to Gigi or Beth or worse—Emma—and I knew I couldn't wait any longer to destroy it.

The photo of me holding the soap on Courtney's phone was worse than the drawing, but I couldn't do anything about that until Courtney got her phone back from her parents. They had caught Courtney sneaking out with her boyfriend last Saturday night, leaving her grounded without her phone, and my only chance to get at her diary was when Courtney was asleep.

Yesterday was Emma's first day back at school, and she'd been crushed to learn that a volleyball scout from UW had watched our playoff game that we'd won while she was still in the hospital. Emma told Beth and me that her mom was looking into suing the school over her hospital bill.

I stepped on a pair of jeans on Courtney's floor as I moved toward her nightstand. My eyes had adjusted enough to the dark for me to make out the outline of her bed. Courtney continued to snore softly as I opened the nightstand drawer. I held my breath, but thankfully, it slid open without a sound.

I felt inside but couldn't find anything that resembled her leather-bound diary. I swept my hand around the drawer, knocking around what felt like two bottles of nail polish and a ChapStick. I glanced at Courtney, making sure the noise hadn't roused her. She rolled over, turning away from me. I froze until her snoring resumed.

I exhaled and pulled my phone from my sweatpants pocket and used the glow from the screen to see inside the drawer. There was hand lotion, nail polish, ChapStick, and a *Seventeen* magazine. But no diary.

I shone my phone on top of thc nightstand before sweeping the light toward Courtney's bed. I leaned over to see her face. Her mouth was open, and a fuzzy sleep mask covered her eyes. I shone the light over the bed and spotted the purple leather diary tucked under her arm. Biting my lip, I reached over Courtney and slowly slid it out from under her elbow.

Spit caught in Courtney's throat, erupting in a sharp sound. Courtney cleared her throat and twisted to the side, draping her arm over my hand gripping the diary. I held still, turning off my phone light, afraid she would be jarred awake by my cold hand beneath her forearm and demand to know what I was doing. If she *did* wake up, I had planned to say I couldn't sleep and had come in to talk. But how would I explain my hand on her diary?

But she remained still, and her snores resumed. I pulled the diary out from under her arm. Using the light from my phone, I flipped through the pages until I found the drawing. My face flushed with anger seeing the uncanny mirror of myself, squirting the dish soap that broke Emma's ankle. I set my phone on Courtney's bed and ripped out the page as quietly as I could.

Courtney coughed. Startled, I dropped the diary. I flicked my gaze toward her. She turned onto her other side but appeared to stay asleep. I needed to get out of her room before she caught me. Courtney would probably realize at some point that her drawing was missing, but as long as she didn't find me in her room, I could deny it was me.

I grabbed my phone and used the screen to light up the diary. Spotting Courtney's distinct bubbly handwriting, I paused to read the page it had opened to.

October 19, 2004

Dear Diary,
Today I learned that one of my "friends" has been trash-talking me behind my back. I'm crushed. I've

> been such a good friend to this person for almost our entire lives. It's more than disappointing. It's . . . sad.
>
> I shouldn't be surprised. Some people can't handle it when others are better than them.
>
> I guess my parents are right. No matter how kind you are, there are people who can't handle having less and think tearing you down will bring them up. Instead of becoming better themselves, they try to hurt you instead.
>
> I'm not ready to share who this traitor is yet. I'm too upset. Plus, I have a plan on how to get her back.
>
> I need to make sure she regrets this. Teach her a lesson. And I know exactly how to make her pay.

I looked over at Courtney, resisting the urge to slap her awake and demand to know who she was talking about. I dropped my gaze to the date at the top of her diary entry. It was the same day Emma broke her ankle from our prank gone wrong. I closed the diary and stared at Courtney sleeping peacefully in her four-poster bed.

Had Courtney *planned* to hurt Emma? *No,* I think. That would make Courtney a monster. Plus, she's Emma's friend. It was why she was always giving her clothes. Just like how she was letting me stay at her house. And there was no way Courtney could've known Emma would break her ankle. I carefully replaced the diary on her bed where I'd found it.

I crept out of her room, crumpling the stupid drawing in my hand when I got to the hall. I tucked the balled-up paper into my backpack to throw it away at school tomorrow so Courtney's mom wouldn't find it in the trash. Then I crawled back into my bed and worked to convince myself that Courtney had to have written that diary entry about someone other than Emma. Courtney could be a spoiled brat, but she wasn't evil.

Because if Courtney *had* wanted to hurt Emma, she'd used me like a pawn to help her do it.

Chapter Eleven

Present: Day Three at Sea

Gigi hits the ocean with a splash, her hoodie disappearing beneath the waves.

"Man overboard!" Adam yells.

He rushes past us in a blur as Emma and Beth call out for Gigi in panicked screams. Gigi's life vest inflates with a whoosh and her head breaks the surface. She gulps for air as we speed away, the distance between her and the stern rapidly increasing.

"Gigi!" I scream.

Beth covers her mouth.

Behind us, Captain Nojan swears. I spin to see him emerge from the companionway while zipping up his shorts. He shouts at Adam: "Release the dan buoy!"

"Releasing the dan buoy," Adam yells. "I need a spotter."

"I'll do it," I say, standing on the bench and gripping the bar of the cockpit cover as I point at Gigi. "She's about thirty feet behind the boat."

"Shit, this is why I said not to sail by the lee," Nojan barks at Adam as he takes the helm. "So we wouldn't risk an accidental jibe. And why the hell wasn't she tethered?"

Beth and I remain in the cockpit while Emma tosses a flotation sling into the water near the rear pulpit. But with the wind at our back, the flotation device lands in the sea only a few feet behind the boat. Emma's top half topples over the pulpit railing as the stern rolls over a swell. Adam grabs her arm, pulling her backward onto the deck floor as Nojan spins the wheel.

"Get a tether on," Nojan orders Emma.

Adam tosses something lime green into the water. When it hits the surface, it inflates several feet in the air, reminding me of the inflatable Air Dancers used for advertising outside of car washes and used-car lots, only thinner.

I keep my eyes and finger trained on Gigi's bobbing head, as Captain Nojan instructed us before we departed. The lime-green buoy made it farther than the life sling Emma tossed, but Gigi can hardly stay afloat in these powerful waves. My heart thuds against my chest as I assess the distance between the buoy and Gigi. At the top of the buoy streams a long bright ribbon. *There's no way she can reach it.* A wave crashes over Gigi's head.

My mind flashes to that day twenty years ago. Courtney, falling into the Sol Duc. Gigi screaming her name. I step onto the upper deck and teeter toward the lifeline when Beth's fingers dig into my upper arm, pulling me back onto the cockpit bench. Gigi disappears beneath the rough sea.

"She's gone under!" I shake out of Beth's hold, scouring the rolling waves for a sign of her blond hair as Emma gets to her knees and hooks a rope to her life vest.

Gigi emerges amid the swell, flailing her arms frantically and gulping for air before going under again.

"She's sixty feet directly behind the boat," I shout as Nojan turns the boat around. "But she's gone under again. I can't see her."

With a fixed jaw, Nojan studies his navigation screen. "I see her beacon on her life vest. She's one and a half boat lengths dead astern." He glances at me. "Keep your eyes on her."

Beth scrambles to the rear of the cockpit, connecting her life vest to the tether ropes lying near Nojan's feet. She clips one to mine as I strain to find a sign of Gigi's blond hair amid the powerful waves. The boat heels from Nojan's sharp turn.

Nojan turns to Emma. "Get on the starboard side or you'll fall in too."

Emma moves unsteadily to the other side of the boat and crouches beside Adam who holds a long boat hook over the side.

I slip my sunglasses above my head, squinting from the midday sun streaming through the patchy clouds, scanning the roaring waves for Gigi.

"You sit down," the captain tells Beth before turning to Emma and Adam behind him. "Be ready to throw her that rope and hold out that boat hook to her when we get close." He glances at his navigation screen. "Gigi should be coming up on the starboard side one boat length ahead."

I don my sunglasses as I search the rolling waves, deciding I see better with them on. But I don't see Gigi. Only the bright-green buoy with its long ribbon flapping in the wind as it bobs over a swell. Then I spot her.

"There she is," I shout, pointing at Gigi's blond head to the right of the bow. Even with the life vest, she's struggling to stay afloat. "Hang on, Gigi!"

Her cheeks are streaked with mascara as she spews out a mouthful of water.

"Throw her a line," Nojan shouts. "And have her grab the boat hook."

"It's okay, Gigi," I yell from the back of the cockpit. "Get ready to grab a rope!"

"*We need to slow down*!" I call out as the middle of the boat sails past her.

Gigi coughs before gasping for air while we speed by.

"We're going too fast." I'm filled with the same helplessness I felt when my raft carried me away from Courtney when she was swept under by the Sol Duc's current. I move to the edge of the deck and grip the stanchion with one hand as a wave pushes Gigi away from the hull. Within seconds, she's more than ten feet from the boat.

I scoop up a coiled blue rope near my feet and toss it over the side. "Grab this line!"

The end of the rope hits the water a few feet from Gigi. She reaches for it as Adam extends the boat hook over the side. Emma throws another line, but a gust of wind catches it, tossing it back at the boat before it hits the water.

Adam turns to the captain. "Turn thirty degrees starboard. I can't reach her."

As Nojan turns the wheel, my eyes widen at the large swell growing in height beyond where Gigi is struggling to reach the sinking rope.

"Big wave coming—watch out!" I shout seconds before the swell engulfs the top of Gigi's head.

"Court—" I hear myself scream as she disappears beneath the waves. "Gigi!"

"Shit." Beside me, Emma stares into the water. "She hadn't reached the rope yet."

I hold my breath as the wave crashes against the side of the boat.

"Hang on," Nojan yells.

I clench my grip around the metal stanchion, sinking to my knees for stability as water sprays onto the deck. Beth cries out behind me as she's thrown back. She catches herself on the table as the boat rocks to either side from the wave that just pummeled us.

"Who has eyes on Gigi?" Nojan asks.

Through my salt water–sprayed sunglasses, I scour the rolling waters for a sign of Gigi surfacing. "I can't find her."

"Wait, there she is!" Emma points beyond the back corner of the boat.

My eyes follow Emma's finger to see Gigi's wet hair and inflated life vest rolling over the top of a swell. "Oh, God."

Gigi's previously flailing arms are no longer moving, and her eyes are fluttering closed. She looks to be on the brink of unconsciousness, her life vest the only thing keeping her afloat.

Adam sucks in a deep breath before he dives off the rear starboard pulpit.

Chapter Twelve

Present: Day Three at Sea

Transfixed with horror, I watch Adam swim after Gigi through the rough ocean, my breath stagnant in my lungs. Captain Nojan steers us closer to the two in the water, and the boat tilts.

"Keep eyes on them," Nojan orders.

Beth joins Emma and me on the edge of the deck.

"We're coming for you, Gigi, just hold on!" Beth yells as Nojan turns sharply in their direction.

Gigi disappears under a swell. Beth squeezes my hand, and I grip the shroud beside me to keep my balance as we watch Adam dive to reach her.

As the swell rolls beneath our boat, I spot Adam surface with Gigi tucked under his arm.

"There they are!" Emma stands, pointing.

Adam turns onto his back and swims toward the boat while Gigi coughs, spurting water before gulping for air. A wave nearly tears her out of Adam's grasp. He stops swimming to grab hold of her with his other arm. Gigi chokes as a whitecap hits her face.

"Hang on, Gigi," I call.

"Throw another line out for Gigi in case Adam loses her," Nojan shouts.

When they get a few feet from the boat, I toss a second rope over the side. Adam snatches the line and helps Gigi loop it around her hand. Nojan moves beside Emma, and together they pull Adam and Gigi closer.

"Come around the stern," Nojan tells Adam as he guides the rope over the stern platform.

We move to help as Nojan lowers the ladder. Nojan and Emma pull Gigi up first. On her hands and knees on the rear deck, she sputters salt water.

Beth and I help Gigi to her feet while Emma and the captain pull Adam on board.

When I wrap my arm around her wet waist, Gigi's entire body shivers.

"We need to get you dry," I say.

"I'll grab towels." Emma lets go of Adam's arm once he's on deck and untethers her life vest before turning and heading down the companionway. Beth and I slowly lead Gigi toward the lower deck, careful not to let her feet slip.

Emma emerges from her stateroom with two white towels as Beth and I guide Gigi down the companionway steps. Emma wraps one around Gigi's shoulders while I help her sit down.

"That scared the shit out of me," Emma says, her eyes on Gigi.

I take a seat beside Gigi and assess her drenched, trembling form. "Do you think you lost consciousness at all out there?"

She shakes her head. "No."

Her large eyes are raccooned with mascara, and her quivering lips have taken on a blueish hue.

Nojan's voice drifts down from the cockpit. "An accidental jibe is one of the most dangerous things that can happen on a sailboat, especially if the boom preventer wasn't installed properly. You were supposed to check it before we departed."

"I'm sorry, it won't happen again," Adam says.

"Hell, she could've died!"

We all turn toward the sound of the captain's shout.

"Go get changed," Nojan says, the calm returning to his voice. "After I make sure Gigi is okay, I want to go over some things with you."

Our gazes are already fixed on the companionway when Adam comes below, dripping wet, followed by the captain.

"Are you all right?" Adam asks Gigi after taking the towel Emma extends to him.

"I am now. Thank you." Her lips shiver. "For saving me."

The captain shoots Adam a sharp look.

"Don't thank me," Adam says, dropping his gaze to the floor as he rubs the towel against the back of his head. "That was my fault that we jibed. And I should've made sure you had a tether on."

I place my palm against Gigi's shivering back as Adam gives Gigi a remorseful glance, then disappears inside his stateroom.

The captain holds an uninflated life vest in his hands. He folds his arms, his face grim when Beth sits next to Gigi.

"You could've drowned," Nojan says.

"I'm fine." Gigi's voice trembles. She lifts her gaze to the captain's. "Really."

Nojan frowns. "We should go back to port so you can get proper medical attention. Have you assessed for injuries."

"No!" Gigi sits tall. "I have to finish this trip, or I'll lose my sponsorship. Please. I promise I'll be more careful."

The captain holds her stare without responding.

"I can't go back now," Gigi continues, her eyes brimming with tears. "I need this."

I turn to her as she shivers beside me, surprised by the desperation in her tone. From the lifestyle she's living, I doubt she's much *in need* of anything.

"I'm a nurse," I offer. "I can make sure she gets warmed up and that she's okay."

The captain's chest heaves with a sigh. He looks from me to Gigi.

"All right," he finally says. He extends the life vest toward Gigi. "Here. You can wear this PFD for now. The one you have on is going to need to be repacked and rearmed with a new CO2 canister before it will work again."

He wags his finger toward Gigi after she accepts the life vest. "I want everyone clipping a tether to their life vest *anytime* they're on deck. And always make sure you're out of the way of the boom. And no leaving the cockpit unless you've asked my permission to go forward. Understood?"

Gigi nods eagerly. "Understood."

The captain grunts before going upstairs, and Emma moves toward Gigi.

"I'm so glad you're okay."

"I know." Beth places a hand on her chest. "It reminded me of—" She stops, her gaze falling to the floor. "Well, you know."

Gigi doesn't move, doesn't stop shivering, but her gaze slides up to meet Emma's, and what I see there makes me draw back. It's the same look I've given Beth countless times since Courtney's disappearance—she's hiding something.

Chapter Thirteen

March 2005

"What's the surprise?" Beside me, Emma looked across the cafeteria table at Courtney as she unwrapped a squished peanut butter and jelly sandwich.

Courtney licked her finger after taking the Tupperware lid off her salad. "Wait until Gigi gets here."

Bryson stood from the table beside ours, the legs of his chair screeching against the linoleum floor. His eyes met mine for a flicker of a moment before he averted his gaze. I set down my string cheese, swallowing my self-hatred for going along with Courtney's lie all these months later. Somehow, Courtney had managed to convince the rest of the school that Bryson and Jake were responsible for the dish soap on the locker room floor.

Over the last few months, Courtney had gone to great lengths to convince Emma of it, too, cozying up to her and laying her charms on thick. I didn't think Emma would've believed Courtney if it weren't for Bryson and Jake being such assholes to us, including Emma, after being wrongly accused. I'd noticed that Emma had started accepting the chai tea Courtney brought her almost every day from Tornado, Emma's favorite coffee shop. I doubted she was 100 percent convinced that Courtney was telling the truth, but I could tell that Emma at least wanted to believe her.

While I was still staying at Courtney's house, I'd snuck into her room another time in hope of deleting the photo she'd taken of me holding the dish soap. But after trying every four-digit number combo I could think of, I'd finally given up. Apparently, when it came to locking her phone, Courtney was smarter than I'd given her credit for.

I watched Courtney take a bite of her salad. If she'd ever discovered someone had ripped that drawing out of her diary, she'd never said anything. At least not to me.

Bryson strode past Emma's seat at the cafeteria table. "Bitch," he muttered under his breath.

Beside me, Emma's head jerked upward. "What'd you say, dickweed?"

She made a move to get up, and I grabbed her forearm.

"Emma, don't."

Courtney met my gaze from across the table. She'd been right. Aside from the two football players hating us, they had faced no repercussions for what we'd accused them of. They'd lost a few friends, but surprisingly, like Courtney had said, most of their male friends didn't seem to care. Even thought their prank was cool. Among most of the guys, they were actually *more* popular now.

"So, what's this exciting news you have for us?" Gigi sat beside Courtney, plopping her backpack on the floor next to her after setting her cafeteria tray on the table.

Courtney turned to Gigi. "You know that prom dress you saw in *Seventeen* that you said was to die for?"

"The one that cost almost two thousand dollars?" Gigi twisted her long hair around her finger. "Of course I do."

Courtney grinned. "I ordered it for you."

My mouth fell open. Even though I knew Courtney's family was rich, it was so different from my own reality that sometimes it still shocked me.

Gigi gaped at Courtney. "You *did*?"

Courtney nodded.

"Wow." Gigi placed a hand over her heart. "I don't even know what to say. Thank you." Gigi smiled, but it looked strained.

I glanced at Beth. She and I had both wondered how Gigi could be so quick to believe Courtney wasn't responsible for the topless photos in the school hallways. But seeing Gigi's reaction now made me suspect Gigi hadn't given Courtney a pass after all.

"You're welcome." Courtney swiped her hand through the air. "But that's not my exciting news." She straightened, swiveling in her seat to face Beth, Emma, and me across the table. "Okay, so I know we're still a few months away from graduation, but I read in a magazine how senior trips can be a great bonding experience and how friends who take them are more likely to stay close when they get older. And since I was our team captain, I thought I should be the one to plan the trip."

Emma's eyes darkened when Courtney mentioned the position she'd taken over after Emma had broken her ankle, despite the volleyball season being over.

"*So,* since Palmer's mom won't let her go to Mexico like I wanted for spring break"—Courtney rolled her eyes—"I thought of another trip we can take that will be really bonding, and something we'll remember forever."

"What?" Beth asked before popping a Dorito into her mouth.

Courtney's eyes widened with excitement. "A rafting trip. On Memorial Day weekend. Down the Sol Duc River. We'll hike in, camp overnight—"

Gigi choked on her Diet Coke. *"Camp?"*

Courtney nodded enthusiastically. "I already bought all the supplies at Swain's."

Beth set her empty chip bag on the table. "Isn't that dangerous?" She shot me a sideways glance, tucking a frizzy, dark wave of hair behind her ear.

Courtney shrugged. "We can totally handle it. My brother did it with some friends a few years ago when he was training for the Marines." Her green-eyed gaze fell to Beth's bag of chips. "It might also help you lose a few pounds. You'll have to work it off somehow if you keep eating like that."

My head jerked toward Beth to gauge her reaction. *Why does Courtney have to be so mean sometimes?* Beth had always been pudgy, even in kindergarten. But she wasn't fat—she just wasn't built with the same lean frame as some of the rest of us. Okay, all of us.

Beth stuck another Dorito into her mouth, and I was relieved to see that she looked unfazed by Courtney's snide remark.

Gigi stared at Courtney. "We're not Marines."

Courtney batted her eyes, turning to meet Gigi's skeptical gaze. "We're athletes."

"I don't know," I said, doubting my mom would allow me to go.

Courtney slapped her palm on the table. "You guys. It's going to be amazing. A wild adventure. We need this. If we can raft the Sol Duc, we can do anything." She gestured to me. "Like go to medical school." Then to Beth. "Or become president of a university." She motioned to Emma. "Or—"

"You two aren't gonna get away with this."

Our heads turned toward Jake scowling at Courtney and me from the end of our table. He turned to Emma. "Your mom should be suing *them*." With a clenched jaw, he pointed his finger at Courtney, then me. "They're lying."

My blood ran cold as I studied Courtney.

"Bryson and I had nothing to do with that dish soap in the locker room," Jake said, "and you all know it." His long pointer finger traveled around our table. "Or maybe you did it yourself?" He cocked his head toward Emma. "For attention. And now what? You're hoping to get rich by ruining Bryson's and my lives?"

"Screw you, Jake." Courtney shot him a sharp, menacing glare.

Gigi scrunched up her face, looking at Emma across the table. "What's he talking about? You're not suing them, right?"

Emma flushed, looking uncomfortable. "My mom is suing the school over my medical bills. But not Bryson and Jake. Our insurance didn't cover as much of my hospital bills as she'd hoped. She didn't know what else to do."

As Jake braced himself on the back of the empty chair across from Emma, a harsh glint lingered in his narrowed eyes, revealing the fury he was trying to contain. "And now the school's coming after *us*," Jake seethed.

Jake looked straight at Courtney, then to me. The accusation in his hazel eyes sent my heart into overdrive.

Jake turned to Emma with a wolfish grin, lips twisting at the corner, sharp and cutting, as though savoring her discomfort. "It's not my fault your dad left, and your mom never went to college."

Emma was out of her seat before any of us could stop her. With both palms, she shoved Jake. He fell backward onto a table filled with freshman. A girl shrieked as Jake landed on the table, spilling milk down the side onto her lap. She jumped from her seat.

"Hey!" Mr. Reynolds, our twenty-two-year-old school-lunch monitor speedwalked across the cafeteria with his hand in the air. "Stop right now!"

Jake sat up, and with gritted teeth, Emma lunged for him, but Courtney stepped in front of her as I reached up and tugged on Emma's arm.

"I said *stop*," Mr. Reynolds yelled. "You're both going to the office."

The cafeteria had gone quiet.

Jake pushed himself off the table. "Shit, Emma."

"Watch your language," Mr. Reynolds snapped.

Emma leaned toward Jake, pulling against my grip on her arm. "Like you'll ever know anything about making money—you've always had everything handed to you. Loser."

Mr. Reynolds stepped toward Emma. "That's enough." His tone was sharp, demanding obedience.

Jake picked his hat up off the floor. "My parents are gonna sue you. And you're going to lose."

"Let's go. *Now.*" Mr. Reynolds put his hand on Jake's back, guiding him toward the door. "Come on, Emma."

Emma turned to Courtney and me, the anger in her eyes now replaced with tears. "I asked my mom not to sue. But my surgery bill was so much . . . she didn't know what else to do."

I looked to Courtney, willing her to tell the truth. I'd never expected there to be this ripple effect from one stupid action. Keeping this secret was making me sick. Staring at Courtney, I knew she'd never confess. I had to be the one to do it.

"Emma, I—"

"Good for your mom." Courtney wrapped her arm around Emma, cutting me off. "Those guys shouldn't be able to get away with hurting you like that. What if you'd hit your head? You could've died."

I gaped at Courtney.

"That's all the more why we should do this trip. We'll never get this year back."

Mr. Reynolds whipped around. "Emma! The office. *Now.*"

Courtney lowered her arm as Emma followed after Mr. Reynolds and Jake.

The cafeteria's silence morphed into murmurings as Courtney returned to her seat. While Emma and Jake were ushered into the hall, Courtney lifted her salad fork as if nothing had happened.

"So, who's in?"

Chapter Fourteen

Present: Day Three at Sea

Adam emerges from his stateroom in dry clothes.

"Thank you again for jumping in after me," Gigi tells him, wrapping the towel tighter around her shoulders.

"You're welcome." His expression turns serious. "But let's not do it again, yeah?"

I try not to stare at how his T-shirt clings to his pectoral muscles before he turns to head back up. Instead, I put my hand on the damp towel on Gigi's back. "You should get in some dry clothes."

Gigi's eyes widen as she sucks in a sharp breath. "My phone! What am I going to do?"

"I think they call that being 'unplugged,'" Beth says, making quotation marks with her fingers. "It's good for you."

Gigi presses either side of her temple. "I can't be *unplugged*. I have to be posting regularly. It's why they paid for Starlink." She looks up at Emma and Beth. "You guys will all have to help me film content. Then, I can use one of your phones to post through my account. Or we can send everything to my assistant." She exhales and leans back against the couch. "I guess that will work."

I stand and grab her by the hand. "First, how about you get changed so you don't get hypothermia?"

Gigi allows me to pull her to her feet, her wet hair dripping onto my forearms. "Okay, good idea." She lets go of my hand.

"I'm going up to get some air," Emma says as Gigi goes into her private stateroom and shuts the door.

Beth pushes herself off the couch, staggering to the side as the boat sways. She catches herself on the table before falling over.

"I'm going to finish my book."

"Really?" I say. "You're going to go back to reading after all that?"

She throws me a look over her shoulder when she gets to our stateroom. "Why not?"

I shake my head as she closes the door to our room, a half smile forming on my lips. I knock on Gigi's door.

"You doing okay in there?"

"Yes, mother."

I smile, glad to hear her sounding back to normal. But until I make sure she's okay, I'll stay close. I decide to go to the bathroom while I wait. Who knows how long it will take her to change? It took her over an hour to get ready for breakfast this morning, while the rest of us rolled out of bed and came out in search of coffee and mimosas.

When I emerge from the bathroom, Gigi is still in her room. I hear the zip of her bag, so I don't knock again. I'm getting a drink from the fridge when the door to Emma's room opens and Adam steps out.

He startles at my presence before his face morphs into a smile. "Hey, Palmer."

"That's Emma's room," I say.

"Yeah." He gestures over his shoulder. "I was just replacing the towels we used for Gigi. Hope that's the most excitement we have this trip."

I return his smile. "Yeah, me too."

Another door opens, and I turn to find Gigi wearing a black crochet maxi dress beneath the new PFD Nojan gave her. Her mascara has been wiped away from beneath her eyes, and a normal color has returned to her mouth. Unless it's lipstick.

"Good as new," she says, "Well, except for my hair." She runs her hand down her long braid.

"You still look fabulous, Gigi. You couldn't look bad if you tried." It was the truth.

She grins. "It's too bad none of you filmed my falling overboard. *That* would've been great content." Her smile fades. "I don't know how I'm going to live without my phone for the rest of this trip. I should've brought a spare."

I open my can of sparkling water. "At least it's just your phone at the bottom of the ocean and not you."

"True." Gigi tilts her head. "But it still sucks." She moves toward the deck. "You coming up?"

I shake my head. "Not right now. Don't you think you should have a rest?"

"I'm good."

"Here." I grab my zip-up sweatshirt off the dining seat. "At least stay warm while you're up there."

Gigi eyes my faded hoodie before pulling it on.

"Now that's a look," I say as the shifting floor thrusts my hip against the counter.

Gigi grins, grabbing the wall for balance. "Thanks, Palmer."

I watch Gigi climb the stairs to the deck, then take a drink of sparkling water, shifting my attention to the door to Emma's stateroom. I take unsteady steps across the small living space as the floor sways beneath my feet. Glancing over my shoulder, I push open the door to her room.

Emma's bed is made with one bag on top, along with her purse, zipped closed and lying on its side. There's another duffel bag on the floor at the end of the bed. I open the single cupboard that looks the same as the one I share with Beth.

At the bottom, there's a makeup case and a pair of New Balance tennis shoes. But no towels.

Chapter Fifteen

Present: Day Four at Sea

"We are *live* on day four of our fabulous sailing trip to San Diego!"

Beth grips the dinette table with one hand to keep from falling out of her seat as she films Gigi. The seas were so rough that Beth gave up reading a few hours ago. I stand from the couch and stagger sideways on my way to the deck, nearly toppling onto the table in the middle of Gigi's live stream.

Her heavily mascaraed eyes flick toward me. She returns her gaze to Beth's phone when I recover my stance enough to stay upright.

Her nude-lipsticked mouth turns up into a smile. "The weather is insane. You guys can probably tell the boat is swaying. We're in the middle of a storm!"

I hear Emma hurl into the toilet—again—as I climb the narrow stairway to the deck. Knowing she spent so much time on her grandparents' sailboat as a kid, I was surprised to hear her throwing up this morning. When Beth said as much, Emma reminded her these open waters are much rougher than anything she experienced sailing around Sequim. When I push open the door, it flies out of my hand from the wind and slams against the boat. My hair swirls around my face as I close it behind me.

Yesterday's sun is nowhere to be found. Instead, dark-gray clouds loom overhead, making it feel much later than five o'clock. I pull my hood over my head. When a wave pummels the boat, I'm immediately sprayed with salt water. The helm is unoccupied. I turn to the sound of Captain Nojan shouting orders at Adam from the middle of the boat.

"Hoist the storm jib," the captain calls over the wind as he struggles to adjust one of the lines on the mainsail.

My gaze darts to the large swell rolling toward the boat and my heart leaps to my throat. I'm thrown onto the bench behind me as the wave hits the hull, spilling cold ocean water onto the deck and soaking my feet through my Converse. I pull myself up on the bench as thunder claps in the distance.

How the hell did I let Beth talk me into this?

Adam ducks low and moves from the foredeck to the cockpit, keeping one hand on the boat with each step. He unwraps a rope from a winch and tugs. "It's not going, Captain."

Nojan looks over his shoulder. "Release the furler line first," he shouts, pointing behind Adam.

I watch Adam release the clamp on his left before he tugs again on the rope in his hand. This time, the rope gives easily. As Adam pulls, a small sail unfurls at the bow. A lump forms in my throat. His inexperience didn't seem so worrisome yesterday when we weren't in the bellows of gale winds. But now . . .

Fear stabs my chest at the thought of my girls, who are probably sitting down for dinner with my sister right now, while I imagine what it would be like for them if I never returned home.

Once the headsail is up, Adam starts to wrap the rope counterclockwise, then stops himself before wrapping the rope in a clockwise motion twice around the winch. He gives it a tug. I haven't said anything to the others about how I found Adam in Emma's room yesterday, lying about replacing the towels. At the front of the cockpit, the captain eyes our stormy surroundings with a grimace, squinting as wind beats against his face, then turns back toward Adam.

"Get below deck!"

I tear my gaze from Adam and see that the captain is pointing at me. "It's not safe for you out here now!"

Captain Nojan grabs the mast as the boat tilts. As we dip to the left from a rolling swell, I slide against the bench on the wet deck. I manage to pry open the companionway door, but it flies out of my hand, smacking against the wall of the cockpit.

When I get below, Emma is out of the bathroom, sitting beside Beth and Gigi at the table, her face a pale green.

"How was it up there?" Beth asks.

I pull off my hood and look down at my soaked shoes. "Wet. And scary as hell."

"I think we should go home," Emma says as I sink onto the couch.

Gigi, who sits across from Emma and Beth, shakes her head. "The weather will calm down. It's just a squall. It will blow by tomorrow, I'm sure."

"What are we doing out here?" Emma asks. "This is miserable."

I spot fear beneath the attitude on Emma's stricken face. She's terrified. And so am I.

"It's fine," Gigi says. "Sailboats are made for this kind of weather. The captain warned me we would hit some rough weather, but he assured me it won't last long. I thought you'd be used to this after all that sailing you did with your grandparents."

Emma shakes her head. "It was never like this. I want to go back. I came here for a vacation, not to die out here."

I can tell by her tone she's only half serious about the dying part, but I'm worried too.

"I agree," I say, looking at Gigi as the boat heels to the side, tilting the floor to a forty-five-degree angle.

Gigi rolls her eyes. "No one's *dying*!"

Emma moans, resting her elbow atop the table and cradling her forehead in her palm. "I did *not* bring enough seasickness pills for this."

Gigi stands from the table. "I should probably take one of the pills I brought. I'm starting to feel pretty queasy myself."

Emma moans again as Gigi unsteadily makes for her stateroom. She emerges a moment later, gripping a prescription bottle in her hand. I sit up, surprised Gigi has prescription seasickness pills since you can buy them over the counter. And she hasn't seemed the slightest bit sick this whole time. *Although she is a diva,* I think. *Everything she does is over the top.*

Gigi zigzags toward the fridge, grabbing the counter for support as she moves past. She reaches the fridge and withdraws a bottle of water just as the boat heels sharply to the side. Gigi yelps, reaching for the counter as the pill bottle slips from her hand. White pills spill across the floor along with the contents from the fridge.

"Oh no," she shrieks, dropping to her hands and knees, scrambling to recover her splayed pills on the moving floor.

I slide off the couch and crawl toward her to help, grabbing a few white pills as I go.

"Here." I open my palm to give Gigi the pills I've recovered, noting the two capital letters imprinted on the round tablets.

"Thanks." Gigi's fake nails scratch my palm as she snatches them.

She swiftly plucks the rest from the floor and returns them to the bottle as I pick up the drinks and put them back in the fridge.

I watch Gigi take two before she screws on the lid. Those weren't seasickness pills. Those were opiates. Prescription opiates.

"Did you guys bring the pocketknives?" Gigi asks, interrupting my thoughts.

"Yeah." I look at Beth, not sure how I feel about Gigi's idea to throw our engraved pocketknives from Courtney into the ocean. Gigi's request had come via an email from her assistant before the trip, which added to the strangeness of the whole thing. The email said Gigi thought it would be akin to spreading Courtney's ashes, since the pocketknives were all we had left from her.

Beth nods, and I can tell she's trying not to roll her eyes. She's convinced Gigi wants to do it only for content to help build her platform. But now that we're all together, I'm starting to come around to the idea. In their search for Courtney, rescue divers had recovered my knife from the bottom of the Sol Duc. Maybe tossing the pocketknives overboard will help me let go.

Without a word, Emma pulls hers out of her pants pocket.

I swallow, staring at the shiny red pocketknife, identical to the one Courtney gave me before we set out on our rafting trip. It was morbid to think back on that now, how Courtney thought she was so tough, so prepared, yet the knives did nothing to save her. Emma remains quiet as she stares at the knife, holding it over the table. I wonder if she's too nauseated to speak, or if she's thinking the same thing I am.

"I didn't actually hurt my knee on that trip," Emma says, still staring at the knife. "I faked it."

I gape at Emma, stunned by her confession.

"What?" Gigi asks. "Why?"

Emma shifts her gaze to the floor beside the dinette. "This sounds crazy, but after Courtney fell in, I thought she'd done it on purpose. For attention. She always had to make everything about her, even if that meant she had to be the victim." Her voice wobbles, and she lifts her gaze to mine. "I was sick of it. So, I pretended to hurt myself on that rock so I wouldn't have to keep looking for her." She turns toward Beth. "It was so stupid, I know, and I'll never forgive myself for it. I had no idea we'd never find her." Emma shakes her head slowly, her eyes distant. "I'm sure you all saw the video of me screaming at the contractor that went viral on social media. I've been seeing a therapist about it, and she thinks a lot of my anger stems from my guilt from that trip."

Gigi puts a hand on her heart, looking wounded. "Why didn't you ever tell me? I can't believe you kept it a secret for so long."

Emma's eyes brim with tears as she twists in her seat. "Because she *died*." She heaves an exasperated sigh and turns back around. "This isn't about you, Gigi. I swear, sometimes you're just as bad as Courtney."

Beth slides me a glance, and I know what she's thinking: *Can't argue with that.*

I put a hand on Emma's arm. "What happened to Courtney isn't your fault." *It's mine.* I try to push down the guilt welling up in my chest before it swallows me whole—something I've had a lot of practice with over the years.

"I think we should throw the pocketknives into the sea tonight," Gigi says, seemingly unaffected by Emma's slight. "It's time that we all let go." Gigi widens her stance to keep her balance as the bow pitches over a swell, her gaze turning to the stairs.

"The captain said it wasn't safe for us to be on deck right now," I say.

She cocks her head. "But you were just up there."

"I know, and that's why I came down."

"Oh, please. It'll be fine. We won't be up there for long."

Emma twists in her seat at the dinette to face Gigi. "We've got over a week left in this trip. Why don't we wait until the seas are calmer?"

Gigi puts her hands on her hips, pursing her lips as if Emma just doesn't get it. "I already announced to my following that we'd be doing it *live* tonight."

Beth's gaze meets mine, her eyes widening as if to say *I told you so.* She turns toward Gigi. "I'm not risking my life for your live stream, Gigi."

Gigi's face falls, seemingly stunned by Beth's refusal, making me wonder when the last time was that she didn't get her way. "We have to. It's the whole reason we're here."

I study Gigi. Is she referring to honoring Courtney's memory or posting "content"?

"This might be a vacation for you, Beth, but I actually have to work."

I shake my head for giving Gigi's intentions the benefit of the doubt. Of course that's all she's concerned about: her following.

Gigi glances at Emma, then me. "I'll meet you all on deck. I just need to grab my pocketknife and touch up my lipstick."

Beth looks between Emma and me after Gigi disappears into her stateroom, the door slamming closed behind her as the floor heels to an angle.

"Did she not hear me?" Beth asks. "I said I'm not going up there. Not toni—"

A scream erupts from inside Gigi's stateroom.

Chapter Sixteen

Present: Day Four at Sea

Gigi stumbles out of her cabin before I can get up. She's staring at a small piece of notebook paper in her hand. All the color has drained from her face, and there's a flicker of terror in her eyes, like she's seen a ghost.

"What is it?"

"You scared me," Beth says, clearly annoyed. "It sounded like you were being murdered in there."

"Look." Gigi holds out the paper with a tremoring hand as she moves into the middle of the salon.

Emma snatches the paper and holds it over the table. I get to my feet and lean over Gigi's shoulder to see what it says.

My breath catches in my throat as I read the note, penned in round, neat handwriting I haven't seen in twenty years.

> I know who killed me, and it's time for you to confess.
>
> XO, Courtney

A haunting silence comes over us as we all stare at the ripped paper. The floor moves beneath me, but I'm not sure whether it's from the rolling sea or Courtney's words. I grab onto Gigi's arm to keep my balance.

Beth looks up at Gigi. "What the—"

"It's Courtney's handwriting," Gigi says.

I stand frozen, my eyes glued to the note. *It's impossible. She couldn't be.*

"You guys don't think she's . . ." Gigi's petrified eyes travel between mine and Beth's. "You know. *Alive?*"

My pulse races as Beth takes the note from Emma's hand.

"Where did you find this?" Beth asks.

"In my bathroom. It was taped to the mirror."

Beth frowns, letting the note fall to the table. "You're making this up. *You* wrote this."

Gigi gapes at Beth. "Why would I do that?"

Beth pushes the note toward Emma. "For 'content.' Why else?" Beth rubs her forearms, probably trying to quell the goose bumps beneath her sweatshirt. Despite her calm demeanor, I can tell she's just as freaked out as the rest of us.

Emma turns, her steely gaze boring into Gigi's. She lifts the note. "Tell us the truth. Did you write this?"

Gigi throws her hands in the air. I instinctively lean back to avoid getting whacked in the face. "No! I already told you. It was taped to the mirror in my bathroom. Why would I make that up?"

From the look of affronted shock on Gigi's face, I'm inclined to believe her, as much as I don't want to. She can't be that desperate for content. Faking a note from Courtney and accusing one of us of murder would be a new low, even for Gigi.

But if Gigi didn't write it, who did? Beth and I are the only ones who know what happened in the woods that day. Aren't we? My gaze falls to the note, penned in blue ink, and my blood runs cold, as if every vessel in my body just froze.

Courtney signed my yearbook the exact same way: *XO, Courtney*. It's been over a decade since I've looked at it, but I instantly recognize the small loop at the top of the *C* and the curve at the top of the *T*. The room spins, and I feel like I'm going to be sick. If someone *has* forged it, they've done an excellent job at mimicking Courtney's handwriting. There's no way it could really be her. Could it?

Emma sniffs the note, then lifts it toward Beth's nose. "Do you smell that?"

Beth inhales. "Smell what?"

"Courtney's perfume," Emma says. "The one she was always dousing herself with."

"Let me smell." Gigi snatches the note from Beth and takes a whiff. "I don't smell it."

I lower my nose toward the note until it nearly touches the paper and inhale deeply. It's faint, but Emma is right. I caught a subtle whiff of Courtney's "signature scent" on the paper. *Ocean Dream,* I recall with a shiver. "I smell it too."

Emma swipes the note from Gigi's grip as the door to the deck flaps open and a gust of cold wind fills our small space. I turn as the captain comes down the steps, his hair and shirt soaked. He shuts the door behind him and crosses his arms. His grave expression mirrors the rest of ours.

"This storm is much worse than what was predicted."

"Wait." Beth holds up her hands. "A storm was predicted?" She turns to Gigi. "Did you know about this?"

Gigi shrugs. "Just that it might get rough. But nothing to worry about."

"I wasn't expecting anything this bad, but the Gulf of Alaska spins up storms fast and sometimes unpredictably. Especially this time of year." The captain's mouth turns to a frown. "But I did tell you it could get *very* rough. And you assured me that wouldn't be a problem for anyone."

Beth gapes at Gigi. "And you didn't tell us?"

I remember Gigi's tense words with the captain before we left Seattle, now certain they hadn't been talking about the menu.

"Shouldn't we turn back now?" I ask. "This already seems really bad." Plus, after the note, all I want is to get off this boat and go home.

"We can't go back!" At the table, Gigi's mouth hangs open as if we'd slapped her. "I'm contracted to give my sponsor two weeks of live footage—I don't have nearly enough content yet. I don't get paid unless I do the whole trip. They want to follow us all the way to San Diego with live streams every day. My followers, I've promised them—"

"You won't be giving them any content if we capsize in a storm, Gigi." Emma crosses her arms, the note still in her hand. "You can't risk our lives for your *fashion blog*."

Gigi shoots Emma a sharp look. "I'm a *lifestyle* influencer, not just fashion."

Emma rolls her eyes. "Whatever, same thing."

I don't see how any of them, even Gigi, would want to continue the trip now.

The captain shakes his head, his face serious. "The storm is setting us west and pushing us away from the Washington and Oregon coastlines. If we turn back now, we'll be facing the waves head-on and stuck in this weather—and possibly worse—our entire way back, if we can even make it back. We're better off to stay our course and let it blow over."

As we rock to the side, a spray of white water splashes against the window above the kitchen cabinets. Instinctively, I grab Beth's knee for support. She jumps.

"Sorry," I tell her.

"I'll keep an eye on the weather." Nojan's gaze drifts to the salt water dripping down the outside of the kitchen window. "Depending on what the storm does, we may have to alter our course. If it looks safer to turn back at any time or head for the nearest point, I will. But right now, we wait it out. The boat can handle it. Trust me, I've seen much worse."

Emma looks around. "Maybe we should take it to a vote?"

"My vote is the only one that counts on this vessel," Nojan says, his tone calm but firm. He pivots to face Gigi. "I don't care what you're paying me. I will not jeopardize anyone's safety for your 'content.'"

I turn to Gigi, confused. "I thought your sponsor was paying for this trip? The yacht-rental company?"

Gigi flicks a glance toward Nojan before meeting my gaze. "They are. That's what he meant."

"But I want you all to be prepared. The weather will likely get worse before it gets better," Nojan adds.

I scan the others' reactions. Emma closes her eyes and sinks back in her seat. Gigi's full lips are set in a hard line. Clearly irritated, she clasps her manicured fingers together so tightly her knuckles turn white. Beth looks unfussed, as usual. I don't know that I've ever seen her panicked, except for that day on our rafting trip. It strikes me that I'm the only one who has children at home.

"All right." Nojan turns up the steps. "I need to go help Adam man the boat. I just wanted to warn you."

"Wait!" Gigi calls. "What's for dinner? I'm getting hungry."

Emma slumps forward onto the table. "How can you even be thinking about food right now?"

The captain points to the fridge. "I'm going to need Adam on the deck. Dinner is whatever you want to make. I suggest a sandwich. You don't want to be chopping anything with the way this ship is rocking." He turns after opening the door. "Oh." He raises his voice to a shout over the howling wind. "And stay below until I say otherwise." His gaze flicks to mine. "I don't want anyone else falling overboard. Especially in this."

After the captain returns to the deck and closes the hatch behind him, Emma thrusts the note at Gigi and stands from the table.

"Take your note. I'm going to lie down."

"It's not *my* note." Gigi takes the paper from Emma. "I just found it."

"You want us to believe it *magically* appeared in your bathroom? Minutes after I confessed to feeling responsible for Courtney's death? Please. Don't tell me that's not what sparked your idea. Although, if you spritzed it with Courtney's perfume, that was some pretty sick premeditation on your part."

Gigi's jaw dropped. "I didn't—"

"*And* if you plan on filming that"—Emma pointed at the note—"which I'm sure you are, I don't want any part in it." Emma assesses Beth and me before heading for her stateroom with one hand on her stomach. "Good night, ladies."

She disappears into her room, leaving Beth and me alone with Gigi, all three of our gazes transfixed on the notepaper in her hand.

◆ ◆ ◆

"Do you think there's any way that, you know . . ." Sometimes, I still can't bring myself to say her name. Even after all this time. I exhale. "Courtney wrote that note?"

I lie next to Beth who's scrolling on her dimly lit phone in the dark of our room. Outside, the storm continues to rage. Rain—and sea spray—pelts against the window hatch above our bed. Beth, Gigi, and I found some cheese and crackers for dinner, but Beth and I barely touched ours. All three of us retired to our rooms as soon as the sun went down.

"You mean that she's alive?" Beth looks up at me, her face lit by the glow of her phone screen. She cocks her head, eyeing me sympathetically. "Palmer, no. Of course not. Emma's right, Gigi's doing this all for publicity. She's squeezing every drop she can out of Courtney's disappearance, like she's always done. But that note was lower than ever, even for Gigi. Can't say I'm that surprised. Gigi would do anything to increase her social following."

I roll onto my back and stare at the window hatch overhead. Wrestling to keep my thoughts from running wild and imagining Courtney hiding somewhere on this ship. I shudder, recalling the desperate, haunting entries of the captain's log on the ship, *The Demeter*, in *Dracula*, which Beth convinced me to buddy read with her last October. One by one, the captain's crewmen disappeared while keeping watch in the night until the captain was the only one left, alone on the ship with the vampire who murdered his men. When the ship reached a harbor, the captain's body was found bound to the ship's wheel.

Beneath us, the hull moaned as the boat swayed.

"Palmer."

My heart hammers in my chest as I consider for the first time since our high school rafting trip that Courtney might have survived.

"Palmer." Beth's voice cuts through the darkness, only inches away from me.

I turn onto my side. "What?"

"I just googled Gigi and found an article posted yesterday. It may not be true, but you know how Gigi's husband wasn't at our send-off at the marina and how she was so against us turning around?"

"Yeah?"

Beth lowers her voice a notch. "This article says that Gigi is being sued over allegedly buying more than two million followers. And her social media accounts will likely be taken down. *And* her husband Alex is divorcing her. There was no prenup because Gigi believed he was much wealthier than her. But the article stated he's not really a hotel heir and instead has a criminal record in Europe. According to the piece, he's pushing to split her net worth and demanding some very hefty spousal support."

I draw in a breath. I didn't think it was possible to feel sorry for Gigi, but I do. "Do you think it's true?"

"It wouldn't surprise me. Plus, it explains why she's so desperate to finish this trip."

I think back to the tears in Gigi's eyes when the captain said we might have to reroute. And her painkillers disguised as seasickness pills.

"That's awful about her husband." I think of Matt, then his young girlfriend, before pushing them both from my mind. The boat tilts, and my stomach churns. "I don't know how I'm going to sleep through this," I say, although it's not the storm that has my mind spinning.

I feel Beth sit up, then hear her rustling through her bag.

"Take a Dramamine," she says.

"I'm not that nauseated. I'm more . . . scared."

"The captain said he'll turn back if it gets any worse. He's been sailing for over thirty years. I think we can trust his competence."

It's not just the storm that I'm scared of. "You're probably right," I say, hoping to convince myself.

"I'm always right."

I sense Beth's smile even though I can't see her. "Here." She nudges my arm with her hand. "Take one anyway. It will help you sleep."

I take the bottle from her and sit up. Beth flicks on the ceiling light as I reach for my water bottle beside the bed.

"Thanks," I say after swallowing a pill.

"No problem."

She kills the light, and we lie in silence on our rolling bed until Beth's breathing morphs into soft snores. My thoughts drift back to Gigi. Her seemingly perfect life is just as messed up as mine.

I recall the five of us, setting out on that hike twenty years ago, not knowing we'd come back as four and how it would eat at us forever.

Beneath us, the hull groans. My mind reels with the idea of Courtney on board, back for revenge over what I did to her. A shudder runs down my spine.

When I finally succumb to sleep, I dream of Courtney.

"Palmer, wake up. I think something's wrong."

I open my eyes to Beth shaking me in the dark. Rain pelts against the foredeck above our bed. My head feels fuzzy from the Dramamine I took before falling asleep, and I wipe drool from the side of my mouth.

"Where's Nojan? Have you seen him?" Adam's panicked tone sounds right outside our stateroom door.

"No, we were sleeping." I recognize Emma's gravelly voice. "Why? What's going—"

A fist raps against our door. "Palmer? Beth?" Adam shouts. "Have you seen the captain?"

Beth sits up. I hear her flick the ceiling light on, but we remain in darkness.

Rap, rap, rap.

"Hey, Palmer. Beth," Adam calls.

Beth slides out of bed as I sit up, suddenly wide awake. She opens the door. Adam's flashlight shines on her, illuminating her bed head of dark waves. The rest of the boat is dark.

"Have you seen the captain?" His tone is curt. Panicked.

It sends a ripple of fear down my spine.

"No," Beth says. "We were asleep."

The flashlight beam swings toward me. I squint and shake my head, lifting my hand to block the light shining in my eyes. On the other end of the boat, a door swings open, flapping against the wall as we roll over a swell.

"What's going on?" Gigi calls. "Why aren't the lights working?"

Adam spins around. "I just got up to take my shift at the helm, and Nojan's gone," Adam says.

"Shit," Beth mutters.

Outside our room, Emma gasps.

Heart pounding, I get out of bed and grab onto Beth's arm as the floor dips. This boat is too small for someone to go missing on board. My veins constrict with panic as I tighten my grip on Beth's upper arm. "Oh my—" The boat tilts, and I fall to the side, pushing us both against the wall.

"Nojan must've gone overboard in the storm," Adam says.

"*What?*" Gigi exclaims.

With my heart in my throat, I draw in a sharp breath as the floor sways beneath my feet. *Overboard? But how?*

"All the rope tethers are still on the boat," Adam adds.

"You mean he's . . ." Beth's voice trails off.

"Gone," Adam says.

No. "He can't be." I stare at Adam, thinking of my girls. I have to get home to them. I push past him. "Nojan has to be here somewhere."

Adam blocks my path. "Stop. I've already checked. If you go up there without a life vest, you'll just end up in the water with him."

"We need to call the Coast Guard," Emma says. "They can look for him, hopefully before it's too late. We can't stay out in this storm without a captain."

Adam's flashlight beam swings toward Emma. "We've lost power. Unless I can get it back on, we can't call anyone."

Chapter Seventeen

Memorial Day Weekend, 2005

Courtney's hair blew wildly out the passenger window of Beth's van as we followed the 101 along the shores of Lake Crescent. I sat behind Beth, my backpack wedged between my legs, and sang along with Gigi and Emma to the Ashanti CD playing through the van's speakers. As soon as the song ended, my phone chimed in my bag.

I flipped open my phone and saw a text from my mom. Be safe and have a great time! Don't forget to text me when you get to the trailhead so I know you made it. Love you!

Courtney whipped around. "Let me guess. That's your mom."

I smiled. "How'd you know?"

Courtney shook her head. "I can't believe she almost didn't let you come. Good thing I got my mom to finally convince her."

"I know." I feigned relief even though I was secretly hoping I could get out of the whole thing. I'd had trouble sleeping last night, imagining a bear attacking our tents, clawing its way inside and eating me alive. I hadn't told anyone besides Beth for fear of sounding lame. Especially not Courtney.

I tucked my phone back into my pack as we reached the end of the lake. The CD mixer changed to Avril Lavigne, and I grinned as

Courtney sang off key to the lyrics of "Don't Tell Me." Behind me, Emma and Gigi stopped singing. Instead, they began to argue over who was the hottest actor: Josh Hartnett or Orlando Bloom.

Beth turned to Courtney. "Did you know it's supposed to rain on Monday? The weather guy predicted a downpour starting early afternoon."

Courtney patted Beth's shoulder. "Don't worry, mother. We'll be driving home by then."

I gazed out the window as Beth turned off the 101 onto Sol Duc Hot Springs Road, debating what I would tell the school board when they interviewed me next Tuesday. After Emma's mom had sued the school, the school board had launched its own investigation into who'd planted the dish soap in the locker room. Fortunately, they'd been unable to prove who was responsible, so nothing had come of it so far.

While Emma had been on the bench at our state championship game, Courtney had been scouted by the Elliott Bay University volleyball coach. Last month, Courtney accepted a full-ride volleyball scholarship to EBU, even though her parents could've easily paid the tuition. Courtney's parents were EBU alumni, and Courtney often bragged that they were some of the school's biggest donors.

Without an offer to play for EBU, or any other major university, Emma enrolled in Peninsula College, a community college in our neighboring town of Port Angeles, where she'd gotten no scholarship but a spot on the team. And she'd have to take out loans for what her financial aid didn't cover.

I still felt sick over lying to Emma about what Courtney and I had done, knowing Emma's chances of someday playing pro volleyball were now next to nothing. I'd said as much to Courtney after we'd learned we'd be formally interviewed about the incident. *I can't lie to the board,* I'd said in the passenger seat of her Mazda Miata when we'd driven to Subway on our lunch break.

"What if they find out?" I'd asked her. "We have to come clean."

Courtney had slammed on her brakes at the red light. "I'm not going to let you ruin yourself for no reason. We'll say that we can't be sure it was Bryson and Jake. Just that it was two guys. That way, no one will get in trouble for what happened—including you."

Now, as the van wound along the narrow road, I stared at the thick evergreen forest speeding by. Courtney's plan to deal with the board actually made a lot of sense, and we'd agreed to stick to the same story during our separate interviews next week. I spotted a cottontail rabbit sitting tall along the side of the road and imagined myself in front of the school board, running through my preplanned answers. Wondering if they would see the lie on my face.

"Eww!" Gigi exclaimed behind me. "Kevin Federline? Seriously? He's so gross."

Courtney skipped to the next track as we passed the sign for the Sol Duc Hot Springs Resort. "My Happy Ending" started to play, and Courtney turned up the volume.

I pulled out my phone and used the number keys to tap out a text to my mom.

"Take this right." Courtney pointed out her window.

Beth slowed. "I don't think that's a road." She lifted her printed MapQuest paper from the center console. "The Sol Duc Trailhead is another mile up this road."

"No, trust me. This is where we want to go. It's where my brother went with his friends."

Beth gripped the steering wheel with both hands, craning her neck to see down the unmarked side road. "I don't think—"

"Just do it!" Courtney shouted. "This is it, I promise."

Beth hit the brakes and turned onto the narrow dirt road. "This seems more like a Forest Service road. I don't think we're supposed to be driving on this."

Gigi giggled at something Emma said in the back, seemingly oblivious to our turn off the main road.

Courtney leaned back in her seat. "Relax. There's a trailhead up here. You'll see."

Beth motioned toward a huge evergreen on Courtney's side of the van. "See that spruce tree? It's probably over five hundred years old. Some of the Sitka spruce trees in the Olympic National Park are estimated to be over a *thousand* years old."

Courtney groaned. "Okay, Einstein. No more nerd talk on the trip, okay? I feel like I'm back in botany class."

We kept driving uphill.

I leaned forward. "Are you sure there's a trailhead on this road?"

Courtney pressed the sole of her brand-new hiking boot against the dash. "Yep. This will get us started farther up the Sol Duc River where it's better for rafting."

"Hey, did you guys know that Bryson and Jake are getting expelled over Emma's ankle?" Gigi asked. "They aren't even going to walk at graduation."

"Yeah, I heard." Courtney placed a hand on her thigh, her green-painted nails matching the color of her cargo pants. "That's old news, Gigi."

My jaw dropped open. "What?" I whirled around. "But Courtney and I haven't given our statements yet. We aren't totally sure it was Bryson and Jake." My gaze faltered between Gigi and Emma. "I mean, what if it wasn't?"

"It *was*," Courtney said, her voice firm.

"Yeah." Gigi nodded. "Courtney gave her statement earlier this week."

"But . . ." My heart dropped into my stomach. I turned to Courtney, confused. "I thought we were both talking to the board on Tuesday."

"Oh, yeah." Courtney ran a hand through her hair. "I asked to speak with them sooner. And I told them what we saw, Palmer. Bryson and Jake. They have already gotten away with hurting Emma for way too long."

"Serves them right for doing that," Gigi said.

My eyes met Beth's in the rearview mirror. "But they—"

Courtney whirled around in her seat, shooting daggers at me with her ice-cold gaze.

"You were right," Beth said, braking the van to a stop.

I looked out the windshield to the small dirt parking area where the road dead-ended. A weathered trailhead sign leaned to the side beside a narrow path at the edge of the forest.

"See! There it is." Courtney touched Beth's arm with the back side of her hand. "I told you!"

The van doors slid open. I grabbed my heavy pack and stepped outside. Hearing the Sol Duc's rushing water made my pulse race. The air was cooler against my legs than when we'd left Sequim.

I slung my pack over my shoulder, grimacing at the weight of the two-person pack raft Courtney had insisted I carry. She'd bought three of them for the trip. Before leaving, we drew straws to decide who would carry them first, and I lost, along with Gigi and Emma. But Courtney promised to take turns when the weight got to be too much.

Beth lifted the trunk door. We each grabbed a broken-down paddle and helped each other stick both ends into the straps of our packs. I heard a soft *pssst* and turned, expecting to see one of the others applying bug spray. Instead, it was Courtney misting herself with her blue perfume bottle.

"I wouldn't do that if I were you," Beth warned. "That's going to attract mosquitoes big time."

Courtney rolled her eyes and tucked the perfume bottle into her pack. "It's better than smelling like sweat. Or that disgusting bug repellant you put on in the van."

Beth cast me a look before turning back to Courtney. "Suit yourself. But don't complain to me when you're covered in bug bites tonight." Beth sighed. "I'm tired already," she added as we moved toward the trailhead.

Courtney turned, shaking her head at Beth. "Oh, stop. You're not even packing a raft."

My gaze followed Courtney as she continued toward the trail. I was still stunned that she went behind my back to accuse Bryson and Jake after assuring me she wouldn't. Now, the board would ask me to validate Courtney's story on Tuesday. *But how can I lie knowing it will ruin Bryson's and Jake's lives?*

I took a deep breath, which my heavy pack made difficult, and tried to dispel the betrayal I felt. I couldn't confront Courtney about it now. Not with Emma and Gigi present.

When Courtney got to the trailhead sign, she spun and reached into the side of her pack. "Guys, I have something for you."

As we gathered around her, she withdrew four shiny red pocketknives. She glanced at each one before handing them out to us, starting with Beth.

"I had them engraved." Courtney handed me mine, and I avoided her gaze as I took the knife from her palm.

I flipped it over in my hand. *Palmer Montague 2005* was engraved in cursive on the side.

"Oh, thanks, Court," Gigi gushed beside me.

"These are so cool," Emma said, taking her knife. She turned to Beth, who was struggling to open her blade. "Here." Emma snatched Beth's knife out of her hands. "Open it like this, otherwise you'll get cut."

Courtney put her hands on her hips when Emma handed Beth's knife back to her. "I'm glad you guys like them. Now we're ready for anything."

Thinking the opposite, I slipped my knife into my cargo shorts pocket as we started toward the trail.

"I also got us matching T-shirts." Courtney slipped off her pack and then unzipped the top. She reached inside and, starting with Gigi, handed out rolled-up pink shirts. "I thought we could wear them tomorrow when we start rafting."

"Aww. These are so cute." Gigi held hers up while I accepted my shirt from Courtney.

SENIOR TRIP 2005 was printed in white letters on the front.

"There's more on the back," Courtney said, handing a shirt to Emma.

Gigi flipped the shirt around revealing the five of our names printed on the back.

"Sorry, I couldn't get one in your size."

I turned to see Courtney handing Beth a bookmark instead of a shirt. My jaw fell open.

"But I remembered how much you've always loved bookmarks," Courtney added with a smile. "So, I got you one instead."

Beth looked as shocked as the rest of us as Courtney waved it in the air. "Here, take it."

I wanted to slap Courtney as I watched Beth begrudgingly accept the bookmark, which was already soggy on one side. "How could you not—"

Beth lifted her palm in the air as she flashed me a warning look. "Palmer, stop. It's fine."

I could read her eyes. *Don't make this worse.*

"Thanks, Courtney." Beth turned the bookmark over in her hand as Emma and Gigi looked on in stunned silence.

I glared at Courtney, wanting to wipe the look of smug satisfaction off her face.

"*What?*" she asked.

Her feigned innocence sent a bolt of rage up my spine. I stepped toward her. "What the hell—"

Beth squeezed my arm. "Palmer, stop. It's fine."

"Oh, wait." Courtney pulled her phone from her pocket as if nothing had happened. "Let's get a photo while we still look fresh." She lifted her phone in the air. When none of us moved, she looked around. "Come on, guys. Get in closer."

Emma and Gigi exchanged a look before huddling next to her. Beth followed suit and motioned for me to do the same. "Come on, Palmer."

I took a deep breath, then squeezed in beside Beth.

"Beth," Courtney said. "Hold up your bookmark."

She had to have felt bad for being given a piece of paper instead of a shirt, but Beth obviously didn't want to draw attention to Courtney's slight about her weight, and I didn't want to make Beth feel any worse than she already did.

"Smile!"

I forced a smile as Courtney's phone clicked. She lowered the device to check the photo. Seeming to approve of it, Courtney returned the phone to her pocket.

"I'll lead," she said.

I followed behind Emma, with Beth at my heels, as we moved up the trail toward the sound of rushing water. I fixed my gaze on Emma's short blond curls sticking out from her ponytail, dread weighing me down more than my pack. I was going to have to tell her the truth.

If I said nothing, Bryson and Jake would still get expelled—and lose their football scholarships—based on Courtney's statement. They wouldn't even be able to attend graduation.

I couldn't let that happen. Dread welled in my chest, remembering the photo Courtney took of me with the dish soap. But I couldn't let that stop me from telling the truth. Even if it meant facing consequences for something I hadn't done.

I swallowed, knowing I was just as much to blame as Courtney was. I could've warned Emma before she stepped out of the shower. Instead, I stayed quiet, crouching behind the lockers while her ankle bone snapped. Then I lied about it.

Courtney would be livid—my statement would prove she was a liar too. But deep down, she had to know it was the right thing to do.

But Emma . . .

I watched her step over a log covered with mushrooms lying across the trail, recalling her face back in March, flushed with rage, when she shoved Jake onto the cafeteria table. She would never forgive me.

"Isn't this amazing?" Courtney asked from the front of our line. "I feel like we're the only ones out here."

I pictured Beth's minivan, the lone vehicle in the remote parking lot. *Because we are.*

Through a break in the trees, I caught a glimpse of the river's white, fast-flowing water. My mind flashed to the teenage girl who drowned while inner tubing in the Sol Duc last summer after getting pinned beneath a logjam. It was the reason my mom almost didn't let me come.

I dug my phone out of my pocket, realizing I'd never sent the text that we'd made it. My heart sank when I checked my phone. Two words were displayed in bold letters across my home screen.

NO SERVICE

Chapter Eighteen

Present: Day Five at Sea

"Are you sure you checked everywhere?" Gigi asks through the darkness.

Adam swings his flashlight beam toward the sound of Gigi's panicked confusion.

"I don't understand," I say, gripping the doorframe beside me as the boat pitches forward at a sickening angle. "Nojan was so adamant about our safety . . . How could this happen?" An image of Courtney emerging from a stowage compartment invades my mind, her long red hair swirling in the wind as she pushes Nojan over the side. A strange tightness coils around my chest as I tell myself that's impossible.

"Wasn't he wearing a tether?" Emma asks.

Adam shines his flashlight on Emma. "There weren't any tether lines in the water. That's why I came below, hoping he was down here."

There's a tremor in his voice. A cold, slithering shiver works its way down my spine. *He's panicked.*

"How long has he been missing?" Gigi asks.

Adam runs a hand through his hair. "I'm not sure. I went to bed four hours ago, at the start of Nojan's watch. The last entry he made in the logbook was right after that, even though we're supposed to make a log every hour we're on watch."

Four hours. My heart sinks, recalling Gigi coughing up water, pale and exhausted, shivering with cold, when we pulled her onto the boat after being in the ocean only ten minutes.

"Shit." Panic permeates Beth's voice as she lifts a hand to her forehead. "What the hell are we going to do? We're going to die out here. Oh my—"

The floor tilts in the opposite direction as it did a moment ago. Beth falls into me, sandwiching me between her and the wall. It feels like we're inside a washing machine moving up and down, side to side, and front to back, sometimes all at once. Gigi shrieks as Adam stumbles, his flashlight beam illuminating a wave pummeling the window above her head.

"We're not going to die. We still have Adam," Gigi says, her voice firm. "He can sail us out of this."

"*Adam?* You mean this guy you hired for his looks?" Emma scoffs. "He might be a chef, but he's no sailor. Beth's right. We're in deep shit, and this is all your fault, Gigi." Emma jabs her finger through the air as Adam's flashlight beam swings toward Gigi. "You risked all of our lives by bringing us out here with a photogenic male deckhand who doesn't know the stern from the bow."

I don't have to see Emma's face to know that she's fuming.

"I don't know what you're talking about," Gigi balks, shooting Adam a blank look.

Adam raises a palm toward Emma. "Right now, everyone needs to stay calm. I know how to sail."

Despite his attempt to sound confident, there's a tremor in his tone.

"And I wasn't hired for my looks," he adds.

Emma crosses her arms, keeping her gaze fixed on Gigi as the flashlight's beam illuminates her face. "Whatever the reason, he's incompetent. We need to get the power back on so we can call for help. Doesn't this boat have a generator?"

"This is a brand-new boat. It's not equipped with any extras yet." Ignoring Emma's accusations, Adam regains his footing after the boat heels to the other side. "I need to man the helm. But I'm going to need some help. This storm's getting dangerous. And we're sailing blind with no lights and no radar."

"Is there anywhere else the captain could be?" Beth asks. "You checked the bathrooms?"

"Nojan!" Gigi yells.

"Yes, I checked the bathrooms. He's not here."

My shoulders relax slightly. If Adam has checked everywhere, that means Courtney can't be here either. Unless she's hiding somewhere she knows we won't look. I shake that last thought from my mind. Courtney's not here. She died in that forest twenty years ago.

"I'll help you," Emma says. "Just let me grab my life jacket." She disappears into her stateroom for a moment before following Adam toward the companionway door. "I sailed with my grandparents a lot as a kid. And I'm going to check the tether lines again."

"I'm coming too," I say, praying we'll find Nojan asleep on the deck somewhere Adam overlooked. Or maybe Nojan hit his head and is lying unconscious somewhere on the boat.

"Is there another flashlight?" Beth asks.

Adam turns around when he reaches the stairs. "Not that I could find."

"I'll get my phone." Beth turns for our room.

"I want everyone to clip a tether line to their life vest before getting on deck." Adam turns to Emma before opening the companionway door. "I'll clip my tether and hand you one to clip on before you come on deck."

"Wait for us," I spin around and run smack into Beth as she emerges from our cabin with her phone's flashlight illuminated.

"We need our life jackets," I tell her.

"Oh, right."

She follows me into our cabin, illuminating the small space with her phone while I grab our PDFs and sling them over each of our heads.

"I'm coming up too," Gigi calls from her stateroom while Beth and I move through the dinette.

When Adam opens the door, wind rushes into the interior cabin with a fierce, howling roar. The door flies out of his hand and flaps against the wall until he manages to lock it in place. The floor shifts when Beth and I move past the galley. Water spills through the hatch when I mount the stairs behind Emma.

Adam swears and heads out to tether himself. I stand on the lowest step and grip the handle on the wall. More water spills over my feet. The shock of cold causes me to suck in a breath of salty air. My heart leaps to my throat as wind slaps at my cheeks. Emma presses her hand against the wall to steady herself while Adam hooks a tether line to her vest.

"Everyone, make sure you're tethered *before* stepping on deck," Adam shouts over the wind.

Emma turns to me as Adam unsteadily heads toward the helm. "Stay here. I'll get your tether line," she says.

After she hooks a line to my life vest, I step onto the wet cockpit floor and tell Beth to wait. "I need your phone light," I add.

She hands me her phone, and I reach for a tether from the pile of ropes Emma is sorting through on the cockpit floor.

"Emma," Adam calls from one of the steering wheels. "Hold this flashlight for me while I see if I can get the navigation electronics back on."

Emma drops the lines to help Adam. Hand trembling, it takes me two tries to get the hook around the loop on Beth's life vest. As soon as I secure the tether to her vest, a wave pounds the starboard side. I fall backward onto the wet cockpit floor as salt water sprays over the boat.

"Palmer!" Beth shouts. She crawls toward me on her hands and knees. "Are you okay?"

I sit up as the floor rocks beneath us. "I'm fine." I hand Beth her phone. "Help Gigi get a tether on, and then we'll make sure there are no lines in the water."

I know Adam said he already checked them all, but what if he missed one? My throat clenches around my trachea as I imagine Nojan getting dragged underwater behind the boat.

For a split second, a streak of lightning illuminates the sky. Despite the cockpit cover, cold rain lashes my face, stinging like needles in the wind. I grab onto the bench beside me for support as we roll to the side. Fear rises to the back of my throat. *How the hell are we going to survive this without a captain?*

I get to my knees and turn toward the helm, where rain beats on Emma as she shines the flashlight on the side of the navigation displays while Adam looks to be trying to remove a panel.

"Are you sure you looked everywhere on deck for Nojan?" I ask him.

"I'm sure," Adam calls.

I hear a click behind me as Beth secures a tether to Gigi's life vest.

"What about the engine room?" Beth asks. "Adam, did you check there?"

Adam shakes his head. "No, you can check it."

I feel a spark of hope, thinking of the small room beneath the companionway stairs, right below us. We'd all watched Nojan lift the stairs and check the engine room during our first dinner on our voyage.

Beth grabs my arm and swings her phone light between me and Gigi. "What if Nojan went down there to try and fix the power outage and got knocked unconscious?"

"I'll go check." Gigi starts down the steps. "Beth, shine your light down here while I pull down these stairs."

I kneel beside Beth and hold my breath as Gigi pulls the stairs out.

Above us, thunderclaps.

"Well." Beth leans her head through the companionway door, shining her light into the engine room. "Do you see him?"

Gigi leans forward. "No. He's not here," she shouts up.

I sit back and settle my gaze on the pile of tether lines, straining my eyes to adjust to the dark. I can't fathom Nojan not wearing a tether, especially in this storm. I look up at the sound of the mainsail flapping violently in the wind above the cockpit.

"Beth, shine your phone on these tethers."

I start to sort through them, running my hand along each line as Beth illuminates them with her phone flashlight. There's still a chance

Nojan could be connected to one. Nojan made it clear at the start of our trip that there would always be several tether lines connected to the ship—enough for each of us to hook onto our life vests.

I find each tether that's connected to the five of us on board and move them aside. Then, I run my hand through one more rope until I find the metal hook at the end.

"Have you found him?" Gigi pokes her head out of the companionway.

"No," Emma responds as she and Adam reach the cockpit, "but the radio mic is missing from the helm."

"*Are you kidding me*?" Gigi cries.

"Check the radio inside," Adam tells her. "Is the microphone still attached?"

Gigi ducks inside, and the four of us wait in silence.

"It's gone," she yells, coming back up the steps.

I swivel toward Adam. "What about the life raft? Doesn't it have its own communication equipment?"

"Yes, that's right, it does." He steps onto the cockpit's bench and grips a shroud before moving toward the bow.

I crouch down and lift the last rope tether and run my hand along it until it slips through my grip. I pick it up again and hold it up to the light. Beth gasps, staring at the end.

"The life raft's gone," Adam says, returning to the cockpit.

"Nojan *abandoned* us?" Gigi exclaims from the companionway.

"Guys!" I lift the end of the rope. "I think I found Nojan's tether." Beth shines a light on the cleanly frayed end. "It looks like someone cut it."

Chapter Nineteen

Present: Day Five at Sea

No one says anything as a wave crashes against the starboard hull and the wind howls through the mainsail rigging like a scream—even though we're all thinking the same thing. Nojan didn't fall overboard by accident. And he didn't abandon us on purpose using the life raft. He was murdered.

"Cut it?" Gigi shrieks. "Like killed him?"

Beth and I huddle near the back of the cockpit cover with the others, staring at the frayed tether in silence as another lightning bolt brightens the sky. My mind flashes to Emma holding her pocketknife at the dinette before we went to bed. We all brought them. In the wake of Gigi finding the note from "Courtney," we never tossed them overboard.

"Who would do that?" Adam asks, tearing his wide eyes from the tether to the four of us.

"You would," Emma says.

I turn to Emma, whose narrowed gaze is directed straight at Adam.

"You were the only one up here. We were all asleep when Nojan went overboard. And if Gigi didn't hire you for your looks, then how'd you even get this job? Who are you? You're not a sailor, and don't bullshit me. I sailed enough growing up to see your mistakes."

Adam sighs, lowering his gaze to the floor. My heart sinks.

"Okay. I have a little sailing experience, but not a lot. The first officer who was scheduled for this trip got sick the day before our departure, and Nojan knew I could use the cash. I convinced him to take me as a last-minute replacement." Adam straightens, looking at Emma. "But I didn't kill him! Why on earth would I do that? I needed him here as much as you do." His gaze falls to the cut rope still in my hand. "Someone cut that line. But it wasn't me."

The other women look skeptical, but when I appraise him, I sense a spark of honesty. "His story makes sense," I say. "If he's not a trained sailor, why would he endanger his own life by killing the captain in the middle of a storm?"

My gaze travels to Emma. Of all of us, she's the one with the most sailing experience. I think of the video that recently went viral of her screaming at a contractor. And Emma's argument on the phone that Beth and I overheard through our stateroom wall. Her temper seems to be getting worse with age. But is she capable of murder? And what would be her motive in killing the captain?

"What about Starlink?" Gigi asks. "Shouldn't we still have internet?"

I turn to Gigi and note that Beth seems to be scrutinizing her the same way I was appraising Emma. "Not without power," I say.

Beth groans, bringing her hands to her face.

"I think I'm gonna be sick," Gigi mumbles before turning down the stairs.

The boat drops down the back side of a wave, and I hear Gigi's head smack the ceiling.

I grip the tether in my hand so I don't slide to the rear of the cockpit.

After we level out, I look up at Emma. "So, we have no navigation, nothing?"

The pointed accusation from a moment ago is wiped from her face. Now, she just looks scared. "The compass still works. And we'll be able to see the weather vane in the daylight."

"So, we can make it back to the mainland, right?" Beth asks.

"First, we need to sail out of this storm," Adam says, looking around. "It's coming from the north, pushing us southwest."

I shudder at the surrounding bulging waves that become visible beneath the beam of his flashlight, amazed we haven't already capsized.

"Which means we keep going southwest to get away from it before we turn back for the mainland," he adds.

My jaw drops. "Keep going? With only a compass? That's like skydiving without a parachute. We have to turn back. *Now.* What if we get hit by a cargo ship? Or get knocked over from these waves? Plus, we only have another week and a half's worth of food and water. We have to get back to the mainland."

"I hate to admit it, but I actually agree with Adam," Emma says. "We have to get out of this storm. If we turn back now, we'll be turning into it. We need to keep heading southwest until the weather improves. Then we—"

The boat gets knocked down to the right, lifting the port side off the water. I scream as Beth falls on top of me and we both slide to the other side of the cockpit, slamming into the bench seat. Adam falls, too, sending the beam of his flashlight straight up in the sky. Emma hits the bench above Beth and me with a grunt.

"Keep your heads down," Emma yells. "The boom is swinging."

In the glow of Adam's flashlight, I look up to see the massive sail push out to the starboard side, the force of the wind whipping it 180 degrees.

"Hang on," Adam calls as the boat dips farther to the right.

"We're going to tip!" Beth shrieks, her torso sprawled across my leg on the cockpit floor.

Emma pushes herself off the bench, planting her feet on the deck beside my head.

"I'll take the helm," she says. "We're running straight downwind. We should be on a close reach. Adam, bring down the mainsail, then tighten the storm jib more."

The flashlight beam moves horizontal as Adam gets to his feet. When Emma takes the helm, I feel the boat turn left, leveling us slightly. Adam moves to the front of the cockpit and starts to lower the mainsail as I stand up and help pull Beth to her feet.

Thank God Emma knows what she's doing. Or, at least, I hope she does. But does she know enough to get us out of this?

Chapter Twenty

Present: Day Five at Sea

Cold salt water sprays over the side, hitting my cheek. The companionway hatch flies open.

Beth turns for the companionway as Adam remains focused on lowering the towering mainsail.

"What are you doing?" I ask when Beth unclips the tether from her life vest.

"I think I know who did this."

"Who?"

Beth glances below deck. "Gigi," Beth calls, moving toward the companionway. "Where are you?"

I follow Beth below, careful not to hit my head with the boat's constant rise and fall.

When I reach the bottom of the steps, I unclip the tether from my life vest. After tossing it onto the deck, I pull the door closed.

My ears feel numb from the cold as I sag against the wall, relieved to be out of the violent, deafening wind.

"Gigi," Beth repeats, swinging her phone light around the cabin.

Gigi emerges from the stateroom shared by the captain and Adam, holding a small piece of paper in one hand. She looks startled by our presence.

I open my mouth to ask, but Beth speaks first. "What were you doing in there?"

Gigi's mouth drops open in the bright light from Beth's phone, exposing her straight white bottom teeth. "Nothing. I thought it was my cabin. I got confused in the dark."

I recall her reaction when the captain announced we might have to turn back due to the weather. And what Beth read about Gigi's personal and professional life being upended, how much Gigi has to lose if this trip were cut short.

"Oh, come on, Gigi." Beth juts out her arm to keep her balance as the bow pitches over a swell. "I read about your fake following, the lawsuit, and how your husband's leaving you and taking half of your money with him. That's why you freaked out when Nojan said we might have to turn back."

Gigi's large eyes brim with tears. "Fine. Yes, my life's a mess. Happy?"

"Why did Nojan say *you* were paying him and not your sponsor?" I ask.

Gigi's chin quivers. "I lied—there's no sponsor paying for this trip. I saw that this San Diego yacht-rental company that I'd rented from in the past was paying to have a new sailboat delivered, so I sold my Lamborghini and paid Nojan to take us along. I was hoping the content would boost my real followers and save my career."

"And now Nojan's dead." Beth steps toward Gigi, stopping when their faces are only inches apart. "You're desperate to have your posts go viral. Having our captain go overboard would definitely do it. You'd get millions of views. You want us to believe you didn't have anything to do with that? That you're not capable? You pushed Courtney off the raft that day, and then you tried to make us all think she fell. But I saw what you did."

I gape at Beth, knowing she must be lying, trying to bait Gigi into a confession. Beth and I have spoken about this many times over the years, but neither of us saw what happened.

Gigi throws her hands in the air. "I didn't—"

Beth points her finger at Gigi's face. "You waited until Courtney lost her balance over a rapid, and you leaned to the side, forcing her into the river. Then, when she reached for your oar, you pulled it out of her reach and paddled away."

My gaze settles on Beth's silhouette as Gigi looks between me and my best friend. If Beth's telling the truth, why didn't she ever tell me?

"Fine." Gigi folds her arms. "I wanted her to fall in, okay? To teach her a lesson. But there's not a day that goes by that I don't feel horrible for what I did. I had no idea we would never find her. I just wanted to get even for those photos she spread around the school." Her voice breaks. "I'll never forgive myself."

I tear my gaze from Beth and see Gigi's lower lip tremble in the glow of Beth's phone light, recalling the painkillers she'd disguised as seasickness pills. She looks stricken. I believe her.

"I didn't—" Gigi blinks away tears that brim her eyes. "I didn't mean for Courtney to get hurt." She closes her eyes, her voice lowering to a whisper. "Or to never come back."

"And the captain?" Beth's tone is steady, almost flat, as if she's completely unmoved by Gigi's confession.

I'm reeling from the announcement that my best friend of twenty years *knew* all this time that Gigi forced Courtney into the water that day. And she didn't tell me. I assess Beth's form in the darkness, shrinking away from my lifelong friend. The floor rolls, throwing us all off balance. I stumble backward, slamming into the bathroom door. Beth catches herself on the companionway steps as Gigi presses a steadying hand on the kitchen counter.

"I didn't kill him!" Gigi shrieks.

Beth pushes herself upright and turns to Gigi. "Did you even stop to think what would happen to the *rest of us* if you killed the only person who knows how to sail?" Beth's accusatory tone is no longer calm but now laced with panic.

I survey Gigi, envisioning her making that calculated game-winning chess move on her phone. Could Beth be right?

"Beth, enough, okay? I think I know who *did* kill him." Gigi shines her phone light on the small piece of paper in her hand. An involuntary shiver travels down my arms at the sight of Courtney's note.

"Oh, please." Beth exudes an exasperated sigh. "You want us to believe *Courtney* killed the captain?"

"Listen." Gigi wraps her long fingers around Beth's wrist. "I was trying to see if I could find the rest of the notepad that Courtney's note was taken from. In case Adam wrote it."

Beth looks skeptical. I look toward the cabin Gigi emerged from when Beth and I came below.

Gigi lifts a hand to her forehead. "And I guess I was checking for Courtney." Gigi points to the bottom of the note. "Look at the tail on the *y*. That's exactly how Courtney used to sign her name. Don't you remember?"

I swallow, staring at the paper in Gigi's hand.

I do.

"That doesn't mean Courtney's alive," Beth says. "There's no way after all these years that she could be."

"Plus, we've already searched the entire boat. If Courtney *was* here, we would've found her," I say, as much to convince myself as the others. But my words do nothing to stop the goose bumps forming on my arms.

"Someone's messing with us." Beth tilts her head to the deck above. "Whoever wrote this note must've killed Nojan." She jerks her wrist free of Gigi's hold. "And right now, I think it's you."

Gigi lowers her voice. "I'm not saying Courtney's alive. I think Adam killed the captain. He must've also written that fake note from Courtney. I didn't find the notepad I was looking for in his room, but I found something else. His—"

The companionway door flies open, making me jump. I whip around. Adam fills the opening, shining his light on Gigi, who drops the note to her side.

Chapter Twenty-One

Present: Day Five at Sea

I hold my breath, sure Adam can hear my heart pounding against my chest wall.

"We need some help up here," he says.

A wave crashes against the starboard side, sending a spray of water into the cockpit that spills down the steps. Emma screams from somewhere near the stern.

I exhale as he moves away from the door and disappears from view. Dishes rattle inside the kitchen cabinets as the floor sways over another swell.

I turn to Gigi. "Why do you think it was him? What did you find?"

Adam reappears in the open doorway. "Like *now*," he shouts.

"Okay, we're coming," Beth says.

Gigi makes for the steps, tucking the note into her pocket. "I'll tell you later."

"Gigi." After seeing Adam retreat to the helm, I grab her arm before she gets to the top. "If he *did* kill the captain, he could be planning to kill us next. Don't say anything to him now. If we do confront him, we need to do it together."

The bow pitches down over the side of a swell, lifting the stern enough to knock Gigi off balance. She hits the top of the steps with her knees before crawling forward onto the deck.

I swear under my breath. Beth casts me a look that I can't quite make out in the dark before we ascend the steps.

What if Gigi's wrong and Adam didn't write the note? I try to wrap my head around the possibility that Courtney is still alive. My mind flashes to that day, twenty years ago, when I last saw her in the Olympic Mountains. It's unfathomable that she could've survived.

For Courtney to have written that note, it would have to be her ghost. I don't believe in ghosts, but the thought still sends a shiver through my body.

I think of Beth's accusation that Gigi killed Nojan to save her social media presence and how much Gigi stood to lose if this trip was cut short. And how Gigi supposedly found Courtney's note taped to her bathroom mirror. Gigi probably has old notes from Courtney. Or, at least, old yearbooks that Courtney had signed. With practice, Gigi could've mimicked Courtney's handwriting.

When Beth and I reach the deck, we're alone in the cockpit. My hair whips violently into my eyes from the screaming wind. Before I look around for the others, I rehook my tether and clasp another to Beth's life vest.

The light from Beth's phone sweeps the cockpit, then lands on Emma at the helm.

"Where's Gigi and Adam?" I ask her.

"What?" she shouts.

I take a few steps toward her and cup my hands over my mouth. "Where's Adam and Gigi?"

Emma points above me. "Trying to unjam the mainsail," she calls. "It got bunched up inside the furler, and now it's stuck."

I turn around and see Gigi in the light from Adam's flashlight as they stand on either side of the mast, tugging on the mainsail's fabric that's been let out.

"Beth," Adam yells. "Hold the top button down on the mainsail controls at the front of the cockpit. It's the small black button on the top left."

"Okay." Beth moves toward the controls.

"Palmer."

I turn to Emma's voice.

"I need you to look through these rear compartments and see if there's a sea anchor." Emma points to the floor around her.

I step unsteadily toward Emma, reaching for the mounted table in the darkness while wishing I'd brought my phone. I'm lashed by rain as soon as I step out from beneath the cockpit cover.

"I don't have a light," I tell Emma when I reach the helm.

"Here, use mine." She hands me her phone with the flashlight on.

I take it from her, wanting to tell her about the note and Gigi's suspicions about Adam. But there's no time for that now.

I open the stowage compartment on Emma's left, my mind still whirling over Beth accusing Gigi, and Gigi's suspicions of Adam. "What's a sea anchor?"

"It's basically a parachute that we'll throw into the water from the bow. My grandparents had one that was inside a bright-yellow canvas bag. Do you see it?"

I reach into the deep compartment, rifling through the contents. "All I see are those black-and-blue bumpers that kept the boat from hitting the dock."

"Those are fenders," Emma says. "Try the compartment behind the other wheel."

I hear arguing from the middle of the boat when I stand. I see Gigi's arms moving animatedly as she yells something to Adam that I can't make out. I can't see Adam's face, but from whatever he shouts back at Gigi, he doesn't sound happy.

I envision him unhooking her tether and shoving her off the boat. *Damn it, Gigi. Why couldn't you just heed my warning?*

"Did you find it?" Emma asks.

"Oh. Sorry. I'm looking." I grip the rear stanchions and then carefully move across the stern and open the other compartment. Lightning strikes overhead as I shine Emma's phone light inside and push aside the two spare life vests and mooring pole to find a yellow canvas bag labeled *SEA ANCHOR*.

"I found it!" I exclaim. Thunder roars, drowning out my voice.

"I got it," I repeat, lifting the bright bag in the air.

But Emma's gaze is fixed on the horizon beyond me. She looks stricken.

"Palmer." Her voice trembles. "Did you see that?"

I turn around, shining the phone at the whirling waves beside us. "See what?"

"In the distance, when the lightning struck, I saw a huge wave—much taller than these others—coming toward us."

"How tall?" I ask, gripping the rear pulpit's metal stanchion.

"Adam!" Emma calls. "Shine your light over the starboard side. There's a huge swell coming at us."

My gaze follows the beam of his flashlight, which illuminates the rough seas only within about ten feet of our boat. Over the howl of the wind, I hear a deep, rumbling roar like a freight train speeding toward us. Another bolt of lightning flashes across the sky, and my knees nearly buckle. The biggest wave I've ever seen is rolling toward us, dwarfing the other sizable swells. I freeze and grip the railing tighter as it disappears in the darkness.

Terror grips my throat, making it hard to swallow. It has to be nearly fifty feet high.

Chapter Twenty-Two

Present: Day Five at Sea

"Get below," Emma shouts.

As she steers the bow toward the wave, I stand still, paralyzed with fear. I stare into the darkness, envisioning the massive wave continuing to grow in size as it comes toward us.

"Palmer." Emma tugs on my arm. "Come on. Get inside."

She takes her phone from my hand. I tear my gaze from the water and allow Emma to pull me toward the cockpit.

"Beth," Emma calls.

Beth spins around at the front of the cockpit. Emma points at Adam and Gigi who are working to unjam the mainsail.

"Tell them to get inside. There's a huge wave coming!"

Beth whirls around and shouts at Adam and Gigi to get below.

"Hurry," Emma yells, fumbling to unhook her tether.

Adam's flashlight sweeps toward us.

"Here, shine this on mine." Beth extends her phone to me.

I hold the light on Beth's life vest while she unhooks her tether.

Adam and Gigi reach the back of the cockpit.

"What is it?" Adam asks.

"There's a huge wave coming," Emma says.

The boat rocks sideways on a swell. I reach for Beth, taking her with me as I fall to the floor.

"Shit," Emma exclaims. "We've turned away from the wave. We need to hit it straight on! Go below," she says to Beth and me while she shakily reattaches her tether. "I'm going to turn us one more time."

"Emma, don't! There's no time," I yell. But Emma is already halfway to the helm.

Adam's flashlight shines on Beth and me, still on the cockpit floor. I get up and start down the companionway, praying Emma makes it back in time before the wave hits.

I turn when I reach the bottom of the stairs. "Come on, Beth!"

"My foot's stuck," she screams.

I press my palm against the wall as we heel over forty-five degrees. My gaze darts to Beth's ankle, lit up by Adam's flashlight. It's wrapped twice in the mess of tether lines at her feet. I start to come up, but Adam holds up his hand. Gigi crouches beside Beth and works to untangle it.

"Everyone else get below," he shouts.

Emma steps past them. I move aside as she comes down the steps. She pulls me toward the dinette.

"Sit down and hold on," she says.

I cast a look over my shoulder. "Beth," I call, relieved to see her figure start down the companionway.

"I'm coming," Beth says.

The boat tips, sending Adam's flashlight to the angled floor.

"Are we all here?" I ask.

"Yes," Beth replies.

"Close the hatch," Emma yells, lying against the wall beside me. "This is it!"

Cupboards fly open, sending dishes crashing to the ground as we heel over, now perpendicular to the water. I grip the table, but it slips out of my hold, and I'm thrown against the window. It's as if I'm a part of the ocean, at the mercy of where it will take me. Like swimming, but without any control.

I hear something slam, and I pray it's just the hatch as the boat flips, throwing Emma and me against the skylight window hatches when the ceiling becomes the floor. Pots and pans are thrown about the cabin while water spills over me.

I squeeze my eyes shut and think of my girls, realizing with horror that we're completely upside down, submerged. My mind flashes to the luxury sailboat that sank last summer while at anchor in the Mediterranean, taking several people down with it. I suck in a breath, preparing for the water pressure to break through the windows.

Adam grunts. Beth screams. The boat sharply tilts again. My back hits the dinette table, knocking the breath from my lungs.

Glass shatters when a window bursts. Water rushes over my head while we begin to flip upright. Emma cries out. My heart hammers into my throat as I roll off the table onto the dinette cushions.

This is it. We're sinking.

The cabin goes eerily quiet as water stops pouring inside. Adam's flashlight shines against the wall in the corner of the room. I glance around the space in awe. It feels like we're bobbing on the surface. *Could the boat really have righted itself after capsizing?*

I sit up carefully, grasping the edge of the table in case we flip over again.

"You guys okay?" Emma asks from the floor beside the dinette.

Beth groans near the companionway steps. "I think so, but I hit my head pretty hard."

"I'm okay," Adam says.

"Palmer, Gigi, you guys all right?" Emma grabs Adam's flashlight and swings the beam toward the window above my head.

"Yes," I say, still in shock that we didn't sink. My heart thumps against my chest.

"We need to patch that window before we get hit by another swell," Emma says.

Another swell. The words send a bolt of panic up my spine. There's no way we can fix that window to make it watertight. If we get hit by another huge wave while we have a broken window, we're sunk. Literally.

"Gigi?" Beth asks. "Are you okay?"

No response. Emma swings the flashlight beam around the cabin, illuminating me, then Adam getting to his knees beside the couch, and finally Beth sitting upright on the floor in front of the steps.

"Gigi?" I say, my chest tightening with fear.

We all made it inside. Didn't we?

"Gigi!" Emma calls, whirling the light around the room for a second time.

"Didn't Gigi come inside with you two?" I say to Adam and Beth.

"I thought she came down before me," Beth says.

"I did too," Adam adds.

Emma steps over the broken dishes to shine the light inside the two open stateroom doors on either side of the companionway. "Gigi," she calls.

No, no, no, I think. She had to have made it down. She was right behind Adam. Wasn't she? I thought the three of them had come down together.

I strain to recall the order in which all of us came down, but after Beth's ankle got caught, everything seemed to happen so fast.

"Gigi," I echo. *Please let her be down here.*

I thought I'd heard Gigi's voice below, but now I can't be certain. We were all so panicked, I must've mistaken Beth's or Emma's cries for—

Emma whips the light around the enclosed space. Above the glow of her flashlight, her eyes double in size. "She's gone."

Chapter Twenty-Three

Memorial Day Weekend, 2005

"Did you guys hear about the two cyclists who were attacked by a cougar on the Pacific Crest Trail earlier this spring?" Beth asked from behind me on the trail. "There were three of them, all women," she continued without waiting for an answer. "The cougar tackled one of them, throwing her off her bike, and started eating her face off, until the other two women wrestled the cougar, choking it and hitting it with a rock until they were finally able to pin it down beneath one of their bikes while one of them called for help."

In front of me, Emma groaned. "I want to go back."

"Yeah," Gigi added. "You're freaking me out."

She was freaking me out, too, but I was glad to hear Beth return to her normal fact-sharing self after Courtney had given her a bookmark in place of a T-shirt.

"I've done a lot of research on cougars," Beth continued. "They're pretty fascinating. They're ambush predators, meaning they stalk their prey, usually attacking from behind. They kill with either a bite to the neck or the throat."

Gigi whirled her head around. "Isn't that the same thing?"

"No." Beth quickened her pace, having piqued Gigi's interest. "When they bite the lower neck, they snap the top of their prey's spinal cord, the cervical vertebrae, breaking the neck and suffocating the animal. Sometimes, they also bite the head to crush the skull, along with their prey's neck bones."

I scrunched up my nose at the visual.

"Eww," Gigi said.

Emma shook her head. "That's some dark shit, Beth."

Beth was now beside me on the trail. "When they bite the *throat*, they crush their prey's windpipe. They can also jump as far as twenty feet, and their jaws are powerful enough that cougars can take down prey even bigger than themselves."

I turned to Beth, whose voice sounded almost giddy with excitement.

"Okay, enough," Courtney called without turning around.

"My neighbor works for the Forest Service, and he told my mom recently that cougars in this area are becoming overpopulated. The increase in population also increases the competition for food supply, which is why they're becoming increasingly aggressive. If you see one," Beth continued, undeterred, "you're supposed to make yourself as big and loud as possible. That way—"

"*Beth*, stop," Courtney called from the front of our group. "You're scaring everyone with your stupid facts."

"They're not stupid," Beth quipped. "These *facts* could save our lives."

Courtney cast a sharp look over her shoulder. "Whatever. You're probably just making it up so you don't have to keep moving so fast. That's why I told you to start exercising before our trip." Courtney turned, taking a long stride over a puddle on the trail. "Plus, your ass is never going to get smaller if you're not willing to put in the work. If you had, you might've also gotten a prom date."

"Courtney!" I stopped in my tracks, gaping at Courtney's long red hair, which swayed with her steps as she hiked. Beth had never done anything to her. How could she be so heartless?

"What?" Courtney whirled around.

"Do you even hear yourself sometimes?" I asked.

Courtney's gaze shifted from mine to Beth's, and her face softened. "I'm just trying to be helpful. Beth knows that."

I turned to Beth, not buying Courtney's act of innocence. Especially not after she went to the school board behind my back. "Are you okay?"

Beth waved her hand through the air dismissively. "Yeah, I'm fine."

I studied my friend's face before turning around. Even though Beth acted like Courtney's "unintentional" jab didn't bother her, I knew it did.

"Beth knows I'm looking out for her," Courtney hollered from an incline up ahead. "Right, Beth?"

"Yeah, I know," Beth called from behind me.

Yeah, right, I thought.

Gigi moved in step beside Courtney. A moment later, Courtney burst out in obnoxious laughter at something Gigi said.

I paused and shot Beth another look over my shoulder. Her expression was unreadable, but I knew she had to be affected by Courtney's insults. How could she not?

I picked up my pace to keep up with the others, fixing my gaze on the back of Courtney's head, cocked to the side as she giggled. She was the most generous person I knew, but she was also the most cruel.

The trail inclined as we hiked on. Somewhere in the woods to my right, a bird chirped. Our group's conversation waned as we worked to keep up with Courtney's pace. Behind me, Beth's breathing became audible as the trail grew steeper.

"I have to pee," Emma said.

Courtney spun and put her hands on her hips. "Already? Can't you wait a bit longer?" Courtney swatted a mosquito that had landed on her neck, leaving a smear of blood on her smooth skin.

"No." Emma shook her head. "I've been holding it for a while. I have to go now."

"Ugh." Courtney threw her head back in impatience. "Okay, that's fine, but I'm going to keep moving. We still have another seven miles to go before we make camp."

"We need to stay together," Beth called out from behind me, her voice stern.

"It won't be for long." Courtney turned to Emma. "Just catch up as soon as you're done."

"Remember what I said about the cougars," Beth warned after Emma as she stepped off the trail. "You shouldn't go off very far by yourself."

"I'll go too," I said, following Emma. I didn't have to pee that bad yet, but I knew I'd have to go before too long, and I had no desire to deal with Courtney's dramatic attitude if we had to stop for a second time.

"Gigi, do you want me to carry the raft now?" I heard Courtney ask after I stepped off the trail into the woods.

After making sure we were far enough from the trail not to be seen if other hikers came along, Emma and I squatted behind large trees, several feet apart. It took me a few minutes to relax enough in the quiet woods before I was able to go. When I finally did, a rustling in the fern beside me made me jump to my feet. A small bird fluttered out of the fern as my heart hammered inside my chest. I exhaled, glad for the large spruce stump that blocked Emma's view of me freaking out with my shorts around my ankles.

I crouched back into a half squat as my pulse slowed. By the time I was able to go again, I sank into a full squat to relieve my tired thigh muscles and accidentally peed on my shorts. I swore, searching for the small amount of toilet paper I'd packed in my bag.

Emma was waiting for me when I emerged from behind the tree a few minutes later.

"Ready?" she asked.

I tried not to dwell on my urine-soaked shorts as I stepped over a log. “Yeah.”

“Wait.” Emma reached for my arm when I moved beside her. “Before we go back, tell me the truth. Did Bryson and Jake really put that dish soap on the locker room floor?” She lowered her voice. “Or was it Courtney?”

My face grew hot as Emma’s hazel eyes searched mine. Now was my chance to come clean. In my periphery, a squirrel scampered up a large tree trunk.

“Come on, Palmer. I can tell something’s bothering you,” Emma prodded, crossing her arms. “I deserve to know—that prank ruined my future. Years of hard work down the drain just like *that*.” Emma snapped her fingers. “I’m playing volleyball at *community college*,” she added. “Whoever did this to me is going to pay. But first, I need to know the truth. Don’t you think I deserve that?”

I drew in a deep breath, steeling myself for my long overdue confession. “Actually, Emma, I . . . um . . . there’s something—”

“Hey, guys.” I spun to see Courtney less than ten feet away, her eyes bright with excitement. “We found a hot spring just off the trail. We’re going skinny-dipping. Last ones into the hot spring have to carry the rafts for the next two miles.”

Emma and I exchanged glances. Emma made no effort to move, and I could tell she was eagerly waiting for Courtney to leave so I could finish my sentence.

“We’ll be right there,” Emma told her.

But Courtney didn’t retreat. “Come on. Let’s go.” She motioned for us to follow, pivoting to the side while she kept her gaze on us. “Don’t make me use my team-captain voice.” Her mouth lifted into a half smile. “What are you waiting for?” Courtney’s green eyes landed on mine, and I wondered if she’d overheard what Emma had asked me.

Emma appeared to study Courtney for a moment and then me. "Nothing." She cast me a knowing look before she followed Courtney back to the trail without another word.

I stood in the woods, watching Emma stride away. She was smarter than Courtney gave her credit for. Courtney may have fooled the school board, but Emma wasn't buying it so easily. I blew a breath out of my mouth and trudged after them, knowing it would be up to me to set things right.

Chapter Twenty-Four

Present: Day Five at Sea

The companionway door rattles before Emma manages to yank it open. Water spills down the steps as she climbs onto the deck.

"Gigi!" she calls.

Beth and I hurry up the stairs behind her. When I step outside, faint daylight filters through the clouds on the horizon, allowing us to see without a flashlight.

"Gigi," Emma hollers again, moving toward the stern. "Where is she?" Her voice is panicked.

My heart catches in my throat. There's no sign of Gigi. Above us, the cockpit cover is ripped in two. One of the poles hangs loose from where it had been attached to the top of the bench seats, which are all missing their cushions.

Water comes up to my ankles when I take a step back to make room for Beth and Adam to come on deck.

"Gigi!" I call, turning around. "Emma." I stretch my arm behind me toward the helm, looking at the mast, which is surprisingly still upright. "Give me the flashlight."

She places the light in my palm, and I sweep its beam across the foredeck. Miraculously, our dinghy is still secured upside down near the bow. The storm jib is a tangled mess around one of the shrouds. But there's no sign of Gigi.

I stare at the foredeck beneath the mast where Gigi had argued with Adam before the wave hit us. She must've confronted him about whatever she'd found in his room.

Beth and Adam call out her name.

I scan the surrounding waters with the flashlight but see only the dark, rolling swells.

"Check the tethers," I tell Beth.

She drops to her knees beside me, and I shine my light on her hands as she tries to untangle the mess of lines.

I squat beside her. As Beth separates the ropes, I try to recall where Gigi was when I went below. When Beth's leg got caught, Gigi was right here at the back of the cockpit. I'm sure of it. I thought she came below after she'd helped Beth free her leg from the tether line.

Keeping my light on Beth's hands, I glance at the companionway door. It's only a few feet away. How could she not have made it inside?

A shudder travels down my spine. Was it possible? Is Courtney somehow alive? Here, on this boat?

I shake the thought away and return my gaze to the deck floor. I hold the light still on one of the tether lines, which is pulled taut and extends back toward the helm. "Check that one."

Beth grips it and pulls. "It's tight, I can't pull it."

"Emma," I call, shining the flashlight on the deck beside her. "Check the tether line by your feet."

Hope builds in my chest as Emma lifts the line.

"It's in the water," she exclaims, lifting the tether with both hands. She lets out a grunt. "Someone help me pull. It's heavy!"

Thank God, I think.

Adam rushes past me to Emma's aid, grabbing the line behind her and pulling it in from the water. Beth comes to my side as I keep the light on the tether as steady as possible while the boat rocks.

"Be careful," I call out, realizing none of us have tethers on. I turn to Beth. "Get tethers for them. We should all have one on."

Beth turns and gathers the tethers without a word.

"I see her," Emma shouts. "Keep pulling."

I direct the light over the side. The hope that had surfaced in my chest sinks when I spot Gigi bobbing—lifeless—in the water. Her long blond hair swirls around her unmoving form, face down, kept afloat by her inflated life preserver.

Beth clips a tether onto Adam and Emma as they pull Gigi's tether to the side of the boat. I take Adam's place, holding tension on the rope, as he leans under the lifeline and drags her onto the deck.

"Roll her onto her back," I instruct him as Beth clips a tether to my life vest.

"Here." I tuck the flashlight into my armpit and grab Gigi's arms. "Help me drag her into the cockpit so she doesn't roll off the boat."

Adam lifts Gigi's feet as I tug her by the arms and pull her inside the cockpit, which feels instantly cramped with Gigi's long form lying on the floor. I extend the flashlight to Beth, who gasps after shining the light on Gigi while I feel her neck for a pulse.

A deep gash runs across the middle of Gigi's forehead to her temple, which is swollen to the size of a golf ball.

"She must've hit her head," Emma says as I continue to wait for a pulsation beneath Gigi's skin.

Or someone struck her, I think. She's deathly pale, her mottled skin nearly the same color of the white fiberglass beneath her, only her pallor has more of a blueish-gray hue.

"Dear God." Beth shakes her leg. "Gigi, can you hear me?"

"She doesn't have a pulse," I announce, withdrawing my hand from her neck and placing my palms, one on top of the other, on the middle of Gigi's breastbone. "Someone check the time."

I inch my knees closer to her torso, cursing the tight space as I press my weight into her chest, feeling the cartilage of her sternum crack beneath my palms. I count aloud as I compress, finding it nearly impossible to be effective while we roll over a swell. My knees slide to Gigi's legs, and her limp body slips toward the helm.

"Hold her steady," I order the others, a calm authoritative assertiveness in my tone from my years of working at a hospital. "Beth, move around and get ready to give her two breaths when I get to fifteen."

A moment later, I pause to allow Beth to blow into Gigi's mouth after pinching her nose. After the second breath, I immediately resume compressions. The early morning sun spills over the horizon as Gigi remains unbreathing and unmoving beneath my hands.

"How long has it been?" I ask when I notice I'm out of breath and the depth of my compressions has decreased.

"Eight minutes," Emma says.

"I'll take over."

Out of breath, I allow Adam to take my place at Gigi's side after I check again for a pulse.

"No pulse," I tell him. "Continue compressions."

Beth continues to give Gigi breaths in between Adam's rounds of compressions. I sit back on my knees, thinking of the survival statistics for going into cardiac arrest outside of a hospital. It's less than 6 percent. And even if we do get Gigi's pulse back, we have nothing to stabilize her with: no ventilator, IV fluids, or medications. Nothing aside from a first aid kit. There's no way to assess the extent of her head injury without diagnostic imaging.

The bow lifts over a swell. I grip Gigi's ankles, struggling to keep her from sliding atop the angled boat. Emma moves to the helm.

"I need to make sure we don't get hit sideways by one of these," she hollers.

Adam counts as he continues compressions, but I can see that he's tiring.

"Emma," I call over my shoulder. "How long have we been doing CPR?"

From behind the steering wheel, she glances at her watch. "Fifteen minutes."

I turn back to Gigi, her lifeless form jerking beneath Adam's compressions.

"Stop," I say, crawling past him to feel Gigi's neck for a pulse. Still nothing. I withdraw my hand, assessing the woman I've known since I was a girl. Normally, it's recommended to do at least twenty minutes of CPR before calling a time of death. But there's nothing we can do to save her. I run my gaze up and down her limp, pale form. She's already gone.

Beth rocks back on her heels beside Gigi's head, looking defeated as a whimper escapes her throat. "Gigi," she mutters, wiping a tear from her cheek.

Adam leans forward, returning his interlaced hands to Gigi's chest.

I lay my palm on his forearm. "She's beyond our help."

A violent clamoring overhead makes me tear my gaze from Gigi's body. A metallic groan emits from the boom as it swings over the side, its end lifting away from the boat. Above the boom, the exposed mainsail that Gigi and Adam didn't manage to furl flaps violently in the wind.

Emma steps into the cockpit, hovering over Gigi's feet. "Is she breathing? Did you get a pulse?"

I shake my head. "There's nothing we can do to save her."

We all go silent as I stare in disbelief at Gigi's lifeless body while the mainsail continues to flap from the raging wind. When my gaze travels to Gigi's wet hair splayed across the deck, my mind flashes to Courtney's long red waves the last time I saw her, soaking wet from the river.

"Shit." Emma slams her fist onto the table beside us, making Beth jump.

"We need to conserve our energy," I add, lifting my gaze to the source of the metallic clamoring. The weather vane's gone, and the Starlink satellite dish hangs by a cord above the middle of the mast, smacking against the metal pole.

So we can try to save ourselves.

Chapter Twenty-Five

Present: Day Five at Sea

"Watch her head," I tell Beth when I get to the bottom of the steps, holding Gigi's lower legs between my arms.

My words are too late. The floor dips when Beth steps onto the top stair. I wince at the sound of Gigi's head smacking against the companionway wall.

"You got her?" I step backward, keeping hold of Gigi's long legs as Beth descends the rest of the steps with her arms hooked beneath Gigi's armpits.

"Yeah," Beth grunts.

Despite being pudgy in high school, Beth is now much fitter than I am. She started working out regularly after graduation, and unlike me, she never stopped.

Once everyone accepted there was nothing more we could do for Gigi, Emma and Adam went to reattach the boom vang and bring down the rest of the mainsail, tasking Beth and me with untangling the storm jib. But first, Beth and I had argued over what to do with Gigi's body.

When Beth reaches the cabin floor, I pivot so she can carry Gigi headfirst into Gigi's stateroom.

"This is going to be even harder if we have to carry her body back up," I say, already regretting our decision.

"It just doesn't seem right to stuff her into the bench seats or a compartment on deck."

"I know." I lay Gigi's lower half onto her bed as Beth lays her head to rest on her pillow.

Beth wipes a bead of sweat from her brow.

"But we may not have a choice if she starts to smell." I already warned Beth about how quickly Gigi's body would decompose, which was why I thought we should stow her somewhere on deck.

"We'll be back to the mainland or rescued by then." Beth tears her watery gaze from Gigi.

I don't share Beth's optimism, but I don't see any point in saying so.

I glance at Gigi's corpse. Noting my lack of emotion, I worry that something is wrong with me. As a nurse, I'm used to compartmentalizing while I do my job. But this is different. I feel numb, in disbelief that our childhood friend is dead.

"Wait," I say when Beth backs away from the bed. "Let's tuck her in so she doesn't roll off."

Beth exhales before nodding.

"I'll turn Gigi on her side while you adjust the bedding." It's not my first time moving a dead body, although this is much more difficult than dealing with a stranger. But Beth is visibly more shaken than I am.

"Let's switch places." I slide past Beth. When I turn Gigi onto her side, I'm finally hit by a wave of emotion. I tear my eyes away from her pale, lifeless face and try to stay focused on the task of properly storing her body rather than thinking about my beautiful childhood friend being gone.

I see a bulge in the zipped pocket of Gigi's sweatshirt. I look at Beth as she reaches over and unzips the pocket, taking something out. "Palmer." She stands, opening what looks like a man's wallet.

I inhale sharply, recognizing the man's face on the driver's license photo. The man in the photo is unmistakably Adam except that his hair is red, not brown.

"His name's not Adam," Beth says, staring at the ID. "It's Russell."

I flick my gaze to the name, sucking in a breath.

"Russell Vance," I read aloud.

"He's Courtney's older brother." Beth taps her finger on the license photo.

"No, he can't be. It has to be a coincidence. Vance is a common name, and . . ."

"Palmer, look at him."

I do, but I've already realized she's right. None of us had seen Courtney's older brother since we were in grade school. He was seven years older and had been deployed in Iraq through our middle school and high school years. I recall his hair being a matching shade of red to Courtney's, just as it was in his license photo. He must've dyed it brown so we wouldn't recognize him. But now that I look at him, I can see it. He even has Courtney's eyes. "You're right." I cover my mouth with my hand.

"Courtney got the idea for us to go on that rafting trip from him, remember? I saw an old family photo of him in Courtney's parents' house once. I thought he looked familiar, too, after you said so, but I couldn't place it until now."

I stare at the driver's license. I should've known when I saw his Marine Corps tattoo.

Beth grasps my arm. "Gigi must've found this when she was in his stateroom earlier, remember?"

I nod as a myriad of questions flood my mind. What the hell is he doing here? Had he come to avenge his sister's death? To off us one by one? The boat creaks as we tip to the side. I keep hold of Gigi until we level out.

My eyes widen in the morning light streaming through the window hatch above our heads. "Adam—I mean Russell—and Gigi were arguing about something before the wave hit. I thought they were fighting over how to unjam the mainsail, but what if she confronted him about being Courtney's brother?"

Beth gasps, lifting her gaze to the boat deck above. She lowers her voice. "He must've locked Gigi out on purpose when we all came below."

I replay the chain of events in my head. Beth was the last one to come down, and Russell was the one who'd shut the door.

"He must be here seeking revenge for Courtney's death," Beth continues. "If he wrote that note, he obviously thinks one of us killed her. What if we're all next?" Her last word comes out louder than the rest.

"Shh!" I warn, raising a finger to my lips. "He'll hear you."

"Hey."

I startle and turn, finding Russell standing in the doorway. "We need some help up top."

Beth holds up the wallet before I can stop her. I inwardly curse her as she waves it toward Courtney's brother.

"You lied to us," she says. "You're Courtney's brother. That's why you can't sail."

Russell clenches his jaw, appraising Beth and then me.

"Beth," I warn.

"Why? Out of some sick revenge for us coming home from that trip without Courtney? We tried to find her! So, what's next? You're gonna kill the three of us too?"

I'm vaguely aware of Emma's bare feet treading down the wood steps as Beth steps toward Russell. I grab Beth's forearm, envisioning Russell, as muscled as a linebacker, striking her down with a single blow.

"What's going on?" Emma asks pushing past Russell, looking between him and Beth. "Adam, I still need—"

"His name's not Adam." Beth whips around to face Emma. "It's Russell." She thrusts the wallet at Emma's chest. "He's Courtney's brother. And now the captain and Gigi are dead." Beth folds her arms, shooting an icy glare at Russell over her shoulder. "I say we push him out in the dinghy."

Russell straightens, his pectoral muscles visible through his shirt. "I'm not going anywhere."

"What?" Emma's face flushes with anger when she looks up from Russell's ID.

"Gigi confronted him," Beth continues. "And he locked her outside."

"That's a lie." His jaw tightens, the muscles rippling beneath his skin as he clenches his teeth.

Emma's gaze settles on Russell, her expression darkening. "I'll kill you myself."

"Stop!" I scream as Emma pummels forward, slamming Russell against the kitchen cabinets.

He grips Emma by the shoulders and pushes her back. "I didn't kill anyone!" He holds up his palms. "I'm just here for the truth—that's all I want." When Emma raises a fist in the air, Russell lifts a forearm in front of his face. "I swear on my sister's life, okay?"

She keeps her fist raised but makes no move to hit Russell.

He lowers his forearm, keeping a palm in the air. "After my parents died last year, I had to go through their things before putting their house on the market. I found an old diary of Courtney's. I knew my sister could be cruel, and her diary proved it." He flexes his jaw and looks between the three of us. "But it also proved that every one of you who went on that trip with her had a motive to kill her."

Emma lowers her fist.

"I know that area where you hiked—very well. I went back there after reading in Courtney's diary about the things she'd done to all of you. If she really went missing where you said, I don't understand why her body was never found. Tracker dogs traced her scent to the river's edge near where you said you got in the rafts. The search and rescue teams believed she drowned, likely pinned beneath a logjam in one of the seventy miles before the river hits the Pacific, but I don't buy it. Not after reading the things in Courtney's diary that she'd done to each of you."

I look away from Russell, my muscles tensing as my gaze drifts from Emma to Beth, trying to gauge what they're thinking.

I fold my arms and turn back to Russell. "So, you came on this trip for revenge? Is that why you killed Gigi? And the captain?" Fear explodes in my chest as Russell's eyes lock with mine. Is he planning to kill us all?

"Yes, I lied about who I was, but I'm not here for revenge. I just want to know what happened to Courtney." He shakes his head. "I didn't kill anyone."

"What about the note from Courtney that Gigi found in the bathroom?" I ask, feeling stupid for believing Courtney could've still been alive after all these years, knowing what had happened to her in those woods.

"What note?" Russell asks.

Emma narrows her eyes. "Don't act like you don't know. The note accusing one of us of murdering her."

He shakes his head. "I don't know what you're talking about."

My eyes meet Beth's. She looks as unconvinced as I am. He had to have written the note—it makes perfect sense. He was hoping to force a confession out of one of us. I drop my gaze to the floor. Out of *me*.

Russell's expression goes hard. "*Did* one of you murder her?" He looks between the three of us.

My insides scream with guilt the moment Russell's eyes lock with mine. I feel Beth's eyes on me too.

"Of course not," Emma says.

He folds his arms. "Then what really happened that day?"

"We already told the police, and the press, and everyone what happened." Emma throws up her arm. "How'd you manage to get on this boat?"

Somewhere below, the hull groans. I exhale a silent breath as Russell returns his attention to Emma.

He runs his hand through the top of his hair. "A month ago, I found out about your trip through Gigi's Instagram when she posted a photo of this boat docked at the Elliott Bay Marina. So, I went down there, found Nojan, and told him about Courtney's disappearance, and paid him to let me replace the first officer on the trip. I promised not to cause any trouble; I just needed to know what happened to my sister. And now there are only three options." Russell closes his palm and holds up one finger. "Either you all killed Courtney." Two fingers. "Or one of you killed her and the rest helped cover it up." Three fingers. "Or—" He pauses, looking between the three of us. "Since there's a murderer on board, maybe one of you killed Courtney on your own and lied to the others about it." He gestures toward Gigi's stateroom. "And you're killing again to keep your crime a secret." Russell lowers his hand and steps toward Emma. "I'm going to find out which of those it is."

"Why would any of us kill the captain?" I ask him. "It doesn't make any sense."

Emma shoots Russell an accusatory look. "Unless it was you. Making sure no one would stand in your way of offing us, one by one."

Russell shakes his head. "Whoever killed the captain put all our lives in jeopardy. I didn't come out here to die—or to kill anyone. I just want to learn the truth about my sister."

Beth scoffs. "You really want us to believe that's—"

A wave slams against the side of the boat. Beth falls to the floor, landing on the mess of broken dishes, while Russell and Emma are thrown against the galley cabinets. I stumble sideways, slamming into Russell.

I teeter off balance, and he wraps a strong arm around my waist. I envision Gigi's corpse in the next room and try to pull away, but the motion of the boat keeps me glued against him. I push off his muscular chest with my palms, but he tightens his hold on my back. My pulse races as I anticipate his hands moving up to my neck, snapping it while Emma and Beth are distracted by the wave pummeling us.

I'm about to cry out when he loosens his hold. His hands move to my hips. I sway to the side, my eyes meeting his. Russell steadies me as water pours in through the broken window before he lets go. A clunk resounds from inside Gigi's stateroom. I cringe, realizing her body must've fallen off the bed. I back away, gripping the countertop beside

Emma, hearing myself shriek as I brace for us to tip over for a second time. Instead, we level out, and the water stops pouring.

I exhale and stand up straight, assessing Russell's unreadable expression before checking the floor behind me. "Beth? Are you okay?"

Beth nods, getting to her knees beside the couch. "I'm good."

"Shit," Emma mutters, pushing off the kitchen cabinets. "I have to get back to the helm. We've lost our autopilot, so we'll need to tie a line to the wheel to maintain our course when no one's at the helm."

"I'm going to cover that window." Russell brushes past me. "Then, I'll see if I can figure out how to get the power back on."

Emma casts a glance over her shoulder on her way up the companionway. "I need someone to untangle the storm jib while I steer."

"I'll do it." Beth uses the couch to push herself to her feet.

"I'll help you," I say, glancing at Gigi's stateroom, thinking about her head wound before following Beth up the stairs. Did she hit her head or had someone struck her while the rest of us went below? It was dark, chaotic. My mind shifts to the captain's cut tether line, sliced clean with a knife. That was no accident.

"We're turning back, right?" Beth asks Emma.

Emma shakes her head on her way to the helm. "First, we have to get out of this storm. Then I'll head southeast, which should put us on course for southern Oregon or Northern California—south of the storm."

I turn at the sound of a metallic clank. Russell is on his hands and knees beside an open cabinet, rifling through a small toolbox. "Is there seriously no hammer in here?"

I assess his muscular arms, recalling how I thought he was going to hurt me when I fell against him moments earlier, only for him to help me keep my footing.

He looks up, meeting my gaze. I avert my eyes and continue up the steps, mentally replaying Russell's story about his sister's diary. I can't help but wonder what it said about me, and the others, although I have a good guess.

When I reach the cockpit, Beth hands me a tether line as Emma takes hold of the steering wheel. Russell is either a very good actor or he's telling the truth. For some reason, my gut wants to believe him. But I can't allow myself to entertain the implications of his story being true.

Because if Russell isn't a killer, then who is?

Chapter Twenty-Six

Present: Day Five at Sea

"Nice work," Emma tells Beth and me from the helm.

The wind whips my hair back from my face as the two of us step off the foredeck between the wheel and the cockpit.

Below deck, Russell is hammering a temporary cover onto the broken window, using a meat-tenderizing mallet from the galley. There was no hammer in the toolbox, making me wonder if the tool was what caused Gigi's head injury. Her gash wasn't circular, but she could've been struck by the curved two-piece end, whatever that's called, instead of the head.

Emma would know what it's called, I think, studying her behind the wheel. A home renovator would be very comfortable using a tool like that. Before I can stop myself, I imagine Emma swinging the sharp end of a hammer at Gigi's head.

I suppress a shudder and push the thought from my mind as the sun peeks through the clouds above the east horizon. I shade my eyes with my hand as I assess the surrounding seas. In full daylight, the waters appear to be slightly calmer than last night's violent swells. Hopefully, that means Nojan was right about the storm moving west and that we're heading away from it.

My gaze travels to the mainsail, which still protrudes a few feet from the boom furler.

I turn to Emma. "Did Russell and Gigi unjam the mainsail?"

Emma shakes her head. "I don't think so. The winds are too strong to have it up right now, but we'll need to get it fixed so we can sail back in lighter winds."

Beth glances in the direction of Russell's hammering before stepping closer to Emma. "He's lying about just wanting the truth. He's here for revenge." She casts another cursory look behind her as the rhythmic pounding continues. "He's planning to kill all of us." Her wary gaze meets mine before she turns to Emma. "One by one. We need to subdue him somehow. If we work together, maybe we can lock him in his room."

Emma frowns. "You read too many books. You don't know that for sure."

"But what about the captain?" I ask, wondering how Emma could so easily dismiss concerns over Courtney's brother being on board—and two people being dead. "He didn't cut his own tether."

"All I'm saying is, what if he's telling the truth?" Emma asks, verbalizing my earlier suspicions. "I think we should at least consider it."

Beth recoils as if Emma had struck her. "Meaning what? That one of *us* killed Gigi and the captain?"

Emma turns her pensive gaze toward the horizon. "Maybe Gigi's death was an accident."

Beth looks sharply at Emma. "You've spent the most time alone with Russell. Up here on the decks while the rest of us were below." She folds her arms. "I'm surprised he didn't try to kill you."

"Maybe he needed me to help sail the boat," Emma says. "It's possible Russell heard Gigi confess to pushing Courtney out of their raft. And then he killed her."

Beth shrugs, keeping her eyes trained on the home renovator. "Or you've known who he is this whole time. Your new boyfriend you told Gigi about. And you're in on this together."

I stare at my best friend, surprised at her boldness. Although, if there was ever a time to be bold, I suppose it's now.

"You've been violent ever since we were kids," Beth continues. "Senior year, Courtney showed me a part in her diary that said you were the one who threw that rock through that volleyball referee's living room window. The one that made that bad call our first game of the season."

I turn to Emma, whose mouth flies open. Beth had told me this right after Courtney showed her, but Emma's action didn't surprise me. Instead, I was more worried about what Courtney might be telling the others about me.

"Yeah, I threw the rock, but it was Courtney's idea! So what? That doesn't make me a murderer." Emma's cheeks flush as she shoots Beth an icy glare.

Beth raises her dark eyebrows. "Oh, really? Maybe you're the one who fought with Courtney outside our tents the night before she disappeared. I couldn't hear everything. But it was nasty, I know that."

My stomach churns despite the calming seas. I want to correct Beth, but even now I can't bring myself to. I look to Emma for her response.

Emma flexes her jaw, narrowing her gaze at Beth. "*You're* the one who took the brunt of Courtney's cruelty that day. Passively enduring Courtney fat-shaming you with her snide remarks about your weight during our hike." Emma purses her lips, knowing she's struck a nerve. "Even though she pretended to be your friend, Courtney was always cutting you down. It sometimes seemed subtle, but it was cruel. It had to have affected you. Hell, it's probably why you've spent the rest of your life burying yourself in books and academia." Emma rolls her eyes. "And your cat. Rather than living in the real world."

"Like you're any different," Beth hisses, raising her voice. "Hiding behind your renovation career, obsessed with creating a new, false image of yourself. Putting a sweet, beaming photo of yourself on a billboard on the 405."

I cringe at Beth's mention of the billboard. After Emma's volatile video went viral, someone had graffitied **BITCH** on the billboard in red letters. The last time I'd driven by, it was still there.

"Just like Gigi, you're addicted to being in the limelight, trying to erase what it felt like having everyone look at you like you were a murderer. And your anger problem is clearly worse than ever. It's why you needed this trip. To repair your shattered public image. Without that, you have nothing."

Emma's knuckles whiten around the wheel. She flexes her jaw.

"Look," I say, trying to defuse the situation, afraid of what Emma might do if Beth keeps poking at her. It wouldn't take much for Emma to throw Beth overboard. I jut out my arm in between them, only partly aware that the hammering below deck has stopped. "Why don't we just calm—"

Beth steps toward Emma, pushing my arm to the side. "You were consumed with jealousy when Courtney replaced you as volleyball captain after you broke your ankle from Bryson and Jake's prank. Especially after we won the championship and Courtney got a full-ride volleyball scholarship instead of you. That's why you had it out with Courtney that night outside our tents. You hated her for it, and you still do."

A wave of guilt washes over me, like a heavy weight on my shoulders.

Beth jabs a finger at Emma's chest. "Maybe that's why you—"

"I didn't fight with Courtney that night," Emma shouts. "Palmer did."

"What?" Beth gapes at me.

"I woke up and heard Courtney say something about Palmer's mom never getting hired again, then Gigi came out asking Courtney if she was okay and Palmer what the hell had happened." Emma squared her jaw and locked eyes with mine. "You decked her, didn't you? Over what she said about your mom."

"Courtney and I spilled the dish soap, not Bryson and Jake," I say, releasing the lie I'd been holding for two decades.

Emma and Beth stare at me in silence, finally at a loss for words.

"I was with Courtney when she put the dish soap on the floor. She tried to get me to do it, but I chickened out at the last minute," I continue. "Then we lied about seeing Bryson and Jake in the locker room." I exhale, meeting Emma's gaze. "I'm sorry, I should've told the truth a long time ago. I was going to—"

Emma's palm impacts my cheek before I have time to react. My flesh stings when she lowers her hand.

Emma's steely gaze sears into mine. "You bitch."

She lunges at me, letting go of the wheel to grab me by my life vest with both hands. "I always knew it had to be Courtney. It was the only thing that made sense. But I trusted you. *You* said it was Bryson and Jake! I even asked you on our rafting trip. And all these years, you pretended to be my *friend*. But you're just as bad as her," Emma seethes.

I'm worse, I think. *Emma doesn't even know what I did the next day.*

Beth tries to intervene, moving between us. The boat tips, and she falls backward, smacking her head on the cockpit table on her way down.

"Beth!" I yell, shoving Emma back.

"Hey," Russell shouts from the companionway. "What the hell's going on? Stop."

"It's her fault." Emma glares at me, shoving me backward before letting go of my life vest.

"Enough," Russell calls as Beth gets to her feet, rubbing the back of her head.

He points to the navigation screens mounted above the wheel. "Look."

Emma and I turn to the screens, which are lit up, displaying the depth gradients around us in shades of blue, and appear to be fully functioning.

"I got the power back on."

Chapter Twenty-Seven

Memorial Day Weekend, 2005

I lay awake in the tiny tent I shared with Gigi. It was barely big enough for one person, let alone two.

"This is our *tent*? It looks like a coffin," Gigi remarked when we had unfolded it on the ground before setting it up.

"Don't be morbid, Gigi." Courtney rolled her eyes. "You guys should be thanking me for finding these lightweight tents. Like you could've carried anything heavier. I just hope none of you are claustrophobic," she added, driving her tent stake into the ground with a large rock.

Our camp wasn't really a campsite, just a clearing between the trail and the river. Courtney had been on a power trip since we'd gotten here, telling us who to bunk with and how this was all part of the team-building exercise.

Now, inside my sleeping bag, I turned on my side atop the uneven ground, trying to get more comfortable. Outside our tent, the only sound was the Sol Duc River's rushing water less than thirty feet away. I closed my eyes, but it was impossible to sleep.

My legs and back ached from carrying the pack raft seven miles uphill, and I longed to be home in my own bed. A fly buzzed inside our tent. Beside me, Gigi snored loudly.

We were all too tired to stay up around the fire much after it got dark, especially knowing Courtney planned to wake everyone at dawn to get a head start on tomorrow's hike and would demand we get our rafts in the water by noon.

I twisted inside my sleeping bag, wishing I would've had the guts to tell Emma the truth after Courtney interrupted us earlier. There was no way I could lie to the school board on Tuesday and destroy Bryson's and Jake's futures. Which meant I had to tell Emma the truth before then. Even though she—and Courtney—would hate me for it.

Maybe I would wait until the trip was over. Except I knew it was going to eat at me until I got it off my chest. I'd seen Emma's temper fly enough times to clearly imagine the names she'd call me when I finally confessed what Courtney and I had done.

Outside, someone unzipped their tent. Feet crunched atop leaves and twigs as they moved past. I sat up. From the heavy footfall, I guessed it was Emma.

I unzipped my tent, pausing to see if I'd woken Gigi. Her snoring continued, and I grabbed the compact flashlight beside me and stepped outside. In the dim glow of our campfire embers, I slid my feet into my hiking boots.

I needed to tell Emma alone. Get her to believe me without Courtney around. If Courtney heard my confession, she would try to make me out as a liar, insisting it was all my idea, including covering it up and placing blame on Bryson and Jake. She even had a photo on her phone to prove it. I darted my gaze toward the tent Courtney shared with Beth, knowing I wouldn't be able to sleep until I told Emma myself.

I zipped my tent closed and flicked on my flashlight, aiming the beam in the direction of the footsteps.

"Emma?" I whispered, moving around the side of my tent.

"It's me." Courtney squinted from my light, blocking the beam with her hand. "Can you lower your light?"

"Sorry." My lungs deflated with disappointment as I lowered the flashlight to my side. "Is it just you?"

"Yeah, I had to pee. Which I usually like to do alone."

I envisioned the sarcastic deadpan expression on Courtney's face even though it was too dark for me to see her with my light shining on the ground.

"Beth's out cold." Courtney snorted. "I know it's the offseason, but she really needs to keep in better shape. I mean, have you noticed how *big* she's gotten this spring?"

Inside me, something snapped. I stepped toward Courtney. "I'm sick of you bullying all of us while pretending like you care. All you care about is yourself. I'm not lying for you anymore."

"Palmer. Geez, calm down. What are you even talking about?"

I gritted my teeth at her feigned innocence. *What am I even talking about?* "On Tuesday, I'm going to tell the school board the truth. I'm not going to let Bryson and Jake's futures be ruined over something you did." I crossed my arms. "And I'm willing to take the blame for my part in it too. I should've told the truth a long time ago."

"You can't do that," Courtney hissed, closing the gap between us so that I could feel her breath on my face. "I lied to protect both of us, not just me. I risked everything. Because I'm your friend, Palmer."

A puff of air escaped my chest. "Ha! You're nobody's friend."

Courtney's green eyes narrowed in the glow of my flashlight, which because my were arms crossed, shone sideways into the woods. "You ungrateful bitch. I could ruin you, and your mom."

My mom? I was taken aback at her mention of my mother. Then I realized what she was getting at. My hand closed into a fist.

"If you throw me under the bus, I'll make sure my parents find a new Realtor for their house," Courtney spat.

"You can't do that. My mom has nothing to do with this." My shoulders tensed, thinking of how hard my mom had worked to become a Realtor after losing her job at the dental office when she had to take so much time off to care for her sister. Courtney's parents recently decided to downsize, and getting their listing was huge was for my mom. Selling it could make her career in a small town like Sequim. Not to mention cover our bills for an entire year.

"You don't think they'll fire her immediately if her daughter publicly accuses me of being a liar? This whole time, I've only been trying to help you." Courtney waved her arms in the air. "My parents have enough connections to make sure your mom never gets a good listing again. Word travels fast in a small town. They only hired your mom out of charity anyway." Courtney brought her face within inches of mine. "The same reason I've tried to be generous to you and your fat friend."

A smile spread across her face, and I finally lost it. I shoved her in the clavicles. Courtney stumbled backward, and I raised my fist in the air. A second later, my knuckles impacted her face.

Courtney cried out in pain, her hands flying to her nose.

I lifted my fist a second time. "You—"

"Palmer! What are you doing?"

Courtney sank to her knees in the dirt, her hands still covering her mouth and nose. I spun to find Gigi, wide-eyed and open-mouthed, her gaze moving from me to Courtney on the ground.

"Courtney!" Gigi rushed toward her. "Are you okay?"

Courtney lifted her palm in front of her face. "I'll be fine."

Gigi spun toward me before pulling Courtney to her feet. "What the hell's going on?"

"It was just a misunderstanding. Right, Palmer?" Courtney added, "No hard feelings."

Gigi gasped. "You're bleeding."

Courtney swiped away the blood on her lip with the back of her hand, leaving a red streak across her cheek. "It's nothing."

Gigi glared at me. "Palmer, what *happened*?"

Shaking with rage, I lowered my flashlight. At a loss for words, I stared at Courtney, shocked by what I'd just done. I'd never felt so enraged in my entire life. In that moment, I'd wanted to hurt her, make her suffer the way she made others suffer. I'd wanted to—

"Like I said, it was just a misunderstanding." Courtney rubbed her palms against her sweatpants, wiping away the dirt and pine needles. "No hard feelings."

Courtney patronizingly patted me on the shoulder as she brushed past, shaking out of Gigi's attempt to help her walk.

"You sure you're okay?" Gigi asked.

Courtney waved dismissively as she moved past the dwindling fire's burning coals. "Yeah, fine. It's been a long day, and I'm gonna get some sleep." She spun around when she got to her tent. "Hey, Palmer. I forgive you. And Gigi? We don't need to talk about this again."

"That was not a misunderstanding," Gigi said in a lowered tone after Courtney disappeared inside her tent. She turned to me. "I've never seen you even come close to attacking anyone. It looked like you were about to beat the crap out of her." She moved in front of me to assess me head-on. "What did she do to you?"

I heard Courtney's tent zip closed. "Courtney's right. It's nothing."

"Yeah, right." Gigi glanced over her shoulder at Courtney and Beth's tent. "You don't want to talk about it, fine. I'm here for you, though, whenever you're ready to tell me the truth. And your secret's safe with me. I've been wanting to hit her for several months now."

Gigi turned, and I followed her back to our tiny tent in silence. Apparently, Gigi hadn't been as quick to accept Courtney's innocence over those topless photos as she'd led on. Before climbing inside, I cocked my head toward the sound of the Sol Duc's swift torrent. *Gigi was wrong,* I thought as I lay down beside her. I hadn't wanted to beat the crap out of Courtney.

I'd wanted to kill her.

Chapter Twenty-Eight

Present: Day Five at Sea

"Thank God," Beth breathes.

Emma rushes to the navigation panel mounted beside the wheel. After seeing Beth is unhurt, I hurry across the slippery deck and then lean over Emma's shoulder to peer at the lit-up screens.

Emma points at the largest screen on the bottom of the panel. "The storm blew us way off course. We're more than three hundred miles off the coast of Northern California. But if we can sail six knots an hour going back, then we could get there in just over two days."

I scan the map display for a sign of other vessels. "Are there any other ships in our area?"

"Doesn't look like it." Emma zooms out.

"They're probably avoiding this area due to the storm." Russell places his hands on his hips, his demeanor visibly cooler now as he stands beside Beth on the other side of the wheel. I remember that Russell spent a lot of time in the military, and I can see it now, in the way he reacts to a crisis. He barely shows a hint of the emotion I saw below when we accused him of murder.

I point to a black dot on the corner of the screen. "What's that?"

"That's a ship. Probably cargo. But it's over two hundred miles northeast. We'd have to sail into the storm to try and reach it. Even if we made it, we wouldn't catch up to it."

I lift my gaze to Russell. "Is there any way we can make contact with other boats through this?"

He shakes his head, gesturing to the empty mouthpiece holder on the side of the mounted screen. "Not without the radio mic."

I tilt my head, squinting to assess the Starlink satellite. It's facing down, hanging by a cord more than halfway up the mast. "Check your phones." I fumble for my device inside my sweatshirt pocket. "Does anyone have a Starlink signal?"

"My phone's dead," Russell says.

"Mine too," Beth adds. "I should go charge it."

My phone screen lights up in my hand. Relief floods my insides as I tap the internet icon at the top left of my screen to connect to Starlink. If I can contact my sister, the Coast Guard could be on their way to us within a matter of minutes.

I bite my lip, willing my phone to connect faster. After a moment, two words appear. *No signal.*

"It's not working," Emma says, staring at her phone.

I drop my phone to my side and look up at the clank the satellite dish makes as it smacks against the metal mast. Russell turns and then disappears below deck, returning less than a minute later with a pair of binoculars.

He aims the lenses at the dish as Emma takes a photo of the navigation display.

"What are you doing?" I ask her.

"I'm noting our location. We should write it down also, in case we lose power again."

Beth frowns, furrowing her brows at Emma. "Why would we lose power again?"

I turn to Russell. "How'd you get the power back on?"

Russell squints into the binoculars. "The battery-selector switch for the two battery banks in the engine room had been switched off, so I turned them back on."

I study him, wondering if that was true. It seems too easy of a fix. Unless he caused the power outage, then knew exactly how to fix it.

Russell lowers the binoculars. "I think I can see the problem. There's one cord hanging loose. The wires may have gotten torn, or it may just need to get plugged back in. Then we need to resecure it to the mast with a bungee cord to get the dish facing back toward the sky."

My confidence evaporates like mist in the sun. I stare at the top of the mast, towering taller than the length of the boat. "There's no way we can get up there."

"Actually," Russell says, "we can climb it."

"Climb it?" My jaw drops as I stare at the pole. "With no steps?"

"We'll use a bosun's chair," Russell says. "We have one on board. Nojan showed me how to use it before we set sail. We can secure it to the spinnaker halyards and use the winches to crank someone to the top of the mast."

I swallow, tearing my gaze from the tip of the mast, which tilts at a sharp angle with every roll of the boat. "Sounds dangerous."

"It is," Emma says. "Especially in this weather. I've watched my grandparents do it, but only when the boat was docked on a calm day."

"I don't think any of us should risk going up there." Beside Russell, Beth stares up with her hand shading her eyes. She turns to Emma. "We have the power back on. Why don't we use the navigation to get back to the mainland? We have plenty of food for three more days."

Russell folds his arms, turning to Beth. "The covering I attached over the broken window isn't watertight. All it would take is one more knockdown to flood the boat."

"He's right," Emma says, her eyes darkly serious. "If we can get the Starlink working, we can call for help now, before something else goes wrong—or we get knocked down a second time." Her gaze drifts to the boom. "Plus, if we can't get the mainsail unjammed, we might not have enough sail to make it back to the coast, depending on the wind. We could get stuck out here and run out of food and water. The weather could also get worse before it gets better. There are a thousand things that could go wrong if we stay out here."

I look up at the mast tip again as it sways with each swell that rocks the boat. It must be at least fifty feet high.

"One of us has to go up there," Emma says. "We don't have a choice."

"I'll go," Russell says.

"It would be safer to have Beth or Palmer go up the mast," Emma says. "You and I have more experience using the winches and steering the boat."

I gape at Emma. Maybe Beth was right to suspect her. Was she trying to get one of us killed? *"What?"*

"That way," Emma explains, "Russell and I can keep the boat afloat and help get you down if there's a problem."

"I'll go," Beth says quietly.

"No." I shake my head, recalling Beth's panic attack when we rode the glass elevator to the top of the Space Needle our junior year.

Courtney had driven all five of us to the Bainbridge Island Ferry on Beth's seventeenth birthday, keeping the destination a secret from us until we got to the Space Needle. When I realized where Courtney was taking us, I tried to talk her out of it, reminding her of Beth's fear of heights. Courtney feigned unawareness of Beth's phobia, saying how the tickets were nonrefundable, even though we all knew that Beth couldn't so much as climb a stepladder without hyperventilating. Since we were kids, Beth hated even sitting at the top of the bleachers, and we'd always make sure to find seats down below.

Beth's not wanting to appear ungrateful turned to sheer terror when she passed out in the glass elevator. For a moment, I thought she'd had a heart attack and died. I called 911 as soon as we reached the top. Beth had regained consciousness by the time the medics arrived at the observation tower's revolving glass floor. They had to give her a Xanax for the elevator ride down.

Now, Beth places her hand on my shoulder. "Think of your girls. I'm not letting you risk your life while I stay down here and watch."

"You can't. What if you have a panic attack at the top?"

"You don't do great with heights either," Beth adds.

That's true. But I'm not as bad as Beth.

"I found the bosun's chair," Russell calls from the stern. "Who's going up?"

I look up at the teetering mast, then lower my gaze and turn to Russell, swallowing the lump of fear that swells in my throat. "I am."

Chapter Twenty-Nine

Present: Day Five at Sea

"Are you sure this will hold?" I cautiously shift my weight against the bosun's chair as Emma clips the shackle onto the end of her bowline knot. She then tests the second rope, which she refers to as a halyard, attached to my seat.

She avoids my gaze, and I know she's still livid after learning I lied to cover up Courtney's being the one who spilled the dish soap on the locker room floor.

"I'm sure." Emma tugs on each halyard. "I trust the knot more than the shackle, because shackles can break. But I did both just in case." She clips a short yellow rope that looks like a dog leash to the halyard.

Russell had tied the first line to the chair before Emma insisted on doing the second one while he steered the boat.

"We can't trust him to do both," she whispered as she checked his knot while he retreated to the helm.

At least she doesn't want me to die, even though she's pissed. I lower my gaze to the knot Emma tied before comparing it to the one Russell tied. Or what if Emma made a faulty knot and that's why she'd stopped Russell from tying both? I swallow, lifting my weight from the chair as

I think back to Beth accusing Emma of conspiring with Russell to kill Nojan and Gigi.

"What's that?" I ask as she clips the other end of the yellow rope to one of the lines suspending my chair.

"This will keep you from swinging out too far and slamming into the mast." The boat rocks, and Emma wraps her arm around the mast for support. "Especially in this weather," she adds. "Ready?"

I adjust the heavy strap of my shoulder bag filled with the various tools we guessed I might need at the top: a screwdriver, a wrench, pliers, a bungee cord, and a few spare screws. I glance above at the swaying mast as the satellite dish clamors against it, hoping for an easy fix when I get to it. I'm not great with a screwdriver on solid ground. How the hell am I going to screw something in on a moving target while I'm suspended over forty feet in the air?

I lower my gaze to the rolling seas. They're calmer than they were earlier but still speckled in whitecaps. Water sprays across the surface from the wind. I tear my eyes away, my mind wildly envisioning the boat getting knocked down a second time while I'm secured to the mast.

I lower my weight into the chair, ignoring my racing heart. "Ready."

The seat feels surprisingly secure, especially with the shoulder and crotch straps connected to it.

Emma nods, patting me on the shoulder on her way to the cockpit. "Just keep calm and focus on fixing the Starlink. Keep your eyes up. Don't worry about anything down below. Wouldn't want you to break something." Seeing the fear in my eyes, she adds, "I won't let you fall."

"She's ready," Emma calls to Beth, who's waiting in the cockpit, gripping the end of one of the halyards wrapped around a winch. "Russell, keep us as steady as possible."

Behind the wheel, Russell gives Emma a thumbs-up. I take a deep breath as I wait for Emma to get in position behind the other winch. Beth warily meets my gaze. I look away, closing my eyes in a futile attempt to quell my nerves.

"On three."

I open my eyes to Emma's voice.

She turns to Beth. "One. Two."

I wrap my hands around each of the halyards.

"Three."

The winches crank as my feet leave the boat. The boat tilts, and I swing out as far as the leash allows while I'm lifted higher in the air. I continue upward, holding my breath while the boat heels to the other side. I stick my bare feet out against the mast as I'm propelled toward it.

My seat lifts above the top of the partially protruding mainsail. I keep my gaze straight ahead while Beth and Emma continue winching me toward the top. *Don't look down,* I remind myself. I can practically hear my pulse throbbing in my ears.

"Big swell coming," Russell yells from the helm.

I drop my gaze to the rolling waves, instantly spotting the wave he's referring to. My head spins and my breath sticks in my lungs when Russell steers us toward the towering swell. I smack against the mast, berating myself for taking my eyes off it as my breath is knocked from my chest.

Below, Beth shrieks when the bow lifts over the swell. One of my ropes goes slack in my hand. Panic rips through my veins until I realize the other lines are keeping me secure. I look down to see Beth on the floor of the cockpit, scrambling to regain her hold on the halyard freely spinning loose on the winch.

Emma stares up at me, holding her line steady while Beth gets to her feet and grabs the end of her line.

"You okay, Palmer?" Emma shouts.

Despite the churn of my stomach, I give her the okay signal with one hand, keeping the other on the taut line. Beth pulls her line tight as we roll over the top of the swell. A scream escapes my throat as I watch the tip of the bow soar down the side of the wave, heading straight for the sea.

I'm suspended higher up the mast while white water sprays over the bow onto the foredeck. The leash is pulled tight when I'm thrown sideways. We roughly level out at the bottom of the swell. I exhale before being jerked backward toward the mast, then stick out my feet to keep from ramming into it.

I look up and see that I'm less than ten feet from the satellite. *You're almost there. You can do this.* I have a clear view of the cord hanging loose from the satellite, and I force myself to take a deep breath, trying to relax my stiff lungs. The end appears to be intact. With luck, I'll just need to plug it into the satellite and use the bungee cord in my bag to secure the device and stop it from banging against the metal mast. Hopefully it hasn't already incurred too much damage.

I feel for the tools in my shoulder bag, making sure they're all still there. My hands are clammy with sweat. When I'm a few feet from the top, I slip the bag off my shoulder. I reach for the swaying cord. It takes me two tries before my hand closes around it. A whitecap in the distance catches my eye, and my head spins. I close my eyes for a moment, steadying myself against the mast with my other hand.

Don't. Look. Down.

I open my eyes and let go of the mast to wrap my hand around the black base connected to the dish, willing myself not to think about how high I'm suspended in the air. Or what would happen if my knots failed.

I run my hand up and down the base until I find the spot to plug in the cable. I'm about to plug it in when I hear Russell shout something from the helm.

I glance down to see a large wave crash against the side of the sailboat. I force myself to look up and thrust the cord into the base of the dish. My swaying movement makes me miss the plug-in's connection by an inch. The mast veers sideways with such force that I'm sure we're being knocked down again. I grapple for a line to hold onto, inadvertently dropping the cord. The tool bag slips off my arm. Seconds later, it hits the rolling waves with a splash.

I swing out from the mast, my panicked gaze glued to the waves below. A snap sounds as tension is suddenly released from my harness. The yellow leash floats loose through the air as the shackle falls to the water. I'm propelled farther over the edge of the boat, my feet dangling fifty feet above the raging sea.

I catch a glimpse of Beth pointing at me from the cockpit when the mast begins to tilt in the opposite direction. I cry out, pulled over the boat as the mast rights itself.

I tighten my grip on the lines, preparing to be swung out over the other side. Below, Emma shouts something I can't understand. I strain to read her lips to no avail. All I can decipher is the terror-stricken look on her face.

When I lift my gaze, I'm heading straight for the mast. I stick out my foot, but it misses the pole, leaving me with just enough time to turn my head before my temple smacks against the mast and everything goes black.

Chapter Thirty

Present: Day Five at Sea

"Palmer!"

When I open my eyes, Beth is leaning over me, shaking my shoulders. I'm lying on the foredeck, staring straight up at the mast. The bosun's chair is still strapped around my shoulders. A sharp pain stabs at the side of my head above my left ear, and my climb up the mast comes flooding back to me.

Beth rocks back on her knees and places a hand over her heart. "Thank God. For a second, I thought you were dead."

"We need to go back up," I say, staring at the satellite swaying above.

Emma kneels beside Beth and looks down at me grimly. "You hit your head on the mast really hard. It was so loud we could hear it from the deck. You were knocked unconscious the whole time we lowered you down. I'm not sending you up a second time for that to happen again."

I sit up, feeling the blood drain from my head. Emma and Beth blur in my vision.

"Plus," Emma says. "We lost all the tools, remember? Your bag fell off your shoulder into the water."

"We don't need them. If I can go up again, I can—" I wince at the sharp pain that stabs at my temple. I lift my hand to it, feeling a tender bump.

"You need to lie back down," Beth says. "I think you have a concussion."

"How long was I out for?" I ask, knowing Beth is probably right.

"At least a few minutes while we hoisted you down." Emma eyes me warily. "We're lucky you weren't hurt worse."

Is that disappointment I detect in Emma's voice?

Water sprays the side of the boat.

"We should get you inside," Beth says. "Do you think you can stand if we help you?"

"I think so."

I try to ignore the painful throb on the side of my head as they help me get unsteadily to my feet.

"You okay, Palmer?" Russell calls from the helm as Beth and Emma guide me through the cockpit.

"Yeah," I say, offering him a weak nod, although I wonder if, like Emma, he could be disappointed I didn't die, making one less person for him to have to kill. Or am I starting to lose it, imagining every person I look at might be a killer? I lift a hand to the growing bump on my head, feeling lucky to still be alive.

Emma holds onto my arm as I descend the narrow companionway steps, then hands me off to Beth who waits at the bottom and helps lower me onto the couch.

I lay my head on the armrest and close my eyes.

"Wait," Emma says, rushing toward me. "I thought people with concussions aren't supposed to sleep. What if you go into a coma?"

I open my eyes to see Emma towering over me. "That's an old school of thought," I say. "Now, it's been proven that it's fine to rest after a concussion. It helps the brain heal. The risk of sleeping is for when there's a suspected brain hemorrhage—a brain bleed. In those cases, you need to wake the person to make sure they aren't worse."

Beth and Emma exchange glances. "How do we know you don't have that?" Beth asks.

We don't. "If my speech slurs, or my balance is off, or—"

Beth's eyes widen. "Your balance *is* off."

"I don't have a brain bleed."

Beth looks unconvinced. "And how else do we know if you're worse?"

I yawn, then grimace at the sharp pain that rips through my temple. "If my headache gets drastically worse or my cognition changes, like I'm unaware of where I am and what's happening. Or if my pupils become unreactive to light, but that can also be a sign of a concussion, which I'm sure is all this is. I just need to rest."

Emma looks between me and Beth. "And what do we do if you *do* get worse?"

I sigh. "Take me to a hospital."

Emma frowns.

"I'll climb the mast," Beth says.

"No," Emma and I chime together.

Emma turns to Beth. "Remember what happened at the Space Needle? There's no way you could go up that mast without panicking. I'll go." She peers out the window above my head. "I don't want to speak too soon, but the seas seem like they might be calming."

"I'll help Beth winch you up." A wave of nausea washes over me as I try to sit up. The room spins, and I grip the edge of the couch for support.

"You need to rest for a bit," Beth says. "Another hour or so isn't going to hurt anything. I'll wake you in a while, and you can help me winch Emma up."

Emma nods in agreement. Reluctantly, I sink against the leather couch. Emma puts her hands on her hips and twists toward Beth.

"I'm going back on deck to see if Russell needs help with anything. Can you see if you can get a weather report on the radio?"

"Okay." Beth moves to the small desk in the corner and then flicks on the radio while Emma goes upstairs.

From the couch, I watch Beth spin a knob while static bleeds through the speaker. She turns up the volume and changes the frequency until a man's voice crackles through the radio. Another voice comes through the radio, but it's hard to make out what they're saying.

Beth sits up straight and reaches aimlessly for the missing radio mic, then swears.

The sounds cut out, leaving us in silence aside from Beth's continual flip of the switches.

I sit up, fighting the nausea that rises with me. "What happened?"

"Shit," Beth mutters, throwing me a distressed look. "The radio stopped working."

Emma comes down the companionway. "We lost power at the helm. Do you guys have it down here?"

Beth whips around. "No, it just went out."

Emma comes down the steps, looking over Beth's shoulder at the radio. "One of the fuel tanks was running low, so I switched to the second tank. But then I lost power."

Russell appears at the top of the companionway. "Second tank?" His brows furrow in confusion. "I only filled one before we left."

Emma turns toward him, placing a hand on her hip. "The controls said there were two."

Beth twists in her seat, giving Russell a sidelong look filled with quiet skepticism.

Russell shakes his head. "Nojan didn't tell me that."

Emma frowns. "Why the hell would he not tell you that?"

Russell comes down a step. "I don't know, but Nojan only told me to fuel the boat when we stopped at the fueling station on our way out of the marina. You were there, remember?"

I rack my brain, trying to recall if Nojan told him there were two tanks. I remember Nojan telling him to fuel up, and I heard nothing about a second tank. But I'd been distracted by the thought of leaving the girls and still having to tell them about Matt's leaving me. I study him, looking between Beth's and Emma's wary gazes. Maybe Beth was right. We need to incapacitate him before it's too late. Pain stabs at my skull, and I sag against the couch, wishing we had formed a plan to subdue Russell before I went up the mast.

"Maybe Nojan didn't realize it either. This boat's brand new. He'd never sailed it before."

Emma crosses her arms. "Where are the tanks?"

Russell motions behind him with his head. "Under the bed in my stateroom. I'll check them."

Beth trails his movement with a distrusting gaze.

Emma follows after him. "Not alone, you're not. I'm coming with you." She glances at Beth. "Beth, can you keep watch at the helm?"

Beth looks to me before going up. "You okay down here without me?"

I try to get up, hating my helplessness. But the galley spins. Begrudgingly, I collapse against the couch cushions. "Yeah, I'm fine."

"Try to rest," Beth adds.

I close my eyes as Beth pads up the steps, meaning to close them for only a moment. Beneath me, the hull creaks. What if Courtney really *was* the one who penned that note? Could it be possible that she's somehow survived? I try to imagine her hiding somewhere in the belly of the boat, waiting to kill the rest of us, one by one.

Or just me, I realize, now that Gigi is gone. Gigi and I would be the two Courtney would be seeking revenge on most, except that we'd all left Courtney behind to search for Beth's van. I catch a whiff of a familiar scent, one that takes me back in time. A flowery scent mixed with sandalwood fills my nose. *Courtney.*

I should get up. Tell the others. But my body doesn't respond to my commands. I must've hit my head harder than I thought. Before I can dwell on it, I'm pulled into a dreamless, listless sleep.

When I open my eyes, it's dusk. I look around the small space as my memory of climbing the mast comes back to me in a terrifying blur. Beth sits across from me at the table, reading her novel in the dim light. I sit up. A throbbing pain still stabs at my temple, but my dizziness is gone.

Beneath us, the waves feel calmer. I wonder how much closer we are now to the coast.

Beth lowers her paperback. "How are you feeling?"

Looking at Beth, I suddenly remember our plan to winch Emma up to fix the dish after I got some rest.

"What time is it?" I ask. "Why didn't you wake me?"

Beth glances at her watch. "It's eight thirty."

I get up unsteadily.

Beth comes toward me as I sway on my feet, easing me back onto the couch.

"I'm ready to help winch Emma up. We need to hurry," I tell her. "We don't have much daylight left."

"We don't have power, Palmer. Both fuel tanks are empty."

I remember the power cutting out a second time before I fell asleep. "But isn't there another way to charge the batteries? Like a generator?" Surely, a boat like this would have one.

Beth shakes her head. "It's a brand-new boat. We don't even have solar. Gigi told me the yacht company in San Diego is going to install solar panels, and she was glad the boat didn't have them yet because she thinks they're ugly and that it would look better on social media without them. It's probably the same with the generator."

With a sickening feeling, my eyes dart toward Gigi's cabin at the sound of her name, and I envision her lying dead on the floor of her stateroom. *How did this even happen?*

"Where's Emma?" I ask Beth.

"She's asleep in her cabin. We decided to take shifts keeping watch. Russell's taking the first shift, and she's going to relieve him at ten. Then, I'm going to take over at two in the morning." Beth crosses the room and retrieves a bottle of water from a kitchen cabinet. "The weather has calmed down a lot," she adds. "We've changed our course and are heading southeast. Hopefully, we'll be south of the storm. If we run into worse weather, we'll have to turn around again." Beth hands me the bottle. "Drink this."

I sit up and twist open the cap. "Is the mainsail still jammed?"

"No, we got it fixed."

I take a drink. At least one thing's going right. I glance at the closed companionway door and lower my voice.

"It had to be Russell who killed the captain. He lied about who he was. He planned this. Plus, how did he get the power on so easily before? Like he knew exactly what the problem was." I grab Beth's arm as an idea enters my foggy head. I should've thought of it before. "Wait. What if we can fix it? We took Russell's word for it when he fixed the power. Has anyone checked the engine room? What if he just unplugged something?"

Beth frowns. "After Emma went with him to confirm the fuel tanks were empty, she went into the engine room to make sure nothing was tampered with. But like Russell said, both battery banks were dead."

"But how can we trust them? What if they're teaming up, and lying about the batteries, like you said before?" I take another drink of water, my gaze drifting in the direction of Russell's empty cabin. "How do we even know he's telling the truth about Courtney's diary?"

"We don't," Beth agrees. "More likely, he's been stewing over his sister's death for the last twenty years and is here to get revenge."

"How long was he in Iraq for?"

Beth shrugs. "I have no idea."

I shift in my seat to face her. "What if he has severe PTSD or some other mental health issue from the war trauma? I saw a documentary recently about an ex–war veteran who came home and killed his neighbors, believing they were a hostile enemy he needed to protect his family from."

Before Beth can respond, the companionway door flaps open, making me jump.

Russell meets my gaze as he tromps down the steps. "Hey, Palmer. Feeling better?"

My mouth feels suddenly dry. "Yeah," I croak.

He nods, but from his expression I can't tell whether he's relieved or disappointed. He opens the bathroom door. "Just using the head."

Beth and I stare at each other in silence until Russell emerges and retreats up the companionway. I wait until he closes the door before getting up.

"You stay here and keep watch," I whisper.

Beth's brows knit together in confusion. "Keep watch for what?"

"For Russell. I'm going to search his cabin. See what I can find. If he really *did* find Courtney's diary after all these years, maybe he brought it with him. Let me know if he comes down," I add before turning for his room.

"How am I supposed to let you know?" Beth asks from the couch.

"Just greet him really loud. Or you'll think of something."

Chapter Thirty-One

Memorial Day Weekend, 2005

I adjusted my grip on the back of the blown-up raft Beth and I carried awkwardly toward the riverbank, trying to stifle the bad feeling that whirled in my gut like a tornado. Emma led the way down to the clearing toward the water, with Gigi and Courtney taking up the rear. Above Courtney's near constant chattering, the roar of the Sol Duc's rushing water grew louder with each step I took; it felt like an alarm was going off inside me, telling me to go back.

I'd hardly slept last night, partly in shock that I'd been so fueled with rage that I'd punched Courtney, but mostly because I'd been unable to stop the growing anger inside me at Courtney's unrelenting insistence on ruining other people's lives. All day, Courtney had been glued to Emma's side. The two of them led our hike, giving me no chance to speak to Emma alone.

"Look, I know I agreed not to bring it up," Gigi said in a low tone from beside me, carrying the front of the raft she was sharing with Courtney. "But what was going on with you and Courtney last night? In all my life, Palmer, I've never seen you act out like that."

"Oh, so you think her hitting me is *my* fault?" Courtney said from behind us. "Just like you assumed I was the one who spread those photos of you around school?"

I glanced at Gigi, whose face burned red. I'm not sure whether it was from the reminder of her school-wide humiliation or the fact that Courtney had overheard her. Or both.

"What are you guys arguing about?" Beth asked over her shoulder a few feet in front of me.

"Nothing," Courtney called from the rear.

Gigi stopped. Turned. "Were you?"

"Was I what?" Courtney asked.

"The one who spread those photos around."

Gigi wasn't usually this bold. We all suspected Courtney was to blame, knowing the things she was capable of. But I hadn't seen Gigi stand up to Courtney about it since that day in the school bathroom when Courtney seemingly convinced Gigi she was innocent. Since then, Gigi had appeared to get over it, and I'd assumed she believed Courtney was telling the truth.

Guess not. Throwing a look over my shoulder at Gigi, I spotted the stone-cold accusation in her eyes as she glared at Courtney.

"I already told you I didn't." There was venom in Courtney's tone now. "You know what I think, Gigi? *You* were the one who put those photos up of yourself. You secretly relished the attention, even though you pretended like you hated it. Then, you got to play the victim afterward. You've always been jealous I get more attention from guys than you do. You can't handle it."

Gigi dropped her end of the raft. I stopped, looking behind me as I felt Beth tug on the other end of the raft.

"You're a bitch," Gigi hissed.

"Whatever you guys are arguing about back there," Emma called from the front, "just stop."

"Yeah," Beth added. "We don't need anyone frazzled before we get on the water."

"Tell that to Courtney." Gigi plucked up her raft as I followed Beth over the river rocks that lined the Sol Duc's shore.

"Easy, Gigi. I was only kidding."

Behind me, Courtney's tone was now light, the venom completely gone.

"But it's nice to know what you really think of me," Courtney added.

On the opposite side of the Sol Duc, a deer lapped water from the river's edge. Seeing us, its head shot up. It turned, disappearing into the woods.

I dropped my raft on the rocky shore. "That's enough, Courtney. Just stop."

"Whatever." Courtney shrugged, lowering the back of her raft into the water. "Like you're one to talk, Palmer."

Beth dragged our raft to the river's edge, and it took all my willpower not to respond.

"You guys ready?" Emma already had one foot in the water and plopped her backpack into her raft.

Gigi warily assessed the fast-flowing water. "Shouldn't we be wearing life jackets?"

"We're in *rafts*," Courtney said. "No one's going in the water. Plus, we would've had to carry them, and none of you guys would've wanted that."

Beth climbed into the back of our raft as I held onto the side. "Did you guys know that on this side of the river is the Olympic National Park and the other side of the river is the Olympic National Forest?"

"So?" Courtney asked.

"So, missing persons investigations are handled by completely different authorities depending on which side of the river you go missing on. If one of us falls out and goes missing *in* the river, it's the luck of the draw whose jurisdiction it would be."

Gigi moaned. "I don't want to think about that."

"I'm just saying," Beth continued as I nudged our raft away from the shore, "that one side has a much better track record at performing in-depth searches for people than the other. Anyone want to guess which side it is?"

"No," Courtney and Emma shouted.

"Let's go," Gigi called, climbing into the back of the raft she shared with Courtney.

I lowered myself into the raft, in front of Beth, adjusting myself in the tight space as she extended her legs on either side of me. I pitied Gigi's being stuck in a tiny raft with Courtney all afternoon.

"Let's do this," Emma called as she started down the river.

I envied her confidence. Emma didn't look the least bit nervous as she paddled downstream.

My blood raced, pulsing with force. The current swept us along, and it struck me how dangerously remote we were. We hadn't passed a single person on the trail, and I hadn't had a phone signal since we'd left the trailhead.

Behind us, Gigi and Courtney pushed out into the river in silence. I shot them a curious look over my shoulder, wondering how they were managing to be in such close proximity without screaming at each other. Courtney was in front, looking blissful as she took in the surroundings. She appeared completely unrattled—disturbingly so—by the argument they'd had on the bank only moments ago.

I faced forward, suppressing the shudder that ran down my spine. The current carried us speedily downstream. Beth and I paddled toward the middle where it was deeper and there was less chance of running into a logjam. The color of the water changed to a dark green. Beneath the moving surface, I could no longer see the bottom.

I used my paddle to steer us away from an uprooted tree, which protruded from the bank and reached nearly halfway across the river.

Up ahead, Emma soared over a steep slope, like a mini waterfall. Her raft disappeared from view before reappearing downstream. Water splashed over both sides of the raft.

"Wahoo!" I heard Emma yell, pumping her paddle overhead.

"Hold on," I said when Beth and I reached it.

I paddled to the left, afraid we might go down sideways and flip. I held my breath as our raft tipped over the edge, grabbing onto both side handles. Beth squealed. I closed my eyes as we dipped forward.

When we landed, I was jerked backward against Beth, the raft bobbing atop the fast-moving water. Water splashed the side of my face, and I opened my eyes.

"That was fun," Beth shouted in my ear.

A laugh escaped my lips as relief washed over me that we hadn't capsized. Beneath us, the current picked up, propelling us toward the next bend.

"Paddle to the left," I told Beth, dipping my paddle into the water to keep us in the middle of the river.

Emma rounded the next river bend as Beth and I sped toward it. Behind us, Gigi screamed as she descended the drop.

"So dramatic," Beth said.

I smiled at her quip.

"Wait! Help! You guys, stop."

I turned, my smile fading when I saw that Gigi was alone in her raft.

"Courtney fell," Gigi shouted, flailing her paddle to one side, trying to stop. Instead, she continued downstream, spinning in her raft until she was drifting backward. Gigi craned her neck toward Beth and me. "I can't stop," she shrieked.

Beth and I held out our paddles on either side of the raft, barely managing to slow down. The river whitecapped around our raft as the current picked up. There was no way we could stop.

I twisted in my seat, looking beyond Beth's shoulder at the small waterfall behind Gigi as she continued toward us, waiting to see Courtney carried over the edge. But there was only water spilling over the drop.

"Look out!" Beth's eyes bulged.

I whipped around, following her terrified gaze. We were heading straight for a cluster of sharp broken branches protruding from the river's surface. I pushed against them with my paddle, and we veered to the right. Behind us, Gigi was still screaming Courtney's name.

Chapter Thirty-Two

Present: Day Five at Sea

I toss a cursory glance over my shoulder at Beth as I open the door to the stateroom Russell shared with Nojan. Beth nods, her signal that she'll warn me if Russell comes below. I step inside the small space, leaving the door slightly ajar. The room is similar to Gigi's but with twin beds.

I blink back the tears that well in my eyes at the thought of Gigi's beautiful corpse decomposing in the adjacent room. I take a breath and steady myself, focusing on what I've come here to find. I don't have time for grief right now.

The twin beds are neatly made, probably an old habit from Russell's time in the Marines. Before I met Matt, I'd dated a guy who'd served two years in the army. He couldn't leave his room in the morning without making his bed.

There's no luggage in sight, so I open the storage compartment beneath the foot of the beds. Inside I find two duffel bags. I put the larger one on the bed and unzip the top. I sift through the stack of blue polo shirts and khaki shorts. When I pull a stack of clothing onto the bed, something rattles inside the bag. I reach in, feeling the sides until my hand closes around an orange prescription bottle. I hold it up to the window and see that it's a cholesterol medication prescribed for Nojan Ahmed.

I stuff the clothes back inside and retrieve the other bag from the storage compartment. Hearing Russell's footsteps on the deck above, I pause. I wait for a moment, making sure he doesn't start down the steps, before unzipping his bag.

I search Russell's bag in the waning daylight coming through the small side window. It's more organized than Nojan's. The same blue polo shirts are neatly folded beside a few pairs of cargo shorts and boxer briefs. I place a stack of clothes on the bed, careful to keep them folded, and feel around the bottom.

I have an idea of what Courtney's diary would've said about the others, but what would it have said about me? While Courtney's phone was never found, her backpack was recovered by divers in the Sol Duc during the search for her body. But Courtney wouldn't have brought her diary on the rafting trip, would she? No, I think. Even if she had, the river would've made her diary entries illegible. The police never brought up Courtney's diary when they interrogated me.

There's no way Russell can know about my fight with Courtney the night before she disappeared. Her threat to end Mom's career and my punching her in the nose. Can he?

Russell can't know what happened on the trip. Without knowing that, he would have trained his suspicion on Gigi and Emma, as they would've seemed to have the strongest motives to want Courtney dead.

I shift the remaining stack of clothes to the side of the bag, finding deodorant and a small toiletry bag, but no diary. I exhale a puff of disappointment. I slide the clothes back to their original spot. With a bag this organized, Russell might notice if something is out of place.

My fingers graze something hard on the bottom of the bag. I close my grip around it. My lungs freeze as I realize what it is. I lift the pistol from the bag by its barrel. My jaw drops as I stare at the weapon in the dimly lit stateroom. *Is he planning to shoot the rest of us?*

"Hey, Russell," Beth calls in a raised voice from the galley.

I whip around and see Russell with his back to me, standing at the base of the steps. I curse myself for being too distracted by finding the pistol to hear him come below deck.

"Where's Palmer?" he asks.

"Oh. She's in our room, lying down."

He turns toward his stateroom. I take a step back, but my calves butt against the end of the bed. I scan the small space, but there's nowhere to hide. My heart beats in my throat as I tuck the pistol into the waistband of my sweatpants like I've seen in the movies.

The cabin door flings all the way open before I have time to return Russell's clothes to his unzipped bag.

He gapes at me in the doorway. "What the hell are you doing?"

There's just enough light for me to see his eyes narrow when his gaze falls to his bag on the bed.

"I—" The gun is cold against the skin of my lower back as I rack my brain for an excuse. "I was looking for Courtney's diary. I wanted to see if you were telling the truth."

He steps toward me, blocking my path to the door. My eyes are level with his muscular chest. My pulse pounds in my ears, knowing how easily he could overpower me and take back his gun. I ready my hand to reach for the pistol if he tries to grab me. If I'm lucky, I can get to it before he can stop me.

Instead, he pivots and points to the galley. "You won't find Courtney's diary in here, because one of you already took it. I found it missing from my room this morning."

Already took it? I think of Emma, supposedly asleep in her room. And Beth, right outside his room. Had she taken it while I was asleep?

"So, maybe you should ask your so-called friends to let you see it. Now get out of my room."

I swallow, keeping my hand at my side, then scurry past him. Keeping my back toward the opposite wall, where the pistol protrudes from my pants, I brace myself for him to grab me before I reach the door. But he doesn't.

He follows me into the galley where Beth is now standing in front of the couch. Feeling Russell behind me, I turn, wondering how long it will take for him to realize his gun is missing. The pistol slides lower down my back, and I'm afraid it will slip down my pant leg and clatter to the floor. I fight the urge to reach behind and grab it and instead take a seat at the dinette before the gun can fall any lower.

"I'm not the one here with something to hide." There's malice in his tone as his hard-set gaze darts between Beth and me. "I've been to the Sol Duc where the search and rescue divers went down looking for Courtney. My sister didn't drown. She was always a strong swimmer, stronger even than me. And if she was attacked by the cougar Palmer supposedly saw—" He turns to face me. "Then why didn't the first-responding search and rescue team find her body?

"No, I don't buy it," he continues before I can respond. "The reason my sister's body was never found is because one of you didn't want it to be."

There's only a trace of daylight left outside, making it too dark for me to read his expression.

"The dogs tracked Courtney's scent to the river as if she never made it out, but I think you all lied to the authorities."

"Russell, we didn't—"

Russell raises his palm at Beth's interjection. "I'm sure of it—don't lie to me. The only thing I'm not certain of is whether one of you acted alone and got the others to cover it up, or whether you were all in on it from the beginning. Maybe all of you left her on purpose after pushing her off the raft, then waited a day to go back to your car and call for help, knowing the longer Courtney was out in the woods without provisions, the lower her chances were of survival." Russell turns toward me. "But after reading Courtney's diary, I think it's more likely that one of you killed her."

I study Beth in the darkness, wanting to tell Russell that it isn't true. But I know my words alone will do nothing to convince him. They might even anger him more.

The pistol presses against my lumbar spine. I shift my gaze to Russell's muscular form. *What was his plan? To off us all, one by one, hoping one of us would eventually crack and confess?*

"The last time we saw your sister, she was alive," Beth says.

"That's what you told the police." Though answering Beth, Russell's silhouette is still looking straight at me.

"It's the truth," Beth adds.

"I'm going back up to keep watch." Russell frowns, his accusatory gaze lingering on each of us before he turns and starts up the steps. "Emma is supposed to relieve me at ten. Can you wake her if she doesn't come out? I'm getting a little punchy up here, and I don't want to fall asleep without anyone on the lookout for other ships."

"Sure," I say as Beth moves into the galley. She rummages through a couple of drawers and finds another flashlight.

After Russell closes the companionway door and the adrenaline that's been keeping me going drains away, I feel suddenly exhausted. Beth doesn't look any better. It couldn't have been much after midnight when we were all jarred awake to find Nojan missing. My gaze flicks to Gigi's stateroom door. That feels like an eternity ago with everything that's happened since then. Maybe Russell stayed awake while the rest of us went to bed so he could kill Nojan as soon as we were all asleep.

"I heard Russell tell you that Courtney's diary is missing. Do you think Emma took it?" Beth asks in a low tone.

"She must have. Unless Gigi took it before she . . . died." I glance at the closed door to Gigi's room. "Once Emma goes up to keep watch, we should search Emma's room for the diary."

"Okay, but first I need a drink," Beth says. "For a minute, I thought he was going to throw us both overboard." As Beth opens a cabinet and plucks out a bottle of wine by the neck, I notice the broken dishes have been cleaned from the floor. "You want one?"

I glance at the door to the top deck, hyperaware of Russell's pistol in my waistband, which feels like its searing into the skin on my lower back.

"Oh, wait." Beth sets the bottle on the counter beside a Solo cup and searches a drawer for a bottle opener. "You shouldn't drink with a head injury, right?"

"Beth," I whisper.

Her fingers go still inside the drawer, and she shines her flashlight on my chest. "What?"

I get up and move to the other side of the narrow counter from where Beth stands. "I found something else in his room." I reach behind me and grip the gun by the handle.

The companionway door opens with a flap. "Hey."

I jump at Russell's voice coming from the top of the companionway.

"Can you guys wake Emma for me? I can't keep my eyes open."

An image of Russell making Nojan stand on the rear platform before shooting him in the chest fills my mind. But that couldn't have happened; we would've heard the gunshot. But there was lightning that night. If he'd timed it right, the thunder would have covered the sound.

"Yeah, okay." I'm glad Russell can't see the look on my face as I shove the barrel back into the waist of my sweatpants, alarmed at how close I came to confessing I had his gun while he was within earshot. I wait until he disappears from the doorway and then lean my elbows onto the countertop.

"Beth," I keep my voice low as she continues to rifle through the drawer. "I found a gun in Russell's bag. A pistol."

Her hand goes still inside the drawer. "Where is it?"

"In the back of my sweatpants. But I need to find a better hiding spot for it in our room before it slides out." I keep one hand on the handle, afraid if I let go it will fall to the floor and go off, shooting a stray bullet God knows where.

Beth looks over her shoulder, lowering her voice to a whisper. "If he's the killer, and he's had a gun this whole time, then why hasn't he shot us already?"

I shrug, my gaze darting to the open doorway to the deck. "Maybe he's waiting for one of us to confess to killing Courtney. Hoping we'll crack."

"He's going to notice it's gone. Maybe you should put it back."

I gape at Beth in the darkness. Is she crazy? "So he can shoot us in our sleep?" I shake my head. "No. We need to incapacitate him. Gigi had prescription opiates that she was disguising as seasickness pills. I recognized what they were when they dropped on the floor. We can use them to drug Russell. Crush some up and put them in that wine."

"Are you saying we *kill* him?"

"No!" I exhale and lower my voice a few decibels. "Just knock him out for a while."

"But don't we need him to help sail? What if we run into bad weather again?"

"We have Emma." I motion toward her stateroom. "She's a better sailor anyway." Unless she's the one we should be afraid of. But so far, I trust her over Russell, and we can't incapacitate the only two people who know how to sail at the same time. Not if we want to make it home. I bite my lip, deliberating. What if I'm wrong?

If Emma and Russell *are* working together, it will be two against one instead of two against two. That should at least help our chances.

Beth goes quiet, seeming to mull it over too.

"Beth, he's an ex-*Marine*. He's been trained to kill. And I think he's planning to kill us all."

"Okay, fine." Beth resumes searching the drawer. "But I can't find a bottle opener." She looks up. "What if he doesn't want wine?"

"Then we'll put it in his coffee when he wakes up." Hopefully, he doesn't notice his gun is missing in the meantime. "Here, I'll look for the corkscrew. You get Gigi's pills." I'm surprised at the waft of emotion that engulfs me at saying her name, even though we'd hardly spoken in the last twenty years. "They're oxycodone, but she might have been hiding them in a different bottle. I didn't see what was on the label. Just bring out all the pill bottles you find, and I'll show you which ones to use."

Beth lifts her flashlight toward me. "You want *me* to go into her room, alone with her dead body?"

She's right. I'm the nurse. "Fine, I'll do it. We need to hurry before Emma wakes up and Russell goes to bed."

I step forward, but Beth raises her palm.

"No, it's okay. I'll find them. You hide the gun. And get the corkscrew. I plugged in your phone while we still had power," Beth says. "You should be able to use it as a flashlight."

Beth goes toward Gigi's stateroom, and I don't stop her. But only because I'm dying to get Russell's gun out of my pants. I've never so much as held a gun before, and I'm terrified Russell will come down and catch me with it. Then what would I do?

I go into my own room to hide the gun before searching for the corkscrew. I can't risk having the outline of Russell's pistol bulging from the back of my pants if he comes back downstairs.

My eyes strain to adjust to the darkness as I scan the small room I share with Beth, trying to think of a place Russell won't look. It won't be long until Russell realizes his gun is missing. And I need to make sure he doesn't get it back.

Chapter Thirty-Three

Present: Day Five at Sea

I shut the door behind me and feel for my phone, finding it plugged in at the end of the bed like Beth said. I turn on the screen, seeing it still has 70 percent battery. My lungs deflate with disappointment at the now familiar words in the top corner. *No service.*

I remove the gun from my pants. For lack of a better option, I slide it under my pillow at the head of the bed, although when I do it, it feels stupid, like I've watched too many seasons of *Jack Ryan*. But I can't think of a more protected hiding spot while I'm asleep. I smooth my pillow and contemplate throwing the gun overboard. I'm no match for Russell's strength—none of us are. At least with his gun we have a fighting chance.

Suddenly, I recall smelling Courtney's perfume before falling asleep on the couch. How could I have forgotten? I need to tell Beth.

I turn for the door when Beth's phone chimes. Seeing her screen light up, my heart leaps. I reach for her phone. Has she somehow gotten a signal? We have different phone carriers, so maybe, just maybe—

I sink onto the bed, recognizing the pop-up from a reminder app: Board Meeting tomorrow 9am. The app must not require an internet connection. I dismiss the alarm and am about to check to make sure

Beth's phone hasn't miraculously gotten a signal when an unsent message notification from Instagram appears in the middle of the screen. Seeing the recipient makes me pause with my finger hovering over the phone. I tap the screen to see the full message. As I start to read, my heart drops into my stomach.

> Unsent message: I'm so sorry, babe. My work has been crazy, and I promised them I would stay for a few more weeks before quitting. I know you'll understand. I love you so much and can't wait to move in and spend the rest of our lives together!

The room sways, and I bite my lip, staring at Beth's typed words to Matt. It has to be another Matt. *But how could Beth be quitting her job and moving in with someone without telling me?*

I swipe up, and the phone prompts me for a passcode. I speedily type in the code Beth's been using since we were kids: 0505. Her birthday.

I hold my breath as it unlocks. I tap the unsent message to see the conversation. Above Beth's unsent message is the last text she received from Matt. It was three days ago. Where are you??? Is everything okay? I'm all moved into our apartment, and I can't wait to see you. I thought you'd be here by now. Please let me know you're okay, baby. Then I see Matt's profile photo at the top of their chat, and I know it's the same Matt that I've been married to for over a decade.

My hands tremble as I scroll up through the previous messages. I keep reading despite the alarm bells going off in my head, warning me I'll never be able to unsee the words I'm about to read. As I read Matt's words, I'm filled with a sickening sense of reliving the moment when I found the topless selfie from twenty-three-year-old Sydney, puckering her lips into an air-kiss above her perky breasts.

I'm out of the house now, baby. I'm free and waiting for you. You can call or text me on my cell now that we don't have to worry about Palmer finding out about us. I love you and can't wait until I can lay next to you all night and feel your naked body against mine . . . The wind leaves my lungs as if I've been hit with an airbag.

A message from Beth. I know I'll see you in a few days, but it's killing me having to wait any longer to see you. My whole body aches for you. I wish I could make the drive from Colorado go faster!

Colorado? I thought these messages were from Beth. Confused, I scroll up past Matt's new apartment address through a lengthy message thread speckled with heart emojis until my finger stops cold on the topless photo that's already seared in my mind from having seen it once. It's the woman from Matt's conference. Sydney. The one he left me for.

Why would Beth have these messages on her phone? Beth is much more tech savvy than I am, but it seems unlikely she could've hacked into this woman's Instagram account. Vomit rises to the back of my mouth. I should stop, but I keep scrolling. I have to know. I move to the top of the chat, which is surprisingly not that far above Sydney's topless photo. I read the first message Sydney sent to Matt. Like Matt had told me, she reached out to him first.

> Hey, Matt! I had so much fun with you in Denver! I just started this Instagram account and was excited to find you! How are you?? This might sound weird, but I miss you. I haven't ever connected with anyone the way I did with you.

I click on the back arrow at the top of the screen and go to Beth's profile. Only it's not Beth's. It's Sydney's. I skim through her posted photos, clicking on the photo of her and Matt at the bar in Denver. I pause, seeing it was posted in April, nearly a month after Matt's conference. I scroll up and see that more than half of the photos were posted within a few days of each other.

With a knot in my stomach, I click *Edit Profile* to view the contact options linked to the account. I gasp, seeing Beth's email and the same phone number Beth has had since high school. The floor sways as my mind reels with what Beth has done.

She catfished Matt by pretending to be the woman he met in Denver. But why?

Tears blur my vision as the screen goes dark in my hand. I toss the phone onto the bed beside me and bury my face in my hands. My friend. My *best* friend. How could she?

I recall the devastating moment when I found that photo on Matt's phone. It was from Beth, not Sydney.

A sob escapes my throat, and it strikes me that her betrayal stings much worse than Matt's. I've known Beth since kindergarten.

Tears slide down my cheeks. Who the hell is she? What else has she lied about? Have I ever known her at all?

"I found the pills."

I whip around at the sound of Beth's voice.

"I know what you did." I raise my phone light to see Beth's expression.

She blinks while pressing her lips together. "I don't—"

My hand holding my phone trembles with rage. "I found your messages to Matt from your *fake Instagram account*." The last three words come out a scream.

Salt water sprays against the cabin window.

Beth flinches.

"Why the hell would you do this to me? To my family? What is wrong with you? I thought you were—" My voice breaks. "My best friend."

I pray for her to tell me that it's not true. That I've somehow gotten it wrong.

When she doesn't, I add, "You were the one who sent Matt that topless photo of Sydney. How?"

Beth frowns. "You can do pretty much anything with AI now. And yes, I catfished him. I've never trusted Matt, and after you told me about him being at the bar all night with that girl in Denver, I wanted to see just how faithful Matt really was. It was a test. To see if he was telling the truth about it being 'nothing.'"

My jaw falls open as Beth makes air quotes with her fingers.

"And guess what? No surprise—Matt failed. I could tell he wanted that woman as soon as I started messaging him." Beth sighs. "Then, I needed to see how far Matt would take it. And maybe I got carried away."

I gape at Beth. "*Carried away?*" I shout. It was the same expression Beth used when she ordered too many books on Prime Day. I stare at her in horrified shock. "You tricked my husband into leaving me!"

Beth scoffs. "Matt left you because he wanted to. All he needed was an excuse. Why would you want to be with a man who would leave you the second a younger woman came onto him? I was only helping you see that."

Her words hit me like a punch to the face. *Is this really the same Beth I've known almost my whole life?*

Beth averts her gaze to the wall, and I want to clench my hands around her throat.

"You were always jealous of Matt, ever since we were dating," I tell her. "You'd complain that he was controlling when he wanted to spend time with me without you. But you're the controlling one." I jab my finger toward Beth's chest. "Thinking you have the right to break up my marriage. Why? So that I would need you the way you *need* me?"

Beth returns her gaze to mine. "I get that you're upset right now. But trust me, Palmer, you'll thank me some day."

I glare at Beth in disbelief. Does she really expect me to just get over it?

"Stop acting like you were being my friend. You wanted Matt to *leave* me." I shake my head, half smiling at the absurdity of it all. "In some sick way, you wanted me to end up just as alone as you." I want to spit. Beth's betrayal is so tangible I can almost taste it.

"You're not seeing things clearly right now, Palmer. I get that you're mad at me, but Matt is the one who betrayed you—not me. I only helped to show you who Matt really is. He lied, by the way, when he said nothing happened with that girl in Denver. They had sex in the bathroom at the bar. He told me in those messages."

"You think that's going to allow me to forgive you? Because I don't. As soon as we get off this boat, you're dead to me. Forever."

"Maybe I went too far, okay? But Matt's leaving was just as much your fault as it was mine." Beth inches closer to me, her finger pointed at my chest. "Ever since that hike, you stopped letting people in. Matt told me how you were always pulling away, busying yourself so you wouldn't have to spend time with him after the girls went to bed. Blame me all you want, but if you'd been a better wife, Matt might not have needed someone else so badly."

It feels like a grenade has exploded inside my chest. I surge forward, fists clenched. "Get out. And stay away from me, you *lying bitch*!"

I slam my cabin door in Beth's face. My chest heaves as I think of how close I was to grabbing Beth by her neck. I double over, resting my palms on my knees.

I find Beth's phone on the bed and throw it against the wall.

"Ahhh!"

How could she? I sink onto the bed and bury my face in my hands as I break into a sob.

Minutes later, the door flings open. I recognize Beth's outline in the doorway. I haven't felt this enraged since that night I punched Courtney. I'm tempted to rip the flashlight from Beth's hand and club her over the head with it. Over and over until blood streams down her face the way tears do mine.

"I told you to leave me alone," I seethe. "Jump in the ocean for all I care. Just stay the hell away from me."

"Palmer, I need you," Beth breathes, her voice coated with panic. "It's Emma. She won't wake up."

Chapter Thirty-Four

Memorial Day Weekend, 2005

"Why are we stopping?" Emma called from her raft after she'd paddled it into the shallows.

Beth and I rowed toward her.

"Courtney fell out," I yelled.

Emma's eyes bulged. "When? Is she okay?"

Emma shifted her gaze to Gigi, alone in her raft as Beth and I made it ashore.

"We haven't seen her," Beth said. "We have to go back."

Emma dipped a leg over the side and into the water. "Where did Courtney fall out?"

I started to stand up, feeling the uneven river rocking beneath the raft. "At the beginning. Before that first drop."

Emma's jaw dropped. "*What?* Why didn't you stop? That was miles back."

I stepped into the frigid water, my foot slipping atop a rock. I leaned forward, catching myself on the raft, thinking of how cold it must've been when Courtney went in.

"We tried," Beth said, getting out of our raft behind me. "We were shouting at you, but you were too far ahead to hear us over the river."

"Shit." Emma stepped ashore and pulled her raft onto the riverbed. "At least she's a strong swimmer."

Emma turned to Gigi, who was still in her raft. "So, you haven't seen her since she fell?"

I looked to Gigi, who shook her head as she climbed out of her raft. "No."

Emma helped Gigi pull her raft onto the bank. "Let's leave the rafts here. We'll move faster without them."

The four of us walked along the uneven riverbed, slowing to step over the logs and boulders that blocked our path.

I turned to the others. "We need to move faster." *How long would Courtney last in that freezing river before getting hypothermia?* I tried not to dwell on how long it had been since she'd fallen from the raft. Too long.

I blamed myself for not being more adamant—like Beth—about us needing to wear life jackets. *What if Courtney got stuck under a logjam or fallen tree? What if she drowned?* I pushed those thoughts from my mind. Like Emma said, Courtney was a strong swimmer, and we were carried downstream fast in our rafts. Courtney probably swam to shore before that first drop-off.

I imagined Courtney, soaking wet, making her way along the river's edge. Pissed that it took us so long to come back for her.

"What if we can't find her?" Gigi asked.

"We will," Beth said. "We need to stay positive."

Gigi was quiet for a few steps. When I glanced at her, her face was starkly pale. Her expression seemed to turn grimmer with each step.

"Do you think she could've . . ." Gigi's voice wobbled. "You know. Drowned?" Gigi looked between the rest of us, appearing desperate for an answer.

While we were all worried about Courtney, the terror in Gigi's brown eyes made me wonder.

Beth turned. "Courtney? No. It would take more than a river to take her down. She's one of the strongest swimmers I know."

"Me too," I agreed. I thought of all the times we'd swum in the indoor pool at the Sequim rec center. Courtney had been beating us at swim races and laps ever since we were kids. Until last year, she had been on the swim team. She'd quit, but not because she wasn't good. She'd held a state record in the fifty-yard freestyle. But some of the meets had conflicted with volleyball. And volleyball was what Courtney was passionate about.

"This is all my fault," Gigi said as we came around a bend.

There was still no sign of Courtney.

"Hang on." Emma started to climb a mossy boulder along the side of the river before I could ask Gigi what she'd meant.

"I'll be able to see a ways upriver from the top of this thing."

The rest of us waited for Emma to climb it. She was nearly to the top when her hiking boot slid on a wet patch of moss. She landed on the rock with her kneecap and cried out in pain.

"Emma!" Gigi yelled as Emma skidded down the side of the boulder, landing on a bed of river rocks.

Blood dripped from Emma's knee as Gigi rushed toward her. Emma got up and grimaced, grabbing her knee as she fell to the rocky ground. She tilted her head toward the patchy sky, where a bald eagle soared overhead, and squinted her eyes shut as she wrapped both hands around her injured leg. "Ahh!"

Gigi crouched beside her as Beth and I exchanged a wary look.

"Can you stand if I help you?" Gigi grabbed Emma's arm.

Emma nodded, wincing as Gigi helped pull her to her feet. Emma planted her injured leg on the ground before withdrawing it into the air. "It hurts to put weight on it."

"I'll help you back to our rafts," Gigi said, then glanced over her shoulder at Beth and me. "You guys go. I'll stay here with Emma. But be careful." Her eyes seemed to send an additional warning: *We can't lose anyone else.*

"Okay," Beth called before she and I continued up the winding riverbank.

We stepped over logs and large rocks and climbed up the occasional boulder, searching the rushing river for a sign of Courtney. I imagined her trapped beneath each logjam we came upon. I suppressed a shudder as I scanned the moving water beneath a fallen tree. *How did this trip go so disastrously wrong?*

I climbed over a fallen tree and envisioned the evil glint in Courtney's eyes in the glow of my flashlight last night. And how her expression remained triumphant with blood dripping from her nose after I'd punched her.

No, I thought. *Courtney's alive, and she's probably enjoying this, knowing we're all looking for her, fearing the worst. Having a laugh at our expense.*

Beth turned to me. "What do you think Gigi meant by 'It's all my fault'? Do you think she pushed Courtney out of the raft? They were pretty pissed at each other before we got onto the water."

"I was wondering the same thing. Gigi looked really distraught, like she felt guilty."

Beth's gaze traveled over the river's fast-flowing current. "Imagine how Gigi will feel if we never find her."

I shot Beth a look, surprised by her morbid words. "Don't you think we will?"

Beth looked away from the river and met my gaze. "Yeah, I do. I mean, it's Courtney we're talking about."

I studied the river as we walked farther, trying to recall rafting through this part, but it didn't look familiar.

"How long do you think we've been walking?" I asked Beth.

Beth checked her wristwatch. "Almost an hour."

Walking along the river wasn't a straight path. We'd had to move away from the shore several times to get around fallen trees and the occasional boulder. I scanned the thick forest to my right. *Had we gone past the place where we'd gotten in our rafts?*

I slowed my pace. "Doesn't it feel like we've been walking farther than we rafted?"

Beth took a wide step over a large rock. "It does, but I think we were just moving really fast in our rafts. We haven't come to the clearing yet where we put the rafts in the water. I'm sure of it."

A bird chirped from somewhere in the trees. My gaze drifted toward the sound as dread sprouted in the pit of my stomach.

Beth motioned to her right. "Let's cut through this way."

Straight ahead, a cluster of large mossy rocks lined the river. Directly behind them, the foliage looked too thick to walk through. I followed Beth away from the water until the woods thinned out enough for us to make our own path.

When we emerged from the forest onto a river-rock shoreline, Beth pointed. "That's the drop-off!"

I saw it, too; the same one we'd watched Gigi raft over alone. My heart sank. Then why hadn't we found Courtney? As I scanned our surroundings, I was surprised to find that a part of me was relieved. What if Courtney was gone forever? No longer able to wreak havoc on anyone's lives, including my own. I started to imagine my life without her, the four of us returning home in Beth's van peacefully without Courtney, then stopped myself.

What kind of monster wishes for someone to be dead?

Beth hurried up the side of a large rock, and I followed. When we got to the top, I saw the spot beside the clearing where we'd put our rafts in the river.

"Courtney!" Beth shouted.

I called her name, too, ashamed of the hope that had surfaced inside me at the thought of Courtney being dead. Atop the rock, I pivoted 360 degrees, yelling her name along with Beth. The only response to our shouts was the echo of our own voices.

I looked to Beth, fearing for the first time that Courtney might never have made it out of the river. "She's not here. What do we do now?"

Despite my disdain for Courtney, my veins constricted with panic. We had no way to call for help. We were at least a day's hike from Beth's van at the trailhead, and it was already midafternoon.

I stared at the glacier water rushing by, imagining Courtney trapped somewhere underneath the surface. "Oh, God." I grabbed Beth's hand. "Beth, this is bad."

Beth appeared calm as she assessed the river. "We need to split up. I'll go back along the river in case we somehow missed her. Maybe she grabbed onto a fallen tree or something."

Or was held down underneath one, I thought as I surveyed the moving water.

Beth turned to face me. "Then you go back along the trail. It wasn't easy to walk along the river, so maybe Courtney went that way. You might also find someone you can ask to call for help."

"Okay." I nodded and then slid down the edge of the rock, glad that Beth could think logically in a crisis. My thoughts felt like they were blurring together. "But wait. Shouldn't we stick together? What about cougars?"

Beth shook her head. "If we're going to find Courtney, this is our best chance. You'll be fine. Just remember what I said about making yourself big and creating a lot of noise if you see one."

I gulped over the lump that formed in my throat at Beth's last words. *If you see one.*

"Meet me back where Emma and Gigi are waiting," Beth added. "You can see the trail from where we beached the rafts, so you should be able to spot them. If you miss it, then follow the river back. Got it?"

I nodded, ignoring my racing pulse. It felt wrong to separate, but I agreed with Beth. It was our best chance of finding Courtney.

"I'll meet you back at the rafts," Beth called before turning down the river shore.

I started through the clearing, taking a deep breath. *How the hell did this happen?* I wondered again if Gigi was to blame.

"Courtney," I called when I reached the end of the clearing and entered the patch of forest that led to the trail.

I searched the trees, not only for Courtney but for wild predators on the prowl for their next meal. *Stupid Beth. Why did she think splitting up was such a good idea?* There weren't only cougars in the Olympic National Park but also bears. I grazed my hand over the hard outline of the pocketknife in my shorts pocket, wishing I had something better.

A branch snapped to my right, and I stopped dead in my tracks. I studied the surrounding woods for movement.

"Courtney?" I swallowed and stepped softly toward the sound, keeping my hand over the knife in my pocket.

I pushed through a stand of blackberry bushes, making my way through a thicket, wondering what the likelihood was of Courtney's still being alive. The Sol Duc was freezing, with powerful currents. We couldn't even paddle to shore for over a mile downriver after Courtney had fallen in. Did we overestimate Courtney's swimming ability?

All my fears about the school board meeting now seemed trivial compared with what was happening to Courtney. But every time I thought of her never coming back, I felt relief, then guilt for being relieved. If she was dead . . .

What if she hit her head on a rock after falling in? What if she—

Another snap. My heart lurched into my throat as I spun in the direction of the sound, preparing to be face-to-face with a cougar. Instead, I spotted Courtney's red hair as she moved between two trees, walking away from me. She was limping, and her hair and clothes were wet.

But she was alive.

Chapter Thirty-Five

Present: Day Five at Sea

"I think she's dead," Beth shrieks.

I jump to my feet, forcing Beth's betrayal to the back of my mind as my medical training takes over. Pushing past Beth, who feels like a stranger to me, I rush to Emma's room.

I flick on the lights, then swear as we remain in darkness.

"Shine a light on her," I order Beth.

I press two fingers to Emma's carotid as Beth shines the flashlight on Emma's pale face. At first, I feel nothing.

"Is she dead? Can you feel a pulse?"

"Shh." I hold my fingers to Emma's neck for several more seconds before feeling a weak, thready pulse. I keep my fingers there for ten more seconds, counting her pulse before withdrawing my hand.

Russell's heavy footsteps tromp down the steps. "What's going on?"

I turn, seeing the beam of his flashlight move behind Beth.

"She's got a pulse, but she's bradycardic—it's only forty-two." I lower my head toward Emma's nose and mouth while I press my palm against her chest. "She's still breathing."

"Thank God," Beth heaves. "But then what the hell is wrong with her?"

I extend my arm toward Beth. "Give me your flashlight," I say sharply.

I take the light from Beth's hand and pull down Emma's blanket, thinking of Russell's gun now hidden in my stateroom. I run the light over Emma's whole body, half expecting her to be lying in a pool of blood. I lift her shirt, but there's no trace of any injuries on her long, toned body. *Of course not,* I think. If Russell had shot her, we would've heard the gunshot.

I shake her unmoving form by the shoulders. "Emma! Wake up."

Her head flops limply to the side. I scan the sides of the bed and turn to Beth and Russell.

"Was she drinking before she laid down?"

"No," Beth says. "Not that I know of."

The only thing on her bedside shelf is an empty bottle of Gatorade. I turn her on her side and stick my fingers into the back of her throat.

Behind me, Beth gasps. "What are you—"

Emma gags and vomits orange liquid as I withdraw my fingers from her mouth. I hold her steady, keeping her on her side so she doesn't aspirate before sticking my fingers down her throat a second time. She gags and vomits again. This time, her glassed-over eyes flutter open as I hold her.

"That a girl. You're okay," I tell her.

I twist toward Beth. "Help me prop some pillows behind her to keep her head up. Russell, get her some water," I add while Beth crawls on the bed beside me.

Emma moans, and I help her lie back on the pillows Beth arranged. Her eyelids close.

"Here." Russell hands me a cold bottle of water.

I take it from him. "Emma. Hey, stay awake. Okay? I'm gonna give you some water."

Her eyelids open slowly.

"I'll help you. Just take a drink."

Emma sighs and opens her mouth as I tilt the bottle toward her lips.

"There you go. That's great," I praise her after she swallows.

I get a rancid waft from Emma's vomit on the bed next to us.

"I'm so tired," she groans.

"I know you are, but you need to drink more water, okay?"

I help her take another sip.

"Did you take any pills before bed?"

"No," she mutters.

I glance at Beth, who stares back at me blankly, then turn back to Emma before I become consumed by Beth's messages to my husband.

"Did you have alcohol?"

Emma shakes her head. "No."

I hold up the half-full water bottle. "I need you to drink the rest of this. We need to flush out your system. You should also have some caffeine. It will help stimulate your heart rate and increase your blood pressure, which I'm sure is low."

"What happened to her?" Russell asks.

As if he doesn't already know. I swing my light toward his face. He stares down at Emma with seemingly genuine concern, then looks to Beth and me for an answer.

"Russell, I think there's an energy drink in the fridge. Can you bring it to us?"

"Sure."

Emma coughs, and I take the nearly empty bottle from her hand. I help her sit up higher, making sure she doesn't choke.

I hold onto her upper arm with one hand and place the other on her back. "I think you might've been drugged."

"Here's the energy drink." Beth shines the light on Russell's hand as he holds out the cold can.

I take it from him and pop the tab before helping Emma take a sip. She takes the can from me.

"You got it?" I ask her.

Beth shifts her flashlight beam onto me. "How did you know it was something Emma drank?"

After making sure Emma has a steady hold on the energy drink, I let go. "Instinct, I guess. After seeing she had no obvious injuries."

"You did this to her. She would've died if I hadn't come in when I did." Beth's voice simmers with hatred. "You killed Nojan, Gigi, and now tried to kill Emma. None of us are safe with you on this boat."

I turn from Emma toward Beth, expecting her to be facing Russell. But she's staring straight at me.

Beth lifts her flashlight toward my face. "Just like you killed Courtney twenty years ago."

Chapter Thirty-Six

Present: Day Five at Sea

I stare at Beth, at a loss for words from her accusation. I think of Russell's gun under my pillow in the next room, wishing I'd thought to keep it on me.

Then I remember I have no idea who Beth even is. Aside from a backstabbing snake.

"I didn't—"

Beth snorts. "Oh, please. Spare us the lies. How did you know what was wrong with Emma so fast if you weren't the one who drugged her?"

"I'm a nurse. I've seen overdoses before."

"It was the exact same thing you were just planning to do to Russell."

"What?" Russell swings his beam at my face.

"Then, after you drugged Russell, you were planning to get rid of me."

"Beth! Shut up." *He's a murderer,* I want to scream. Now, he'll be too on guard for us to subdue him. And I have no doubt he's planning to kill us all before we reach the mainland.

"I didn't drug Emma." I almost add that I have no intentions of killing anyone, but after reading Beth's messages to my husband, I'm not sure that would be true. I stand up and close the space between us, stopping when my face is inches from hers. "Which only leaves two people on this boat who could've done it." I lift my finger toward Beth's face. "You're the one who's a liar with no conscience. Catfishing my husband so he would leave me!"

From the bed, Emma gasps.

"That's not enough for you?" I ask. "Now you're accusing me of drugging Emma? Why? To throw suspicion off yourself? You're the one no one should be trusting on this boat, you *lying, scheming snake*." No longer able to contain my fury, I shove Beth by the shoulders, slamming her into the bulkhead behind her.

Russell juts out his arms between Beth and me. My stomach pushes against his forearm as he holds me back.

"All right, enough," he shouts. "You two can go to therapy when we get home. *If* we get home. Right now, we need to put our energy into surviving. I need to rest, so someone needs to keep watch so we don't run into another ship in the night." Turning to me, he adds, "But first, I need to know what happened to my sister."

Beth pushes his arm aside. "You're right, Palmer. I went too far. I was wrong. But you're a murderer. And I'm not covering up for you anymore. Either you tell Russell—and Emma—what really happened that day when Courtney went missing, or I will."

My breath catches in my throat as I look toward Courtney's older brother, my hatred for Beth growing by the second.

"Go on," Beth adds. "Tell him."

Chapter Thirty-Seven

Memorial Day Weekend, 2005

"Courtney. Are you okay?"

She spun. Rather than relief when she saw me, her expression dampened. "Oh. Did you guys *finally* decide to come looking for me?"

"We've been looking for you this whole time."

Courtney tilted her head back as she let out a short egotistical laugh. "Oh yeah? Then where is everyone?"

I stared at her mascara-streaked face in disbelief. Could she be more ungrateful? "We thought you were dead. Emma busted her knee, and Beth and I have been scouring this entire forest for you. We even split up—even though it's dangerous—so we could find you sooner."

Courtney pursed her lips, and I saw tears in her eyes. "I can't believe all the things I do for you guys, and none of you jumped in after me when I fell. I would've jumped in after you."

Was she serious? "Courtney, I don't think you understand how dangerous these currents are. You're the best swimmer of all of us. We wouldn't have been able to save you if we'd tried. Plus, we were all carried downstream too fast after you fell to be able to get to you. It doesn't mean that we didn't *care*. We got out of our rafts and came back as soon as we could."

She rolled her eyes, and I started to regret coming after her at all. "Whatever. By the time I got out of the river, which wasn't easy, by the way, you were all long gone, rafting without me like nothing had happened." She pointed in the direction of the Sol Duc. "I'm not even convinced it was an accident that I fell in. When our raft tipped, Gigi acted like she was handing me her paddle to grab onto, but the way she shifted her weight made our raft tip more. The next thing I knew I was in that freezing water." She flipped her long wet hair over her shoulder. "And you know what? I'm starting to feel like you guys planned to ditch me all along." Her full lips formed a pout, reminding me of the look she used to make when we were kids and she didn't get her way.

"Courtney, come on. Just stop. I don't know what planet you're on sometimes, but you're the most ungrateful person I've ever met." I was losing the energy to fight with her, although I wasn't sure whether it was due to exhaustion or annoyance. "Beth is on her own looking for you. We need to find her so she doesn't get lost too. Then we need to meet up with the others. We'll be safer in a group." I paused before adding, "Plus, they're worried about you." I turned back for the river.

"You're the ones who are ungrateful!" Courtney shouted. "After all the things I've done for you guys! This is the thanks I get? I buy you guys clothes and let you live in my house, and you can't even jump in after me? Just kept floating along in your rafts, hoping I'd die? I see who you really are."

I whipped around to find her pointing a finger at me.

"Your mask is off, Palmer."

If I wasn't so irritated, I might've laughed. "You know what? Screw *you*. I came all this way to find you—*worried* about you—and all you can do is insult me. Go ahead, find your way back to those damn rafts *you so generously bought* on your own." I turned around and marched toward the river the way I had come, aware of the knife she'd given me inside my shorts pocket. "Good luck with that. *And* you're welcome for coming to find you," I called over my shoulder as the top of Courtney's head disappeared down a steep, densely forested slope. I turned back around, shaking my head, and stopped dead in my tracks.

Ten feet in front of me, maybe less, was the biggest wild animal I'd ever seen. It was huge. I held perfectly still as its wide-set eyes bore into mine. I realized then that when Beth had been talking about cougars, I had been envisioning a bobcat. This beast in front of me, however, was what she'd been referring to. Now I could see why they were also called mountain lions.

It was close enough for me to clearly see the defined brown stripe of fur that ran down the top of its head to the middle of its yellow irises, its long whiskers, and the patch of clean white fur that surrounded its mouth and nose, along with a white patch on its chest. I might've been in awe of its beauty if I weren't so sure it was about to kill me.

It snarled, dipping its head while a vicious sound emitted from its mouth. I staggered backward, stumbling on a rock, but managed to keep my footing as the massive beast took two steps toward me, then crouched low, ready to attack.

I thought of the pocketknife in my shorts and wondered if I should grab it. The blades were only two inches. For it to do any good, I'd have to stab it in the neck, and if it wasn't a fatal blow, I'd only manage to anger the hungry predator. But if I were to get close enough to the cougar to be able to use it, it would bite my hand off before I could plunge it into its neck.

Flooded with adrenaline, I screamed, recalling Beth's advice. I plucked a long stick from the ground beside me and waved it over my head.

Courtney's voice carried from beyond the slope. "Get a grip, Palmer. You're way worse than Emma. You're the one with the real anger problem."

The cougar's head swiveled in Courtney's direction.

"And you're judging *me*?" Courtney continued, sounding as if she'd started back up the hill to make sure I could hear her. "Listen to yourself. You're a total psycho."

The cougar growled, baring its sharp teeth. I froze, keeping hold of the stick with my trembling arm as the cougar stalked toward Courtney's voice with its teeth bared, head bowed, and body crouched.

I knew I should call out to her. Warn her. Jump on top of the stump beside me and try to scare the cougar away from both of us. Do *something*. But as Courtney continued to rattle off insulting jabs about my behavior, oblivious to the target she was making of herself, I stood still, too afraid to do anything but stand frozen in silence.

The cougar moved purposefully through the trees, its body hunched low to the ground. Even as the distance between the mountain lion and me grew, I still couldn't bring myself to breathe a word of warning.

Your mask is off, Palmer.

I could no longer see Courtney, but her voice sounded as though she was close to the top of the slope where I last saw the back of her head. The cougar started down the hill.

"Courtney!" I screamed. "Watch out, there's a cougar."

The animal stopped, cocked its head toward me, and growled. I stumbled backward and fell to the ground.

"Stop trying to scare me, Palmer," Courtney shouted.

I pushed myself to my feet and ran. I shot a glance over my shoulder as I dodged between trees, spotting the cougar disappear from my sight in nearly the exact spot where I'd last seen Courtney. I slowed. *I have to go back. I can't leave her alone.* A moment later, I heard Courtney scream.

I started to turn around when I tripped over an exposed tree root and tumbled down an eroded cliffside toward the river, leaving Courtney to fend off the deadly predator alone.

Chapter Thirty-Eight

Present: Day Five at Sea

"You saw her, and you lied all these years?" Emma sounds wide awake after I finish describing what happened after Beth and I separated from the others. "Unbelievable. All this time, I've been living with so much guilt. And not knowing how Courtney had seemed to vanish into thin air. Wondering if she'd still be alive if I hadn't faked my knee injury, if I'd helped you look for her. When it's your fault she's dead. You lied to the police—to everyone!"

Beth shines her light on Emma who pushes herself upright in bed. Behind Beth, Russell stands in stoic silence. His expression looks more pensive than grave, even though he must be inwardly seething.

"I didn't kill her," I say, even though I've never been able to convince myself of my innocence. While I've outwardly been living in denial of my role in Courtney's death, the weight of my guilt has been crushing me like a tidal wave. Emma's right. It's my fault Courtney's dead.

"Not directly." Beth swings her beam at me. "But you knew that cougar was going for Courtney, and you barely tried to warn her. You could've saved her. If you hadn't run away, she could've had a chance. Instead, you left her alone, leaving her for dead."

Beth's accusation burns. She's the only one who knew the truth of that day, and she's always consoled me over it. Acted like she was protecting me by assuring me she'd never bring it up.

"I—"

"I heard your fight with Courtney the night before outside our tents, just like Emma did. Her threat to your mom. I knew it was you who fought with her."

I stare at Beth in the darkness, seeing her true self for the first time. She's been lying our whole lives. I replay her warning, the ominous threat, about overhearing Courtney fight with one of us the night before we lost her in those woods. *What if they think it was you?*

And all this time Beth knew it was me. She used it against me, making me believe that if I'd told the truth about seeing Courtney—and our fight—that I could be facing manslaughter charges. That everyone would think I'd left Courtney for dead on purpose. A familiar weight of guilt crushes my chest. *Because that's exactly what I'd done.*

Russell speaks for the first time since my confession. "If a cougar got to Courtney, why didn't they find her remains?" His flashlight settles on my neck. "Did you hear the attack?"

"No, not exactly." I think back to those moments after the cougar prowled toward Courtney. "But I heard her scream once. I ran away so fast, toward the river, which would've muffled the rest of her screams. Then, I found Beth getting carried downstream and jumped in to help her."

"It still doesn't make sense," Russell adds. "One of you, or all of you, is lying. The dogs tracked Courtney's scent to the river. It was as if she never got out."

This had bothered me too. And the fact they never found her remains. But that heavy rainstorm had halted the initial search, and at seventeen, I had no idea how much of Courtney would be left after a savage cougar attack.

"If that's really what happened, why didn't you just tell the truth?" Russell's voice has an edge of accusation in it.

"I . . . I was scared." After Courtney was never found, I knew I should've confessed. But how would it look that I had lied in the first place?

Every time I came close to picking up the phone and telling Courtney's parents the truth, Beth's warning rang in my ears. *What if they think it was you?*

"*Scared?*" Russell shouts. "Imagine how my sister felt when you left her to be ravaged by a cougar! My—" He huffs out a breath. "She could've still been alive for a while. Did you ever think of that? If you'd told the truth right away, the search team might've been able to save her."

"I'm sorry," I croak.

We came home to a new reality: being sequestered for police interviews, having news vans surrounding our homes, and being stalked by reporters every time we left the house. Once I realized the gravity of my lie—and that Courtney was never coming back—I knew I was in too deep to revise my statement without looking guilty of murder.

With no body, there was also no way to prove a cougar attacked Courtney. I worried they would think I lied because I killed her, then hid her body. But it's still no excuse for what I did. And saying any of this to Russell will only make him angrier.

"Sorry? You left my sister for dead and then lied about it! Do you know the hell my parents and I went through? Not knowing what had happened to my sister ate us alive. And because of you, they *died* without ever knowing the truth." His voice breaks.

I open my mouth to say I'm sorry again but then close it as a tear slides down my cheek. The pain in Russell's voice is so raw. It kills me to think of how selfish I've been, choosing my own preservation over Courtney's life—and the lives of her family. There's nothing I can say to make it better. Russell's right. It's my fault.

"If what you're saying is true, then you're going to pay for this as soon as we get off this boat." Russell thrusts his finger at me in the glow of the flashlight.

My breath sticks in my lungs. I could go to prison. Not see my girls for years. Just the thought sends a bolt of terror through me. Strangely, it also feels like a ton of bricks has been lifted off my shoulders at confessing what I should've confessed twenty years ago.

Russell turns toward Beth before lowering his gaze toward Emma. "But I'm still not one hundred percent convinced that's what happened."

The floor tilts, and I fall against the bulkhead as a wave splashes against the hull.

"Maybe it's a good thing my parents didn't live to find out that Courtney was mauled to death by a cougar," Russell says, lifting a hand to his head. "I think I need to lie down, but one of us needs to keep watch for other boats."

"I'll go," Beth volunteers.

Good, I think, relieved to have some distance from her. And Russell. For a few hours, at least.

Emma yawns, and I force myself to focus on helping her rather than the worst thing I've ever done. I shine my phone light on her face. "You need to stay awake and drink some more of this, okay? I'll get you some more water and a clean blanket." Fortunately, her vomit landed all on her comforter and didn't seem to seep through to the sheets. "Russell, are there spare blankets onboard?"

"No, but you can use Nojan's."

Surprised he's still speaking to me, I follow him and Beth out of Emma's stateroom as Russell heads toward his room.

"Beth?" he calls when her flashlight reaches the top deck. "I'm going to try to rest, even though I'm not sure I can sleep. I'll set an alarm on my watch for four hours. If you have trouble staying awake before then, just come wake me up to relieve you."

"Okay."

I avert my eyes, my disgust for her too great to even look in her direction, as I wait for Russell to come out of his room with the blanket for Emma. A few hours ago, it would've seemed unfathomable that Beth would catfish my husband and accuse me of murder. Has she secretly hated me all these years? Why bother pretending to be my friend at all? I grab another bottle of water for Emma from the kitchen.

A minute later, Russell emerges from his stateroom. In the flashlight glow, his face is grim, almost sinister. I freeze, suddenly afraid he's about to kill me. I step back as my gaze falls to his hands, expecting to see a knife or some other weapon. Instead, he folds Nojan's blanket into my arms, laying his flashlight on top.

I gulp down a swallow. "Thanks." I hear myself say.

He retreats to his room and closes the door, and I wonder how long it will be before he realizes I've taken his gun. Emma's eyes are closed when I return to her room.

"Hey." I place my hand on her shoulder. "Did you drink the energy drink?"

She opens her eyes. "Half of it."

"Okay, good." I hand her the water bottle. "Drink this while I change your bed."

I roll up the vomit-stained comforter, wrinkling my nose at the smell, before tossing it onto the floor. Although, after fifteen years of nursing, I've smelled much worse.

"Emma," I say as she takes a big drink. "Did you find Courtney's diary in Russell's room?"

She's quiet for a moment, as if debating how to answer. "Yeah," she finally says. "I fell asleep before I could finish the whole thing, but I read where Courtney admitted to being the one who spread Gigi's shirtless photos around school, then I got to the part about the dish soap. How Courtney did it after you chickened out, then blackmailed you with the photo she'd taken. It was obvious that Courtney didn't care about my broken ankle, and she was over the moon about getting to replace me as volleyball captain." Emma peers up at me as I spread Nojan's blanket out over her legs. "Look, it was twenty years ago. And I know how conniving Courtney could be. I forgive you."

This is a side of Emma I haven't seen before, and I wonder how much of it is the painkillers in her system. Nevertheless, I take her hand.

"Thank you. I'm so sorry. You never deserved that."

"But still," Emma adds, "I can't believe you left Courtney to die like that."

I lower my head, air leaving my lungs. "Sometimes I still can't either. You don't know how many times I've wished I could go back and try to save her. I was afraid. I *let* that cougar go after her by running away. After Beth nearly drowned, I convinced myself it was too late by that point to save Courtney, and I was scared that if I told the truth I could be facing manslaughter charges." *Because that's what Beth made me believe.* "I should've been truthful. It's not fair that Courtney's family has had to wonder what happened to her all these years."

"Reading Courtney's diary brought back how . . . almost evil she could be. Ever since that trip, I've been angry at myself for exaggerating my knee injury, wondering if we would've found her if I'd helped look for Courtney rather than make Gigi come back to the rafts with me. Now, after reading how much Courtney enjoyed watching the torment we went through from things she'd done, I wonder if Courtney would've been happy at the way things turned out."

I sit tall. "What do you mean?" *Happy to be dead?*

"Happy with how her disappearance ruined our lives and marred us forever. That we've all had to live with guilt over that trip. You and Beth lying about finding her, me faking my injury instead of looking for her, and Gigi pushing her from the raft. I think Courtney would've loved to see us all called murderers by reporters, and random strangers even."

I swallow, thinking about the last time I saw Courtney. I move the flashlight onto the bed so Emma can't see the guilt on my face.

"We'll never get away from Courtney, or that trip. Ironically, I think it's what she would've wanted." Emma stretches her arm toward the skylight hatch. "The mystery of her death haunting us for the rest of our lives. I mean, look at us *now*. Stranded in the Pacific, wondering which one of us will end up dead next." She props herself up on her elbows. "Maybe it's from reading her diary—or that note left in the bathroom—but it feels like Courtney's here somehow." Emma leans closer to me. "You don't think she could be here, on this boat, do you?"

I recall the look on Courtney's face when I found her that day in the woods. And how much I'd hated her in that moment. Courtney couldn't have survived; I made sure of that for her by running away in silence while that cougar—

"Palmer?"

I turn toward Emma. Unless . . . somehow . . . could it be possible? If Courtney *had* survived being mauled by the cougar, she might've been horribly disfigured. Courtney was meticulous about her appearance, careful about what she ate, always making sure she never had a hair out of place. She even stayed home sick from school once because she had a pimple. Would Courtney have preferred the world think she was dead than be seen as less than perfect?

Were Courtney and Russell working together, planning to off us one by one? "No. Russell seems genuinely convinced of his sister's death. Courtney couldn't have written that note." There's a firmness to my voice, and I'm not sure who I'm trying to convince more: Emma or myself. "But I get what you mean. A part of Courtney has stayed with all of us. How could she not?"

Emma yawns. "Yeah, you're probably right."

But I feel her presence too. "Take another drink and then you can have a rest," I tell her.

Emma closes her eyes after lifting the can to her mouth. "Get out."

"What?"

Emma turns on her side. "If Courtney *is* dead, it's your fault. And you've been lying about it all these years. Just like you lied about being the one who caused my broken ankle. I don't trust you. One of you drugged me. How do I know it wasn't you?"

"Emma, I—"

"Even Beth thinks you did it."

The truth in her last statement stings. "I *saved* you. I'm a nurse, I've seen overdoses before. But I didn't drug you!"

Emma sighs.

"It wasn't me, Emma. I swear. I'm here to help you."

She doesn't answer. Hopefully, that means she believes me. More likely, she's just too drugged to put up more of a fight. If it weren't for those pills in her system, Emma would probably have me against the wall.

I lie beside her in silence, my thoughts consumed by Courtney as I stare up at the darkened window hatch. After a few minutes, I sit up, recalling the smell of Courtney's perfume on the couch.

"Emma?" I sweep the small space with the flashlight. "Where's the diary?" My heart beats with anticipation to read Courtney's words but also at the implication of what the diary's presence means: Russell is, at least in part, telling the truth.

Emma's only response is her rhythmic breathing. I feel the inside of her wrist for a pulse. It's stronger and faster than before. Seeing her second bottle of water nearly empty, I let her sleep, counting her respirations for a full minute before I shine the light around the bed in search of the diary.

I lift up the blanket and sheets, sifting through the fabric with my hand. But it's not here. I shine my light over the edge of the bed, wondering if Emma stashed the diary in her bag. But she said she'd fallen asleep reading it, hadn't she? I check her bag anyway, but it's not there.

Whoever drugged her must've taken it. Probably Russell. But it could've been Beth.

Or Courtney, I think before forcing the thought from my mind.

Chapter Thirty-Nine

Memorial Day Weekend, 2005

I rolled to a stop at the bottom of the cliffside, the air knocked from my lungs when I landed painfully on a bed of river rocks. I stared at the sky as my breath returned to my body. Slowly, I got to my feet near the river's edge and placed my hands on my knees. My heart thudded against my ribs as I caught my breath. *I should go back.*

I turned, looking up at the steep eroded riverbank, doubting I could climb to the top even if I tried. *And what good would I be against the cougar on my own?*

I swallowed, staring down at the fast-flowing water, as it struck me that Courtney could already be dead. I didn't hear anything after her first scream. I closed my eyes, and my mind filled with an image of the cougar tackling Courtney to the ground and gnawing on her neck.

I stood tall, cupping my hands around my mouth. "Beth!"

Maybe if she and I went back together, we could stand a chance of scaring off the wild beast. Hopefully, before it was too late to save Courtney. I moved unsteadily along the riverbank, scanning the rocky shore for my best friend.

"Beth," I called again.

Where was she? I spun 360 degrees, but there was no sign of her. I continued along the river downstream when a branch snapped in the woods to my left.

I startled, my hand hovering over the pocketknife in my shorts. Had the cougar finished with Courtney and tracked me to the shore?

"Beth?"

No response. My pulse quickened as I hurried along the rocky shore, casting a wary glance over my shoulder in the direction of the noise. I moved faster, praying the cougar wouldn't emerge from the tree line and attack.

I called Beth's name again as I followed the river around a bend, downstream from where Courtney fell in.

"Beth." My voice echoed through the woods.

We should never have separated. What if I lost Beth too?

I went a little farther and climbed to the top of a slippery moss-covered boulder, similar to the one Emma hurt her knee trying to climb. I made it to the top and stood, able to see around the next bend in the river. There was no sign of Beth.

I called her name again anyway. Had she already gotten back to Gigi and Emma? I climbed down, deciding to retrace my steps upstream. Hopefully, I would run into Beth. If not, I would go back to where I'd left Courtney alone. I berated myself for not going back to warn her. What kind of person does that?

Courtney's words resounded in my head. *Your mask is off, Palmer.* What if she was right?

I started into a jog. My feet rolled on top of the round rocks, but I kept my pace, pushing myself forward. I had to at least *try* to help Courtney, however I could. I steeled myself for the state she'd be in—or her body would be in—when I found her. Without slowing my jog, I withdrew the knife from my pocket, wishing she'd gifted us bear spray instead.

A splash drew my attention to the river. I spotted Beth being carried downstream. She was gulping for air, her arms flailing above her head before she was pulled under.

"Beth!" I put the knife back in my pocket and waded into the frigid water, my feet slipping on the rocks at the bottom.

Straight in front of me, Beth's head surfaced. She sucked in an audible breath before disappearing beneath the current a second time.

I rushed toward her, falling into the water, the shock of cold taking my breath away. I swam, fighting against the current and the drag of my clothes to get to Beth.

She surfaced again, downstream of me. I recognized the sheer panic on her face as she coughed, water sputtering out of her mouth.

"Hang on," I yelled, allowing the current to carry me toward her.

Unlike Courtney, Beth had never been a good swimmer. She had no buoyancy and wore water wings to the pool until we were twelve. Beth's head sank beneath the water as she was dragged beneath a fallen log.

"Beth." I kicked my legs to pick up speed and wrapped my arms around the log when I reached it. A current pulled my legs forward under the fast-moving water beneath the log, and I struggled to keep hold of its trunk. "Ugh!" I strained to see over the top. When I managed to pull myself up far enough to see the river beyond it, there was no sign of Beth.

Then I felt something tug at my thigh. A hand. I reached below and grabbed Beth's wrist, trying to pull her toward me. But she moved only an inch before my tug met hard resistance.

To my left, a mangled mess of broken branches hung from the log into the water. Beth must be caught on one beneath the surface. I reached down, closed my hand around her forearm, and pulled with all my strength.

"Ahh!" My grip slipped down Beth's arm, bringing her no closer to the surface.

I let go of her and reached for the pocketknife in my shorts. I gripped the log with my armpit and used both hands to open the blade. I sucked in a deep breath as I let go of the log, allowing the current to pull me under.

Chapter Forty

Memorial Day Weekend, 2005

As icy river water rushed over my head, I grabbed hold of a branch protruding from the base of the log. Beth's dark hair swirled around her face as she struggled to free herself. I placed my hand on her shoulder, needing her to hold still so I could see where she was hung up.

She stared at me, her brown eyes bulging with panic as bubbles escaped her mouth. I lifted the small blade in front of her face. She pointed to her shoulder. Then I saw it—a branch had caught the sleeve of her oversize T-shirt. I tugged at the fabric, trying to free her shirt from the branch, but it was pulled tight from the weight of Beth's body being forced downstream by the current.

More bubbles escaped Beth's lips as her eyes closed. I stuck my knife beneath her sleeve and thrust the blade upward, but there wasn't enough tension on her shirt for the blade to cut through the fabric. I released the branch so I could pull her sleeve tight with my other hand, fighting to stay under the log, knowing I wouldn't have long before the current carried me downriver, away from Beth.

I grasped her sleeve and jerked the knife upward and back. It sliced through her shirt, releasing Beth from the branch. The knife jabbed my hand between my thumb and forefinger while Beth was immediately pulled downriver. I dropped the knife as my blood clouded the water around my hand, allowing the current to carry me downstream. My lungs burned for air as I fought to reach the surface. When I did, I gulped in a deep breath. Beth surfaced a few feet away, coughing and sputtering. Relief washed over me. *She's alive.*

My arms were numb from the cold. I swam toward her with slow strokes. As soon as I could touch the bottom, I helped Beth stand on the uneven riverbed. We moved together, shivering as the frigid current swept sideways against our legs. When we reached the shore, we collapsed beside each other on the rocks.

"You're bleeding." She pointed to my hand.

"I'm fine." I rolled onto my back, laying my bloody hand atop my chest. It was too numb to feel any pain from the cut. "For a second, I thought you were dead. That it was too late when I cut you loose."

"Thank you." Beth plopped her cold, wet arm onto mine. "You saved me."

I stared at the patchy sky, shivering while catching my breath. When I turned to Beth, her eyes were closed.

"I found her."

Beth's eyes snapped open. "You did? Where? Is she okay?"

I sat up and told Beth about fighting with Courtney after finding her in the woods. Beth sat up too. She stared pensively at the river while I recounted my cougar encounter and how I left Courtney alone to be ravaged by the beast without so much as warning her.

"And that's when I found you," I concluded. "I never should've left her." I was filled with too much shame to meet Beth's gaze. "We have to go back. What if we can still save her? We have to at least try."

Although if I had stayed to help Courtney, I thought, *Beth would've drowned.* We might all three be dead.

"No." Beth's tone was firm.

I turned to her in surprise.

"We've both almost died already."

I swiped a stray piece of wet hair from my face. Blood dripped onto my leg from my hand.

"Look at us." Beth gestured to my cut. "We need to join the others. Then we'll find the van and call for help."

I gazed upriver in the direction of where I'd left Courtney. "And leave Courtney?"

"If that cougar attacked her, then she's already gone. It could very well attack us, too, if we go back—we have nothing to defend ourselves with. If we stay out here, we could all die," Beth added. "It's too dangerous."

I stared at the river, thinking of my pocketknife at the bottom.

Beth got to her feet and held out her palm. "The best thing we can do for Courtney is call for help—professional, emergency help—as soon as we can."

I bit my lip, studying Beth while debating what to do. Her dark waves hung flat against her face. Water dripped from her clothes onto my legs. The image of Beth closing her eyes under the log while the remaining air escaped her lungs was seared in my mind. She was lucky to be alive. A shudder passed through my upper body as I recalled the cougar's snarl. *And so am I.*

"Okay, fine." I took Beth's hand and looked behind me after I stood, not knowing how much this decision would haunt me for the rest of my life.

Chapter Forty-One

Present: Day Six at Sea

When I open my eyes, bright morning sun gleams through the window hatch above me. I'm alone in an unfamiliar bed. I sit up, remembering drifting off in Emma's bed as last night's events—and Beth's betrayal—come flooding back to me. I slide to the edge, surprised I didn't hear Emma get up.

Emma is in the galley when I emerge into the boat's main living quarters. Like me, she's wearing last night's clothes. She turns from the gas stovetop and pours steaming water from the kettle into a French press.

"Want some coffee?" she asks.

I rub my eyes. "Sure, thanks. How are you feeling?"

She shrugs. "Tired. But otherwise okay."

I assess her as she pushes the plunger to the bottom of the French press. She looks completely recovered from last night. If she's pissed that I stayed in her room after she told me to get out, she doesn't show it. Perhaps she had too many pills to remember. Although, looking at her now, it's hard to imagine she had anything in her system at all.

I glance at the closed door to the stateroom I've been sharing with Beth. "Who's keeping watch?"

"Russell." Emma fills two insulated mugs with coffee and hands one to me.

I exhale, hoping that means Beth is still asleep in our room. I'm not ready to face her again.

Emma follows my gaze. "Beth's still asleep."

She slides me a canister of powdered creamer after stirring some into her mug. I add a heaping spoonful to my coffee, noting that the boat doesn't seem to be rocking as much as it was the last couple of days.

"I told you not to stay in my room last night."

So she does remember. "Sorry. I didn't mean to fall asleep. I only stayed to make sure your breathing and pulse rate stayed normal. I meant to sleep on the couch."

Emma eyes me suspiciously as I lift the mug to my lips and take a sip. I would've rather slept next to Gigi's dead body than Beth. I can't wait to get off this boat, hold my girls in my arms, and never see my backstabbing "best friend" again.

I remember that Russell's gun is still under my pillow in the room where Beth is sleeping. I inwardly curse myself for not bringing it into Emma's cabin. I start to turn for my room when Emma holds out what I was looking for last night.

I instantly recognize the light-purple journal I'd seen Courtney write in nearly every night when I stayed at her house senior year.

Emma sets her jaw in the same way she used to when she stared down our opponents in volleyball. "Why did you rip out the last pages?" She raises her eyebrows. "What did Courtney do to you that you don't want anyone to know about?"

"I don't know what you're talking about. I didn't rip out any pages." I take the diary from her, surprised by the well of emotions that spring up when I run my thumb over the diary's faded cover.

"Where was this?" I lift my gaze to Emma's. "I couldn't find it last night in your room."

Emma sets down her coffee. "Well, someone did. Because it was out here on the couch when I woke up this morning." She folds her arms. "Missing every page after Courtney's cryptic entry that she wrote in the fall of our senior year."

"What do you mean cryptic?"

"You'll see."

I think back to Beth's accusations last night in Emma's room when all four of us were together. Had she taken the diary? Russell didn't come far enough into Emma's room to have taken the diary from her bed. Unless he'd taken it earlier. Like after he knocked Emma out by putting Gigi's opiates in her Gatorade. But why would he go to the trouble of stealing a diary he'd already read?

I stare at the diary as I lower myself to the padded bench of the dinette and wonder what's in here that Russell—or Beth—wouldn't want us to see. I flip through the pages, recognizing Courtney's handwriting in blue ink. It was neat and bubbly, like her personality when she was in a good mood. Just like the note stuck to the bathroom mirror. I swallow, trying to combat the eerie trepidation that washes over me. If someone *had* forged it, they'd done an exceptional job.

"Go to the last page," Emma says.

My coffee churns in my stomach when I get to the last page in the diary. It's from October 19, 2004. I turn the page to see that the rest of the diary has been ripped out.

"Are you sure these pages weren't already missing? Maybe it was like this when Russell found it."

Emma shakes her head. "I'm sure. I didn't read this far, but I skimmed through to see there was more after this, and the last several pages were blank."

I flip back to the final diary entry. It's much shorter than the rest of her diary entries. I stare at the date. I was staying with Courtney at the time. I bite my lip and look up at Emma.

"This was right before we won the state championship."

She nods.

I lower my gaze to Courtney's written words, suck in a breath, and start to read.

Chapter Forty-Two

Present: Day Six at Sea

Emma's eyes are on mine when I set down the diary. "I read this before." The memory came flooding back to me as soon as I started reading. "When I was staying at Courtney's house the fall of senior year, I snuck into her room one night." Looking at Emma, I refrain from telling her why. "And I found this."

Emma furrowed her brows. "Who was she talking about?"

"I don't know. When I saw Courtney had written it on the day you broke your ankle, I worried it was you."

Emma shakes her head. "I broke my ankle on October seventeenth. Two days before she wrote that." She gestured toward the diary.

I cock my head to the side, straining to remember. I recall feeling sure Courtney wrote that on the day of her "prank."

"Trust me," Emma adds. "It's not something I could forget."

She's right. That day had a much bigger impact on Emma's life than it did mine, which leaves me feeling I have no right to argue. But I remember standing in Courtney's room, seeing that date in her diary so clearly and being sure it was the day Emma had broken her ankle. *Had I been confused?* I meet Emma's gaze. *Or is she lying?*

"Maybe she was referring to you," Emma says, seeming to note the skepticism on my face.

"No," I say. Courtney and I didn't have a problem until I finally stood up to her the next summer on our rafting trip. At least, I didn't think we did. Even though Courtney had blackmailed me with that photo over the dish soap prank, I was still her friend. It makes me feel ill now, how I'd let Courtney walk all over me because I somehow thought I needed her in my life. "It wasn't me."

"Then who was it?" Emma asks. "When I skimmed through the rest of the pages, I came across a line in an entry from November about how Courtney's revenge plan was working. How this 'traitor' was totally falling for whatever Courtney was doing to them."

I can't remember Courtney doing anything horrible later that fall or winter, aside from falsely accusing Bryson and Jake of being the ones to cause Emma's broken ankle. I swallow. Which I'd so sickeningly gone along with.

Could Courtney have meant me? Looking back, it was obvious how Courtney had enjoyed watching me squirm and feel responsible over what we did to Emma. But I chalked that up to Courtney's cruel nature, not because I'd done anything to make her feel I'd deserved it.

"It couldn't have been me," Emma says. "Courtney had already gotten you to help her break my ankle."

"By accident. I'm so sorry. I never meant for you to—"

Emma holds up her palm. "What I'm saying is that I really don't think Courtney was talking about me. She never did anything to me after that."

I recall how livid Emma was when Beth and I visited her at the Port Angeles Hospital. When Emma believed it was Courtney who'd spilled the dish soap, not Bryson and Jake. Did Courtney find out Emma was bashing her behind her back?

"If it wasn't you," Emma lowers her voice. "Then it had to be Beth or Gigi."

I steal a glance at the closed door to Beth's cabin. "Courtney never did anything to Beth." *Although that's not true,* I think, remembering the bookmark Courtney gave Beth in place of a T-shirt at the start of our hike. And the fat-shaming comments Courtney used to make to Beth that Courtney tried to pass off as well meaning. "Well, at least not to the extent of your broken ankle or those slut photos of Gigi that Courtney spread around school. Maybe it was Selena." I add, "She started with us that year on the volleyball team."

"I know who Selena is. But they weren't friends for most of their lives." Emma taps her pointer finger on the diary. "It has to be one of us."

"You're sure the rest of the pages weren't ripped out when you found the diary yesterday?"

"I'm sure." She tilts her head toward the deck above. "I'm going to ask Russell what it said."

"Not by yourself. I'm coming with you."

Chapter Forty-Three

Memorial Day Weekend, 2005

I wasn't sure how long we'd been walking, but we had to be getting close to where Gigi and Emma were waiting with the rafts.

"I don't think you should tell Emma and Gigi that you saw Courtney."

I turn to Beth as we continued along the river. "Why not?"

"What if they think you left Courtney on purpose?"

"I did." I hated myself for it now, but it was the truth.

"I know. And I know you were scared. But what if they think you left Courtney on purpose *to die*?"

I slowed my pace.

"Like how you didn't even call out to warn her," Beth added. "Until it was too late."

"I didn't mean for . . ." I kept moving, studying my best friend. Did she think I *wanted* Courtney to die? A ripple of guilt shimmied down my torso as I stepped over a log. Is that what they'd all think? I couldn't explain why I left her, not even to myself. I wished now that I could take it back.

"I . . . panicked. I was too scared to stay and help her after facing the cougar head-on." As I said the words, I wasn't sure they were true. *Had* I wanted Courtney to die when I kept silent and ran away?

Beth frowned. "I mean if Courtney's . . . dead"—her eyes skirted to the trees behind me—"you could be charged with manslaughter."

I stopped. "What?"

"You know how powerful Courtney's parents are. And last night, I heard Courtney fighting outside our tents with someone."

I swallowed, recalling the stream of blood dripping from Courtney's mouth after I'd punched her.

"It was probably Emma or Gigi, but what if they think it was you?" Beth turned to me as she moved around a large rock.

It was me, I wanted to say, but something in the way Beth was eyeing me made me hold back. Gigi already knew. Would she think I'd left Courtney to die on purpose if I told her and Emma the truth?

"I'm just worried how it might look," Beth continued. "I say we tell them everything except for you finding Courtney. Then, we'll get to the van as fast as we can and call for help. Getting a rescue team up here ASAP will be Courtney's best chance of survival."

I gazed at the tree line to our left, noting the late afternoon sun had dipped below the treetops. *That makes sense,* I thought. But just as some tension released from my shoulders, another thought raced through my mind.

"Beth, what if Courtney's alive and she catches up to us? Or a rescue team finds her, and she tells them I found her before we fought, and I left?"

Beth's brown eyes searched mine. "Do you really think she could still be alive?"

I envisioned the huge mountain lion, and the size of its teeth when it snarled. How it was crouched—in hunting mode—when it went after Courtney.

"Come on." Beth tugged at my arm. "We need to keep going if we want a chance to reach the van before dark."

I pondered Beth's warning as we kept walking. Was Courtney's phone still in her backpack or did she have it on her? Was it wrecked by being in the water? If Gigi told the others how I punched Courtney last night, and if the police found the photo on Courtney's phone of me holding the dish soap in the locker room—evidence that Courtney could've been blackmailing me and that we'd lied about what happened to Emma—how would that look?

I stared at the Sol Duc's white water rushing past us. I *did* leave Courtney to die. I did nothing to save her, not even warn her until it was too late. Then, when Courtney didn't believe me, I'd run away rather than convince Courtney she was in danger. Would I go to prison if I told the truth?

Gigi's tall frame emerged from a row of trees up ahead. She waved her arms in the air, making sure we saw her. Beyond her, I spotted Emma perched on a stump with her injured leg extended in front of her.

Gigi jogged toward us. "What happened to you guys? Are you okay?"

"I fell in the river and got caught under a log." Beth gestured to me. "Palmer saved me."

Gigi's hand flew to her mouth. "Oh my—"

"After Palmer nearly got attacked by a cougar," Beth added.

Gigi gasped, lowering her hand. "What about Courtney?" Her worried gaze darted between me and Beth. "Did you find her?"

Beth looked at me, allowing me to answer.

I shook my head, avoiding Beth's gaze. "No. We couldn't find her."

Chapter Forty-Four

Present: Day Six at Sea

I follow Emma up to the cockpit. Russell is at the helm, wearing the same color of navy polo shirt he's worn this whole trip, plus sunglasses and a baseball hat.

Russell doesn't greet us, even though he had to have seen us come on deck. I can't blame him, considering what I did to his sister. I take a seat on one of the cockpit benches, noting the swells aren't as high as they were yesterday.

Emma moves to the back of the cockpit and lifts her gaze to assess the sails. Before we came up, Emma had tucked the diary into her sweatshirt. I take a drink from my coffee, which spills onto my pants as the boat tilts, and wait for Emma to ask Russell about the ripped-out pages.

She turns to him. "We need to let out the sails now that the wind has decreased. Here." She hands me her coffee, which I hold away from my legs while Russell uncoils the line around a winch near the helm and lets out the jib.

As Russell rewraps the line around the winch, Emma goes to the front of the cockpit and lets out the mainsail halyard until the mainsail bubbles out into a taut curve. After securing the line, Emma reclaims her mug from me and takes a drink.

The three of us sit in awkward silence. I throw Russell a sideways glance. He's looking in my direction, but with his sunglasses on I can't tell if he's staring at me.

Either he or Beth drugged Emma. *Or Courtney,* a voice in my head says before I force the thought from my mind. Russell's been lying this whole time: first about who he was, then about the note he left in the bathroom. He had to have written it and probably studied Courtney's handwriting after finding her diary. I watch Emma step around a shroud on the foredeck. Had she drugged herself so no one would suspect her? If Courtney's diary was all about us, then why would Russell rip pages out of it? It makes more sense that Emma or Beth ripped them out, not wanting the rest of us—or the police—to see what was in there.

I take a sip from my mug and wonder if Russell's discovered his missing gun yet. I choke on my coffee, remembering leaving his gun under my pillow.

I cough. Russell watches me, his mouth set in a hard line. I should've kept his gun on me. Now it's with Beth. What if she tries to use it? Or what if he knows that I took it? I warily assess his muscular upper body. I would be no match for his strength if he tries to throw me overboard.

With Emma here, I decide to ask him the question that's been burning in my mind since last night. But first, I hastily clip a tether onto my life vest. Just in case.

I turn toward the helm. "Why is it so hard for you to believe that I left Courtney with the cougar? It's the truth."

Russell squares his jaw and looks out at the ocean. "I actually thought it was Beth who killed Courtney after reading what Courtney did to Beth your senior year."

I rack my brain, trying to recall what Russell is talking about. Emma and I exchange a look. She appears as confused as I am.

Russell looks at me and then Emma, who stares at me blankly. "Beth never told you, did she?"

"Told me what?" Beth's accusing me of murder in front of the others after I'd discovered her online affair with Matt replays in my mind as I wait for Russell to answer. Had I even known her at all? My body tenses, having no idea what he's about to say.

"It was in the diary," he says. "In the pages that someone ripped out."

Of all the things Courtney did, Beth had the least reason of all of us to want her dead. My throat is so tight with anxiety that it takes effort to swallow.

"Courtney could've exaggerated it," I tell him. "She did that, you know."

He shakes his head. "Not this. I was there."

Chapter Forty-Five

December 20, 2004

Dear Diary,

I haven't written much about this before, mostly because I never thought my prank would keep going this long. But here we are, and what's happening tonight is too good not to document. I'm smiling right now at how well—no, freakin' amazing—my plan has worked. I had no idea it could go this far, but Beth is more gullible than I'd given her credit for. For being so book smart, Beth's actually pretty dumb.

I'll start at the beginning. At the end of summer, I sent Beth a message from the fake MySpace account I created pretending to be Russell (she told me in fifth grade that she thought he was hot). It was just for fun, and I'd planned to tell Beth the truth soon after. I wasn't even sure she'd reply. I mean, does she honestly think my brother would remember her, let alone message her?

But she did, and she was so OBVIOUSLY into him. It was so sad and pathetic that I decided to let her live in her fantasy a little longer.

Beth's never had a boyfriend (and probably never will if she doesn't start counting her calories). So it seemed cruel not to let her enjoy what it feels like to be in love, at least for a little while. It's sad to say, but her pretend online fling is probably the best thing that's ever happened to her.

Being Beth's friend, I planned to let her down easy before Halloween, saying that "Russell" was heading into a top-secret op and couldn't contact her anymore. But then, Beth got all jealous of me and Palmer's friendship when I let Palmer stay with me. The chubby bitch went so far as to tell Palmer that I was using her, calling me a fake friend.

Ha! Now that's bullshit. What would I be using any of my friends for? I'm the one who has everything. I should be worried they're using me. Plus, Beth was the one with a fake boyfriend. Hello!

Anyways, I was shocked. I've always been kind to Beth, taken her under my wing. I've stuck up to bullies for her since kindergarten. How dare she?

I'm the most honest one in our whole volleyball team. No one else has the guts to tell Beth she needs to lose weight. But I tell her because it's the truth. And that's what friends do.

When Palmer told me what Beth said about having a boyfriend, I was tempted to gloat, crush the pretend fairytale Beth was living in. But I held my tongue. Instead, I came on even stronger to Beth as "Russell."

I've been told I'm not a good listener, but fortunately Beth talks about books so much that it's impossible not to know what her favorites are. Normally, I space out pretty quick when Beth starts rattling on about books, but lately, I've been paying attention.

And get this: Now, Beth believes that she and Russell are not only soul mates, but that they also read the same books. LOL, picturing my brother with a book in his hand (especially one of those super old boring ones that Beth reads) makes me laugh out loud. My pen is jiggling because I'm LMAO right now writing this.

One night a few weeks ago after I helped myself to some peach Schnapps from my parents' liquor cabinet, I proposed, asking Beth if she'd marry me (Russell) when he got home from his tour in Iraq.

After hitting Send on my laptop, I thought it was game over. I'd gone too far. Beth had to know she was being punked. But she said yes! I couldn't believe it. What a moron. I honestly thought she was smarter than that.

I made Beth promise not to tell anyone about our secret engagement, warning her that not everyone would understand our love connection since she was so much younger than me. She agreed. (I know, shocker.)

The next day at school, Beth was practically floating on air, as if she'd lost those extra fifteen pounds. I caught her smiling to herself three times just in Spanish class.

But I was getting tired of having to keep up the fake messages. While fun, it's also exhausting. I even had to record the last episode of One Tree Hill! I was going to stop responding to her altogether when Russell surprised my parents and me by coming home for Christmas. It couldn't have been more perfect if I'd planned it.

Beth thinks she's coming over tonight to help me pick out a New Year's dress, even though I already totally know what I'm going to wear. She should be here any minute. My parents aren't home, and Russell is downstairs watching football. When Beth gets here, I'll let him answer the door and watch from the upstairs balcony. I can't wait to see the look on her face.

Oh! The doorbell's ringing. I have to go.

We'll see who's fake now.

Chapter Forty-Six

Present: Day Six at Sea

"I had no idea why Beth had acted so strangely that night until I read Courtney's diary," Russell says.

Emma leans against the cockpit table as I sit frozen on the bench, reeling from hearing about what was likely Courtney's cruelest act of all. I can't help but feel partly responsible. *I* was the one who told Courtney what Beth had said behind her back.

"Courtney catfished her," Emma says, taking in what Russell told us.

Just like Beth did to Matt, I think. Her high school trauma must've been what sparked her idea. Beth had everything necessary to make Matt feel like they had a deep connection. Beth knew all about Matt's life—even his marriage—because I had told her. Just like Courtney had known enough about Beth to make her think she and Russell were soulmates.

"I don't think there was a name for it yet, but yeah, she did." Russell leans forward, resting his forearms on the wheel. "When I answered the door that night, Beth looked stunned, then flung her arms around me. She said 'Baby, what are you doing here?' I backed up and had to peel her off me. When I asked her what the hell she was doing, she put her hands on my face. She looked like she was about to kiss me, so I swatted her arms away.

"She looked crushed and said, 'It's me, Beth. Your fiancée.'" Russell shakes his head. "I was confused, thought she was nuts. I wanted nothing to do with an underage girl throwing herself at me."

I glance below deck. Despite Beth's betrayal, my heart breaks for my seventeen-year-old friend, with her frizzy hair and glasses, thinking she and Russell were in love. And how shattered she must've been.

I shift my gaze to Russell, who could pass for an A-list actor all these years later. I can only imagine how attractive he was at twenty-four.

Russell stares at the deck. "I told her that Courtney was upstairs and retreated to the TV room as fast as I could. Beth called after me as Courtney came downstairs, grinning at the scene as I made my escape. I whispered, 'What's with your friend?' while Beth stood frozen in the doorway. Courtney shrugged and told me not to worry about it, saying that Beth was always like that. She said, 'She just thinks you're hot.' So, I said, 'Tell her to keep her hands off me next time, okay?'"

Russell lifts his gaze to mine and Emma's. "Beth said my name again, so I turned and said, 'See you later.' Beth stared at me like she'd seen a ghost, but after what Courtney said, I chalked it up to teenage-girl emotions. Until I learned from Courtney's diary that Beth truly thought we were engaged."

Emma crosses her arms. "That was cruel. Even for Courtney."

I gaze out at the swirling sea. "Beth never told me."

Emma turns toward the bow before she passes me her empty mug. "Hold this. I'm going to take down the storm jib. It's slowing us down."

"Sounds good," Russell calls from behind us while Emma hooks a tether onto her life vest.

Why didn't Beth ever tell me? I wonder as Emma makes her way to the front. Beth must've been too shattered to even tell her best friend what had happened. I close my eyes, envisioning the messages to my husband I found on Beth's phone. The bitterness of Beth's betrayal, dry and acrid, coats my tongue. She was also not the friend I thought she was.

From the foredeck, Emma swears.

"Guys."

I stand up. The horrified expression on Emma's face makes my blood run cold. She covers her mouth with her hand, and she's staring down at the deck. I climb onto my seat to see what she's looking at.

I gasp, seeing the blood smeared across the foredeck. I start to go forward when Russell places a strong hand on my arm.

"Careful," he says before I make my way beside Emma on the foredeck.

I stare down at the dark-red streak across the white fiberglass and wood.

"That's a lot of blood," Russell says, practically in my ear.

The blood on the deck leads to the edge of the boat, as if someone was dragged overboard.

"Beth," I breathe.

I spin, ramming into Russell before I push past him and climb down into the cockpit. The boat rolls, and I stumble forward off the bench seat.

I catch myself on the center table and manage to keep my footing.

"Beth!"

I fumble to unhook my tether and scramble down the steps. I dash past the galley and throw open the door to my stateroom. My heart plummets. Our empty bed is unmade. Beth's phone lies on top of the comforter on her side of the bed.

My knees buckle. I rest my palm against the wall as it sinks in that Beth is gone. My eyes brim with tears, but I'm swarmed with too many emotions to know exactly what I'm feeling. I'd already decided that she was dead to me, but now I'm losing her for the second time.

As much as I want to hate her, I can't stop the tears from streaming down my face.

"No, no, no." This can't be happening. She can't be gone.

Heavy footsteps sound down the companionway steps as I slide my hand under my pillow. I lift it up, staring at the white sheets. I check under Beth's pillow, but there's no gun.

"Is she here?"

I whip around at the sound of Russell's voice in the doorway behind me, snatching my arm out from under Beth's pillow and placing it at my side. Emma is behind him, peering over his shoulder at our empty stateroom.

"Oh, shit," she says.

"Check the bathroom," I tell Emma. "Just in case."

Emma calls Beth's name and opens the door to the bathroom closest to our stateroom. It's empty.

Emma checks the second bathroom—also empty—as my mind swirls with what likely happened, the scenarios making me dizzy. Beth must've taken Russell's gun and confronted him about killing Nojan and Gigi, and then he killed her. But as I stare into Russell's green eyes, I realize that doesn't make sense. Beth accused *me* of killing them.

Did Beth have a change of heart? Did *she* take Courtney's diary from Emma's room, and Russell caught her? Before I can accuse him, Emma does it for me.

She grabs him by the shirt collar and shoves him against the wall hard enough to make me flinch.

"You killed her, you sick bastard," Emma sneers through gritted teeth.

Chapter Forty-Seven

Present: Day Six at Sea

Russell raises his hands in defense. "No, I didn't. I swear."

"You had to have." Emma narrows her eyes. "Palmer and I were asleep. Beth was on watch when we went to bed. You were the last one to see her when you changed shifts. Plus, you just admitted to believing Beth had the most motive to hurt Courtney. There's no one left to blame this time, Russell."

My mind runs wild, imagining their confrontation. Was Beth alive when she hit the water? Where is she now? I picture her lifeless body bobbing face down atop the waves. Or is she lying on the ocean floor? Either way she's alone. And dead.

"I took your gun," I blurt, figuring there's no point in hiding it now. "Beth must've found it and confronted you with it. And you killed her."

Like me, Beth had never held a gun before in her life. I doubt she'd even know how to take the safety off. Given his size and military training, it would've been so easy for Russell to overpower her. He couldn't have shot her—we would've heard it. I picture him bludgeoning her in the head with a winch handle before dragging her body over the side. Inwardly, I curse Beth for being so stupid.

Emma gapes at Russell. "You had a gun? Were you planning to shoot us?"

Russell shakes his head. "No. I mean, yes, I had a gun. I always carry one with me. It's more of a habit than anything, after serving in the military for so long, and I only brought it on board as a precaution since I knew at least one of you is a killer."

"What happened to Beth?" I ask, as Emma seems to be debating whether to believe him.

"I don't know. Get off me." Russell forcibly shakes out of Emma's white-knuckle grip on his shirt. "I woke up to my alarm in the night and called out to her that I was coming to relieve her after I went to the bathroom. When I was in there, Beth knocked on the door and said she was going to bed." He looks between me and Emma. "There was no confrontation. I didn't even see her."

I study Emma after she releases his shirt, recalling how chipper she was this morning after her supposed overdose last night. Could the voice Russell heard have been Emma's? It's not like he knows us that well to tell the difference.

"I've been on watch ever since," Russell adds. "So that blood had to have been there before I went on deck last night. Both of you or *one* of you"—his gaze skirts to mine—"must've killed Beth before I took watch. Which means whoever I heard outside the bathroom was actually Beth's killer."

He has to be lying, I think, as Emma takes a step back and crosses her arms. I face her, but I can't tell what she's thinking. Unless . . . Did Beth take the diary last night and read something damning about Emma? Did Emma kill Beth to get the diary back?

Except that doesn't make sense. *I* was the one who confessed to being responsible for Courtney's death.

If Russell still holds us all responsible for his sister's death, despite my confession, he could've killed Beth while Emma and I slept. Which would also mean he's planning to kill us next.

"You're lying," Emma tells Russell.

"I'm not."

He's either a very good liar or telling the truth.

"I believe Palmer's account last night of leaving Courtney with the cougar," Russell adds. "She's the killer on this boat, not me. Even Beth thought so, which is why Palmer must've killed her."

"I didn't kill Beth!" I'm surprised by the ferocity in my voice as Emma's gaze skirts to mine.

"You killed Courtney." Russell narrows his eyes at me. "Maybe not directly, but you're still responsible for her death."

I lower my head. That I can't argue with.

"I didn't come to kill any of you. I only want justice for my sister, and I'm going to make sure you're held accountable for that when we get back."

I don't have to look at him to know he's only talking to me.

"And for killing the others on this boat."

Before I can refute his second allegation, a loud flapping sound erupts from the deck, causing me to look up.

"The sails are luffing," Emma says, moving toward the deck. "The wind must've changed direction." She calls down to Russell after stepping into the cockpit. "We need to tack."

I warily regard Russell, feeling suddenly vulnerable without Emma nearby. My shoulders tense. If what he told us is true, Beth had the most motive to kill Courtney. Or, at least it would appear that way from Russell's perspective.

"Beth couldn't have killed Courtney," I tell him. "When I found Beth after running away from the cougar, she was in the river. She almost drowned."

"I need some help up here," Emma calls over the flapping sails.

"Maybe Beth was faking it." Russell makes for the steps.

"She wasn't faking it. Trust me. You weren't there."

He turns, looking unconvinced.

My eyes narrow as I try to imagine Beth's final moments on this boat. My gaze runs up and down Russell's khaki shorts. If he's carrying his pistol, I can't tell. If he is, he could shoot me point blank for accusing him. What's to stop him at this point?

"Emma's right. You did kill Beth," I say as he ascends the steps. "Didn't you?"

"I haven't killed anyone on this boat." Russell glances at Gigi's closed stateroom door.

"Prepare to tack," Emma shouts. "I need someone at the helm."

"I'm coming," Russell steps into the cockpit.

I stare at Gigi's door as Russell yells "Helm's a lee" from the wheel.

The boat starts to turn. A moment later the flapping stops. I take a last look at my empty stateroom before going on deck.

Both sails are pushed out in the opposite direction from the last time I was on deck, slightly curved and pulled taut by the wind.

Emma turns to Russell at the helm after wrapping a line around one of the winches at the back of the cockpit. "So, you killed Beth because you think she murdered Courtney?"

Russell looks put out at being asked this another time. "No. I didn't kill Beth. Or Nojan. Or Gigi."

Emma's lips are set in a hard line as she puts her hands on her hips. "Where's your gun?"

Russell shakes his head. "I don't have it."

"Bullshit." Emma turns to me. "*I* don't have it, which means one of you must."

"Beth might've had it on her when she went overboard," I said. "I told Beth about it last night and left it hidden under my pillow in our stateroom when I went to bed in your cabin."

Emma puts her hands on her hips. "Lift up your shirt and turn around."

"What?" *Does she seriously think I killed Beth?*

Emma turns to Russell. "You too."

"I already told you," Russell says. "I don't have it."

"Sorry, but your word's not good enough." Emma points to him, then sweeps her finger around to me, ending with it pointed at herself.

"There are only three of us left, and one of us is a murderer. And it's not me."

"Fine." Russell steps out from behind the wheel and lifts his shirt to expose his waistband and toned abs.

"Turn around," Emma says.

He does, and there's no sign of his gun.

"Now you."

I frown at Emma's command but nevertheless comply by lifting my shirt to expose the waist of my sweatpants. I turn around slowly.

"Now you," Russell says to Emma.

She follows suit, revealing the waist of her skintight leggings which leave nowhere to hide a weapon.

"Satisfied?" Russell asks.

"No." Emma gestures below deck. "I want to see inside both of your bags. Come on, we'll go down together."

I follow her below, even though I still think Beth likely had Russell's gun when she went overboard. Russell comes down, too, and we start with his room first. After he shows us the full contents of his bag, Emma lifts his bedding, and Nojan's, before we continue to my cabin.

We repeat the process in my room and then Emma's without finding the gun. Emma looks relieved, but I don't feel any better. You don't need a gun to kill someone on this boat.

Russell returns to the helm when we go back on deck. Emma uncurls a line from a winch and tightens the jib halyard as I scan the seemingly endless ocean that surrounds us. I wonder how far we are from land. My throat tightens as I think of Beth's body, somewhere in that ocean.

The bloodstained foredeck catches my eye. After tethering myself, I move to the middle of the boat to get a better look. I stop beside the dinghy tied upside down to the deck. With a tight grip on the metal shroud, I study the smeared blood trail that's at least a few feet long, sure now that Beth is already dead. Possibly before she hit the water.

I steal a glance at Russell and Emma, who are both studying the surrounding waters with grave expressions. I follow their gazes toward the endless seas, wishing there was someone on board I could trust. My throat swells when I think of Beth somewhere out there, and conflicting emotions surge in my chest. My grief feels muddled by Beth's betrayal, secrets, and accusation.

I look away from the rippling sea to study Courtney's brother. If Russell killed the others, there's no way he could be planning to let Emma and me live to tell about it.

I carefully make my way back to the cockpit, keeping one hand on the boat with each unsteady step as we roll over the ocean swells. My eyes lock with Russell's for a split second when I step onto the cockpit bench. It strikes me that he could've made up the whole thing about Courtney catfishing Beth. Although, what reason would he have to lie about it?

Emma tilts her head toward the top of the mast. "If this wind keeps up, it'll help push us to the mainland faster than I'd hoped." She lowers her gaze to the water, which seems to stretch forever. "We're probably doing eight to ten knots, which means we might reach land tomorrow."

I stare at the blue horizon. "Let's hope so."

"I have to use the head," Emma says before going below, leaving me alone with Russell.

I shoot a wary glance in his direction as Emma disappears below deck, suddenly afraid of what he might do now that we're alone. But his eyes remain fixed on the surrounding seas, and he doesn't move from his post.

I sink onto one of the bench seats toward the front of the cockpit, wanting to keep a fair distance from Russell. As I hear the bathroom door close below deck, I consider that he might be telling the truth. If he was here for revenge, then why wouldn't he have killed Emma and me already? If Emma's right, we should be close enough to the mainland for him to sail back without help.

I turn to the sound of the toilet flushing below. We've been trusting Emma to steer us toward the mainland. But what if she's not?

I get up and move toward the compass mounted on the cockpit dash. The rounded glass is splintered and cracked so severely that I can't see which way the arrow beneath is pointing. It must've happened when we were knocked down by that huge wave. I feel stupid for not noticing it earlier. I've been trusting Emma blind, not even paying attention to the angle of the sun.

I spin and retreat toward the helm, gesturing toward the navigation controls. "Is there a working compass on those controls?"

Russell shakes his head. "They're all electronic, so not without power."

My heart drops into my stomach as I stare at the endless waters that surround us. *Could we have been heading away from the mainland this whole time?*

"But I have one on my watch," he adds.

"Can I see?" I inch closer to him, leery of getting too close but also needing the assurance that we're heading the right way.

He extends his arm, angling his wrist so I can see the face of his watch. "We're heading slightly southeast."

I lean closer to his watch until I can see that he's right. I exhale as Emma returns to the cockpit. Making my way back to my seat toward the front, I feel only slightly reassured. I can't trust either of them, but if we want to survive, we have to work together—for now.

We are, at least, heading toward the Pacific coast. If we stay on course and Emma's speed assessment is correct, we could reach land tomorrow.

The hard part is going to be staying alive until we get there.

Chapter Forty-Eight

Present: Day Six at Sea

My stomach grumbles as I look across at Emma perched on the opposite side of the cockpit. Beyond her, the sun sinks toward the horizon. Earlier, Russell insisted we eat a proper meal, even though neither Emma nor I could stomach much of anything. Russell pan-fried rib eye steaks before they went bad with no power to the fridge. Russell ate his steak down to the bone, while I picked apart a peanut butter and jelly sandwich and Emma pushed around the meat on her plate.

Now, Russell yawns at the helm. I twist toward him, relieved to see that he looks like he can barely keep his eyes open. Beth's four Dramamines I crushed into his glass of wine at dinner must be kicking in.

"I can take the helm and keep watch with Emma if you need to get some rest."

Russell looks warily between Emma and me. None of us have spoken much since searching the boat for Russell's gun, and we've all been maintaining a safe distance from each other. I've been careful not to turn my back on either of them—even though it's Russell I'm more concerned about—or go near the edge of the boat.

"Yeah, okay." Russell stifles a second yawn. "I could use some sleep."

I stand, and he steps aside for me to take his place. My shoulders brush his as I slide past. His tired eyes lock with mine, and I hold his gaze, imagining him striking Beth with the meat tenderizer he used to patch the broken window.

"Thanks." He turns away, swaying slightly, and adds, "I'll set my watch alarm for four hours."

"Don't worry about the alarm," I tell him. "We'll wake you when we need a rest."

Emma casts me a curious glance before she studies Russell unsteadily disappearing below deck, shutting the companionway door behind him. She doesn't know about the Dramamine, since I couldn't risk telling her without Russell overhearing.

A heavy silence fills the sea air once Emma and I are alone. She fixes her gaze on the surrounding waters as my mind becomes consumed with thoughts of Beth. Why hadn't she ever told me about Courtney pretending to be Russell? Was she too devastated or embarrassed to tell even her best friend? My throat swells at the sight of Beth's blood on the foredeck.

Did Beth really think I'm a murderer? That I killed Courtney, and Nojan and Gigi, in cold blood?

"Beth never told you about Courtney catfishing her?"

Emma stares at me, as if reading my thoughts.

I shake my head, tucking a loose strand of hair behind my ear. "No." Then I remember the thing I never got to tell Beth. "Yesterday, before I fell asleep on the couch, I smelled Courtney's perfume. Ocean Dream, that same perfume that was on the note. It was like she was . . ." I lift my gaze to the mainsail, debating whether to say it out loud. "Here. On this boat."

"That's just your mind playing tricks on you," Emma says. "It happened to me too. When we were searching for the captain, I thought Gigi was Courtney. For a moment, I swear her hair looked red from behind. But it wasn't. Obviously."

Emma turns back to the open waters, and I assess her tight blond curls blowing in the wind.

"Being out here all alone, the captain dying, then Gigi, and now Beth—it's messing with our heads," Emma adds.

I open my mouth to tell her about the Dramamine I slipped Russell but then pause. What if I'm wrong, and I incapacitated the wrong person?

It was unlike Emma to have forgiven me so easily for my part in causing her broken ankle, and for lying about it all this time. The girl I knew would've never let something like that go so quickly.

Like the rest of us, Emma had a motive for wanting Courtney dead, especially with her out-of-control temper. Had Emma heard more of Courtney's and my fight outside our tent than she let on? If Emma *did* hear that Courtney planted the dish soap, she might've wanted to kill her.

But I took care of that. A familiar drudge of heaviness weighs down my chest as I recall the thing that's haunted me for twenty years.

What about Beth? Had Emma woken in the night and come up here to accuse Beth of drugging her? I'd seen Emma's temper in action enough that it wasn't hard to imagine her attacking Beth in a fit of rage.

Emma was the first one to smell Courtney's perfume on the note. I think back to nearly touching my nose to the paper before I smelled the faint but distinct scent. Had Emma really smelled Courtney's perfume, or had she been the one to spray it on the note, forging Courtney's handwriting to make us think Courtney was here?

"Can I ask you something?" Emma says, interrupting my thoughts.

I turn toward her. "Sure."

"The dish soap. Why did you and Courtney do it?"

I exhale as my gaze drops to the floor. "It was Courtney's idea, but I take full responsibility for going along with it. We thought you'd just slip, and it would be funny. We didn't mean to—"

"I lost my scholarship."

"I know, and I'm so sorry." I meet her wounded gaze, hating myself for lying all this time. "I should've told the truth a long time ago."

"Yeah, you should've." Emma's eyes appraise mine. "It makes me wonder what you're still lying about."

I shake my head. "I'm not lying anymore."

Emma stares out at the surrounding waters, leaving me unsure whether she believed my last statement. "I never thought I'd say it, but looking back, I can see how everything worked out the way it was supposed to. If I hadn't been so miserable at community college, I never would've moved to California and majored in interior design. And I love what I do now, wouldn't trade it for anything. If I'd gone to UW on that scholarship, I would've majored in accounting. I would've ended up hating it, but I probably wouldn't have realized it until after I graduated and got some shit job, locked in a cubicle, crunching numbers all day."

I study Emma's pensive profile, taking in what she said. She's built a full life for herself and is on the brink of more success with her housewares line. Why would she jeopardize all that to try and kill us all?

The killer on board has to be Russell, I think. He lied about who he was, then wrote that fake note from Courtney. He's here for revenge. It's the only thing that makes sense.

I stare at the seemingly endless choppy seas beyond the bow and pray that Emma's right about us reaching land tomorrow. I look down below to where Russell is sleeping. Then why hasn't he killed us already? So we can help him sail back? If Russell killed the others, he can't be planning on letting Emma and me live.

Whatever the reason, hopefully those pills will keep him too subdued to hurt us before we reach land. I wonder if we could lock him in his room if we stacked all of our bags in front of his door. Probably not, I reason, then remember Gigi's body in the adjacent stateroom. Maybe with her added weight, we could keep him from—

"Palmer." Emma stands. "Do you see that?"

I look in the direction of Emma's extended arm. My jaw drops with relief at the faint lights in the distance. There's just enough waning daylight paired with tonight's full moon to make out the silhouette of a large ship.

"It must be a cruise ship." Emma speaks fast, excited at the possibility of being rescued.

I move beside her. "Which way is it heading?"

"It looks like it's heading north, coming toward us. We need to send off a flare."

I look around the cockpit. "Where are they?"

Emma turns. "I'm not sure. Ask Russell. I'll start checking these rear stowage compartments."

Without unhooking my tether, I hurry below and grab the pair of binoculars hanging from a hook beside the navigation desk. I sling them around my neck as I bang on Russell's door.

"Russell, wake up!" I pound again. "There's a ship in the distance. Wake up. We need to send off a flare, and we don't know where they are."

He swings open his door, wearing only boxers. As he squints to make out my figure in the poor lighting, his expression seems vacant and confused. My heart drops into my stomach at the stupidity of what I've done. I back away until I ram into the kitchen counter. Russell steps toward me, and I tighten my grip around the binoculars, prepared to use them as a weapon if I have to.

If Russell killed the others, there's no way he'll let Emma and me live to testify about the trip.

"There's a flare gun in the stowage compartment behind the starboard-side steering wheel. It's orange and should have four rounds." He turns. "I'll throw on some shorts and be right up."

He disappears into his cabin, and I hurry up the steps. The bow dips before I get to the top, and my head smacks the ceiling.

"Not there," I tell Emma when I reach the cockpit, ignoring the throb in my skull. I point to the opposite side of the bench where she's searching. "There should be an orange flare gun inside the bench behind that wheel."

As Emma rushes toward the other end of the wood-slatted bench, I step out from beneath the cockpit toward the lifeline. The sky has grown visibly darker in the few moments I was below, making the lights of the distant ship more visible. At the stern, Emma lifts the bench seat and starts searching through the compartment's contents.

I duck beneath the mainsail and step onto the foredeck to get an unobstructed view of the distant ship. I step over the blood smear on the deck as I lift the binoculars. My throat tightens at the thought of Beth not being among us getting rescued.

I stagger sideways as we roll over a swell. The side of my leg bumps into the dinghy, which has come loose from the middle of the ship and now leans against the lifelines beside me. I turn, scanning the deck for how it could've come untied.

Something small and metal slides across the deck, hitting the side of my shoe. I look down. A pocketknife. The blade is extended and stained with blood nearly the same shade of red as the handle. My stomach twists. It has to be the weapon used to kill Beth.

A flash of movement near the stern catches my eye. I whirl toward it, hoping Emma has found the flare gun. Instead, I spot a female figure creeping toward Emma on the other side of the boat. My heart lurches into my throat. *Courtney?* Was it possible?

Emma still has her head down, frantically searching the compartment as the figure moves closer to her. It's then that I recognize the figure's silhouette. Her dark waves blowing in the wind. The dinghy hadn't come loose on the foredeck. Beth had been hiding under it this whole time.

Beth raises her arm toward Emma's back. I freeze when I spot Russell's gun in her grip. I'm too far away to stop her. Russell comes up from below, but even he's too far away to stop Beth in time.

Beth says something to Emma that makes her stand up and turn around, and I see the orange flare gun in Emma's hand.

"Emma! Watch out!" I yell, but the blast from the gunshot muffles my warning.

Chapter Forty-Nine

Present: Day Six at Sea

Emma falls backward onto the deck from the shot to her upper chest.

"Emma!" I rush toward her.

Beth swings the gun toward me as I trip over a shroud. The binoculars clamor against the deck just before my face smacks it. A second shot rings out.

I look up, expecting to see blood on my clothes, but I don't feel any pain aside from the ache in my cheek from hitting the deck. Russell charges at Beth. Beth swings the gun away from me and aims it at Russell's head. He stops a few feet from her and raises his hands in the air. Behind me, air escapes the side of the dinghy with a hiss from being struck by Beth's stray bullet.

The fall saved my life.

"Don't shoot," Russell says.

I get to my feet slowly, careful not to make any sudden movements. Beth keeps the gun trained on Russell and her back to me. My gaze falls to Emma who swears, then groans, lying on her back on the deck floor near Beth's feet. Blood seeps through the fabric of Emma's light-gray sweatshirt. But she's alive. For now.

The flare gun has rolled out of Emma's hand into the cockpit, stopped by the mounted outdoor table.

"You killed Courtney," Russell says.

I inch forward on my hands and knees. Beth angles her head to the side enough for me to see her lips curl into a smug smile as I crawl toward Emma along the edge of the cockpit. A bloodstained dish towel is tied around Beth's forearm. She must've cut herself with her pocketknife, then smeared her blood on the deck during the night when she was supposed to be on watch.

"Yes, I did."

But I was with her. How could she have killed Courtney? I recall Beth being carried downstream, getting pulled under the Sol Duc's currents when I found her.

Beth's steely gaze remains fixed on Russell. Not wanting to draw attention to myself, I refrain from verbalizing my thoughts.

"How?" Russell asks.

I slide onto the cockpit bench.

"Don't move, Palmer," Beth says, not taking her eyes off Russell.

I freeze.

Beth sighs. "I never planned to hurt your sister."

Behind Beth, Emma grits her teeth and reaches for the flare gun, but it's several inches out of reach. I keep my gaze on Beth.

"I was looking for Courtney along the riverbank," Beth continues. "And I found her, jogging along the tree line on the other side of the Sol Duc. I called for her, but she acted like she couldn't hear me. Downstream, there was a fallen tree that went nearly the whole way across the river. I used it to get across. I was out of breath by the time I caught up to her. I told Courtney she had to come back. But she refused. She marched away from me, barely keeping her balance after tripping over a large rock. She told me there was a cougar on the other side of the river. That it followed her until she finally raised a stick over her head and threw a rock at it. Then she pointed across the river and said, 'I saw Palmer.'"

Keeping her gun trained on Russell, Beth shifts her gaze, her eyes boring into mine. "She said you had to have seen the cougar coming after her. But instead of coming back to help her, you left her for dead. Courtney's eyes flamed with fury when she whipped around. She was planning to press charges against you, saying she'd send you to jail for manslaughter." Beth smirks. "I told her she meant prison—not jail—and that you can't press charges for manslaughter if you're still alive." Beth shakes her head. "Courtney could be so stupid sometimes." Her gaze skirts back to Russell, whose jaw is clenched. "No offense."

He glares at Beth, his eyes burning with an unyielding fury.

"Anyway—" Beth swipes her free hand through the air. "I told Courtney I thought she was making the whole thing up. If Courtney *had* seen a cougar, it wouldn't have left her alone. She was easy prey." A faint smile reaches Beth's lips. "Then Courtney narrowed her green eyes at me, saying 'Well, then I hope that cougar eats Palmer alive.' At that point, I was exasperated," Beth continues, returning her gaze to mine. "I told her to stop lying, and Courtney looked as though I'd slapped her." Beth's voice morphs to a high, mocking tone. "'I almost died, Beth.'"

Beth's imitation of Courtney makes my blood run cold.

"Then, she sneered," Beth adds. "She said, 'You think I'm making that up, but you believed my brother could actually be in love with you?' I asked her why she always had to be such a bitch. But Courtney wasn't listening. She'd caught her sweatshirt on a low-hanging branch, going on about how she always stuck up for me and was so kind to let me hang out with her even though I was"—Beth makes air quotes with her hand not holding the gun—"such a nerd." Beth's face contorts in loathing, her gaze unflinching from mine.

Her eyes are hard, staring with a fierce, silent intensity. Even though she's looking at me, I get the sense she's not seeing me but Courtney.

"I pulled out the pocketknife Courtney gave me and told her to hold still. She was flailing her arm, making it worse. I lifted the blade toward the branch and asked why it was so hard for her to believe her brother could've been in love with me." Beth turns to Russell. "Courtney threw her head back and said, 'Do you seriously think my brother would ever like a girl like you?' So judgy. Then she laughed."

There's a distant look in Beth's eyes, like she's physically here, but her mind is back in the Olympic National Park, reliving the moment. She scrunches up her nose as her expression turns painful. "A deep, throaty cackle. Just like she'd laughed when we got to her upstairs bedroom that night when I threw my arms around you. When she told me it was all a prank."

Emma grunts on the deck floor, but Beth doesn't turn around.

My gaze flicks to Emma and the blood pooling on the deck beneath her chest. Her eyes flutter closed. She needs pressure on her bullet wound or she's not going to make it. In the distant waters beyond the stern, the cruise ship is now directly behind us.

"Courtney's eyes bulged with disbelief when I stabbed her the first time," Beth adds, as if relieving her conscience. A slight smile forms on one side of her mouth as she stares at Russell. "Like she didn't think I had it in me. She tried to push me away—and to run—but her sweatshirt was still caught on that tree." Beth shakes her head. "And her screaming only angered me more. Then, the branch snapped, and Courtney stumbled toward the river. I stabbed her in the neck to shut her up. Then I kept stabbing. The next thing I knew, we'd both fallen in the water. Courtney had stopped moving when the current pulled us downstream."

Russell bows his head without saying a word. I assess the woman standing before me that I've known as my best friend since I was five. All this time, she knew what happened to Courtney. Because she was the one who killed her.

I inch along the bench seat, closer to the flare gun on the deck floor as Beth directs her gaze toward me.

"Courtney was face down in the water, and the current moved her body along faster than mine. Then I heard you, Palmer. Calling my name on the other side of the river." She shakes her head as if recalling a normal, nonmurderous memory. "I was afraid you might see her. So, I stuck the knife back into my pocket and called out to you, acting like I was getting pulled under so all of your attention would be on me."

I swallow, thinking how close I must've been to Courtney when I went into the river to save Beth. *She was right there.* She might've even still been alive. If I had seen her, I might've been able to save her. Instead, I'd saved Beth.

Behind Beth, Emma goes still. The flare gun rests against the foot of the table, well out of my reach. If I lunge for it, Beth would have plenty of time to shoot me before I can set it off.

"I had no intention of getting stuck underwater beneath that log, though," Beth adds. "For a second, I thought it might be my karma after what I'd done to Courtney." She smiles, locking eyes with me. "But then you saved me."

Vomit rises to the back of my throat.

"I'm sorry you've blamed yourself for Courtney's death all these years. But I couldn't tell you the truth."

Until now. She's planning to kill us all. In the distance, the ship cruises past us.

"Beth," I coax. "Please don't do this. You'll never get away with it. Think of all your accomplishments. All you'll be losing. Your appointment to university president. And how you want to run for Senate. It's what you wanted your whole life."

"That's exactly why I can't let you live. With all of you gone, there will be no one to refute my story. How Russell came aboard under a fake name, on a killing spree to avenge his sister's death. Especially when I produce Courtney's diary, minus those specific pages about me. It will show his motive to kill all of us."

"You planned this?" I ask her, readying myself to dive for the flare.

"Of course not!" She cocks her head to the side. "I'm not a psychopath, Palmer."

"Then why'd you kill Nojan? And Gigi?"

"I recognized Russell immediately when we came aboard and knew, given his fake name, that he was here to uncover what happened to Courtney. I saw him talking to Gigi alone on our first night at sea. He knew I had the most motive of all of us to kill Courtney. I didn't know what he'd told her, but I couldn't risk it. It was dark that night when I came on deck. I thought Nojan was Russell. He was kneeling near the side, his head down, tying a knot, so I pushed him and cut his tether with my pocketknife." Beth lifts the gun toward Russell's head. "Then, I found his logbook near the helm. When I checked the entries, I realized Nojan had been the one on watch, not Russell. So, I turned the battery banks off to buy myself some time to correct my mistake."

I strain to recall Beth getting up that night but remember the Dramamine she'd given me. I'd been out cold.

"What about Gigi?"

"I saw her arguing with Russell. Right before the wave hit, Gigi pulled a man's wallet from her sweatshirt and waved it in front of Russell's face. I knew she'd figured out who he was. Then, he grabbed her arm and leaned in, probably warning her not to say anything to the rest of us. But I couldn't risk him telling her what Courtney had done to me. After Gigi helped untangle my ankle and you went below, I told her to grab the flashlight that had fallen to the floor behind the steering wheel. Only the flashlight was already below. After I went down, Emma asked if that was everyone, and I said yes. She was too panicked to get the door closed before the wave hit to double-check." Beth shrugs. "By the time you all did, it was too late."

"You drugged Emma," Russell says.

"I saw her come out of your room and saw Courtney's diary in her hand before she had a chance to tuck it behind her. She didn't know that I noticed. So, when she went on deck to tell you she was going to take a nap, I crushed Gigi's pills into her Gatorade."

"But then why did you come and get me so that I could save her?"

I slide an inch sideways on the bench. The cruise ship is getting farther away by the minute. We don't have much time to send off the flare gun to make sure they'll spot it.

"That was an honest mistake. Just like Nojan. I'm not a doctor. I couldn't wake Emma up, so I thought she was beyond saving."

I lower my gaze to Emma long enough to see from the light of the full moon that she's still moving. Beth follows my gaze as the stern lifts over a swell. The flare gun rolls toward me. Beth loses her footing, and I dive for it.

Beth recovers her balance as I hit the deck and grab the gun, turning on my back to aim it toward the sky. Beth lowers her gun toward me. I change my aim and pull the trigger, shooting the flare into her chest. Russell rushes Beth as soon as the flare explodes with a blinding light. The front of her sweater erupts in flames.

Beth screams in pain, clutching the gun with both hands. She doubles over when Russell grips her forearm. He thrusts Beth's arm over her head, forcing her upright as she fires a shot into the darkening sky.

I reload the flare gun with trembling hands and fire another round into the air. Beth and Russell stumble back until Beth slams into one of the steering wheels.

I drop to my knees and press two fingers against Emma's neck. Miraculously, her pulse is strong.

"Ahh!"

I turn to the sound of Beth's cry as Russell forcibly extends her arm holding the gun across her chest, aiming it at the water. A shot rings out as Russell pulls Beth's arm toward the lifeline. Russell slams Beth's arm against the deck, sending the gun flying over the edge.

I hurriedly unzip my sweatshirt and ball it up, pressing it against the bullet wound on Emma's chest. She groans, and her eyelids flutter open as Russell wraps his arms around Beth, lifting her feet off the ground in an effort to subdue her as she claws his face.

"Emma." I lower my face toward hers and pull her hand over my sweatshirt, pushing it against her chest. "Hold—"

The boat dips. I slide sideways on my knees toward Beth and Russell as salt water sprays over the side. Russell stumbles toward the boat's edge as the port side tilts toward the sea. I reach for Russell, but it's too late.

His feet have already lifted off the deck as he and Beth plunge headfirst over the side.

Chapter Fifty

Present: Day Six at Sea

I grab onto the wheel to keep from falling in after them. Emma rolls against my thighs on the deck. I grasp the wheel with my other hand and hang on with all my strength until the boat levels out.

Twisting, I scan the water behind us. A spotlight shines from the ship in the distance, sweeping the water between our two boats. It's too dark for me to clearly make out Beth and Russell in the water, but I hear splashing and spot a white blinking light on one of their life vests. I scan the water for the other light, then remember Russell wasn't wearing a vest. He wasn't even wearing a shirt.

"Russell," I yell.

"Over here." I turn in the direction of his shout, spotting his head bobbing atop the water in the light from the full moon.

Thankfully, he's not too far away. Yet. I frantically feel around the deck for the flare gun, praying it didn't go overboard. I find the orange gun against Emma's leg and shakily reload another flare into the barrel. I shoot into the air, and in the flash of light, I spot Russell treading water directly behind the boat.

"Emma." I shake her by the shoulder.

"Hmm?"

"You still with me?"

"Yeah," she croaks.

I press my sweatshirt against her chest and fold both of her hands over it. "Keep pressure on this and hang on a little longer. Help is coming."

"Okay." Her voice is barely more than a whisper.

I debate leaving the flare gun with her, but she's too weak. She'll likely lose consciousness before she can shoot it.

I reload the last flare and zip the gun into the pocket of my sweatpants as I step onto the portside pulpit. A second spotlight sweeps the ocean from the cruise ship, which looks to be turning toward us.

I need a flashlight, but by the time I find it, Russell will be too far away for me to swim to. Instead, I feel for my tether, making sure it's still clipped to my life vest, and plunge feet first into the Pacific. The frigid water takes my breath away when I surface, reminding me of when I jumped into the Sol Duc after Beth.

"Russell?"

"Palmer. I'm over here."

I swim toward his voice. A cold wave breaks against the side of my head. With the drag of my clothes and the force of the swells, it feels like I'm swimming in place. A wave engulfs my head. I come up, gulping for air, and realize the binoculars are still around my neck, weighing me down. I reach to pull them off when I feel two hands press the top of my head beneath the water.

I thrash to come up and feel Beth's surprising strength holding me down. Her hands move to my shoulders, and I sink deeper. I kick wildly but can't manage to break the surface beneath her hold. Air escapes my mouth as I clench my fist and thrust it into her jaw. Her hands fall away, and I grapple for the surface, spurting water from my mouth between gulps for air.

I swim away but get only two strokes before I'm dragged back by my tether. As I start to go under, Beth climbs onto my back and forces me down farther with the weight of both her forearms.

"Palmer," Russell calls before I go under, but he's too far away to help me.

I flail my arms and legs, air escaping my mouth when I scream at Beth beneath the waves. But she holds me under while the boat tows us behind it. I fumble to unclip my tether. Our momentum comes to an abrupt halt when I detach the tether from my vest. I thrust a fist upward and back toward her face, but this time she grabs my wrist and pins my arm to my side.

I close my other hand around the lens of the binoculars around my neck and pull the strap off my head. With every ounce of adrenaline coursing through my veins, I twist and pummel the binoculars into the side of Beth's face. Her weight falls away. I strike again, impacting the hard bone of her face before I swim to the surface.

I suck in a deep breath as Beth brings her hands to her face in the water beside me. With gritted teeth, I strike her again, this time in the temple.

"You bitch," she seethes as water enters her mouth, muffling the end of her word. In the moonlight, she raises her hands toward my head.

"Ahh!" I hit her in the cheekbone with every bit of strength I have left.

She cries out, her arms flapping into the water as her head recoils from the force of my blow. I waste no time in swimming away from her, dropping the binoculars in my haste.

"Palmer."

Russell sounds less than ten feet away from me. I keep swimming.

"Russell?"

"I'm—"

Splash.

"Here," he spurts.

I turn around and spot the outline of his head bobbing atop the rough surface. When I reach him, a wave splashes over our heads. He coughs when we emerge.

"I brought . . . the flare gun." My lips quiver from the cold.

I feel him grab onto my shirt as I unzip my pants pocket. I withdraw the gun and lift it above the surface, wondering if it will still work soaking wet. Aiming at the sky, I pull the trigger. It shoots into the air with a high-pitched whiz before a bright-pink flash erupts in the dark sky.

I exhale. *Thank God.*

Russell's head sinks beneath the water before resurfacing. He sucks in an audible breath.

I hook my arms beneath his armpits from behind him. "Lie back. My life vest should hold us both."

He does as I say, but his added weight brings the water over my mouth, so I tilt my head back. A swell swallows us. I keep hold of Russell as I swim for the scattered moonlight on the waves, which is a struggle even with my flotation device.

When we break the surface, I gulp for air.

"You need to let me go," he says.

"No." After finally learning that I wasn't to blame for Courtney's death, I can't face being responsible for the death of her brother. "Help is coming," I spurt.

He pushes away from me. "It'll take too long for that ship to get here."

I grab his arm. "Do you hear that?"

I turn toward the hum of a motor, but I can't see anything over the choppy water.

"Let me go."

"Wait. Look!"

In the distance, a green light speeds toward us. It looks halfway between us and the cruise ship, which is now heading in our direction.

"They must've sent out a lifeboat."

I wave my hands over my head. "Hey," I call. "Over here!"

As the light comes closer, the drone of the motor grows louder. A bright beam sweeps across the surrounding water before coming to a stop on Russell and me.

"They see us," I gurgle, lowering my arms.

The orange-encapsulated boat slows. As it pulls up beside us, a life ring is tossed over the side.

Russell and I sling our arms over the sides of the ring.

"Hang on," a man calls from the boat. "I'm going to pull you in."

After being pulled on board, a woman covers us each in a hypothermia blanket and introduces herself as the ship's nurse.

"Is it just you two out here?" asks the man driving the boat.

"No," I tell him. "There's another person in the water, and another on our sailboat. We lost power, so there's no light. The woman on the boat has been shot. She needs to get to a hospital."

"We've already called the Coast Guard. They're sending out a helicopter. I've got eyes on the boat. I'll let them know." The boat driver lifts a radio mic from the dash.

"You said there's another person in the water?" The other man on the boat asks.

"Yes. She's wearing a life vest, and it has a flashing white beacon like mine."

The man scans the surrounding waters with a searchlight beam before turning back to me. "We'll keep looking. But I don't spot anyone."

I huddle against Russell as the ship's nurse asks if we've sustained any major injuries.

We assure her we didn't, and she tells us to keep the blankets on. "We need to get you warm," she says.

I turn to Russell when she goes to help search the water for Beth.

"I'm sorry about Courtney."

"Thanks," he says, his shoulder touching mine. "But it's not your fault."

Across from Russell and me, a small window shows the searchlight sweeping the ocean's surface. Sitting beside Courtney's brother, I'm struck by an eerily unsettling feeling—this moment echoing the day I left the trailhead in Beth's van twenty years ago. Except now I'm not carrying a dark secret.

Although freeing myself from my lie has come at a very high price.

Epilogue

Three Months Later

I stand back to admire the plaque on the trail-marker post after Russell and Emma drive it into the ground at the Grave Creek Trailhead. Emma moves beside me, placing her hands on her hips, as we both read the words Russell had etched onto the metal plate. *In loving memory of Courtney Vance, lost to these woods but never forgotten.*

"Thanks for coming with me." Russell folds his arms, his gaze fixed on the trail marker. "I know my sister had her faults, but it means a lot to be able to remember her with the people who were closest to her."

"I'm glad we came." I turn and gaze at the dirt parking area, vacant aside from our three vehicles, just as it was twenty years ago.

"Me too." Emma shades her eyes with her hands and looks in the direction of the river.

After Russell and I were rescued by the cruise ship's pilot boat, Emma was helicoptered to an Oregon hospital for emergency surgery. Once we were checked out by the ship's nurse, Russell and I were taken to the nearest seaside town to recount the events of the trip to the police. Russell finally admitted to forging the note from Courtney and spraying her old perfume on the boat, hoping it would make us confess what really happened to her. In the days following, another search was conducted for Courtney's remains by a dive team in the Sol Duc, but no trace of her was found.

Beth, too, was never found, despite the Coast Guard's thorough search for her in the waters where the rest of us were rescued.

I cast a sideways glance at Emma. You would never know by looking at her tanned, toned self that she nearly died from the bullet wound two inches below her heart. I gaze up to see a red-tailed hawk soar above us, wings outstretched beneath the blue sky.

Russell lifts his tool bag and looks between me and Emma. "Ready?"

"Yep." I turn to Emma, who takes a last look at the trail, and follow her gaze.

"Ready," she says.

After loading his tools into his truck bed, Russell puts his hands on his hips. "You two up for a drink?"

"Sorry," Emma says. "I've got to film a video of my current renovation project tonight for my YouTube channel."

After Target dropped her housewares line during our trip, Emma started filming her house-flipping projects on YouTube. In only three months, she's grown over one million followers and has offers from three department stores to carry her line.

Russell turns to me. "What about you?"

"Sorry, I have to pick up my girls from my mom's in Sequim and then head home." When I told Mom about Matt's leaving, she was incredibly supportive, moving in with me over the summer to help take care of the girls while I returned to work.

You don't seem surprised about Matt, I'd told her. *I thought you'd be devastated.*

She waved her hand through the air as if swatting a fly. *Good riddance. I never wanted to intrude, but I always thought you could do better than him.*

Once Matt realized he'd been duped and that Sydney hadn't been the one who'd been messaging him online, he asked to move back in with me, begging for my forgiveness, assuring me that it would never happen again. I told him to pound sand.

"I have an early shift tomorrow in the ER," I add. My initial fears about returning to work after my mistake paled in comparison to everything we went through on the trip, making my return to work surprisingly easy. In fact, I felt bored working on the surgical unit. After discovering how calm I could be in emergencies, I had a newfound desire to help save people who'd been through trauma.

"Well, thanks again for coming out."

The three of us hug goodbye before Emma and I turn our separate ways for our cars. I climb behind the wheel of my Bronco and sink against the seat, thinking of Courtney, Beth, and everything we went through on that sailing trip from hell.

"Hey, Palmer!"

I lean out my open driver's door to see Russell jogging toward me.

"How about Friday?"

I must look confused, because he adds, "For a drink. Just you and me."

"Oh." I rack my brain for an excuse, but Matt will have the girls on Friday, and I have the day off. I don't even work on Saturday.

"I'm starting my own tech company, a modern take on the software my dad built, and it's based out of Bellevue, so I'm not far from you." He rests his muscular arm on my doorframe, and I think how Beth was right. He does look like Chris Pratt. "I mean, you did kind of save my life. Seems like I owe you a drink. Or two."

I bite my lip.

"Well?"

My pulse quickens. I can't date him. He's Courtney's brother.

He smiles. My heart flutters. What would be the harm in just one?

"Friday would be great."

◆ ◆ ◆

On my drive back to my mom's house, I find myself turning down the street Beth grew up on. I'd driven slowly through Sequim's quaint downtown, taking in the familiar buildings. It's the first time in twenty years that I've felt at peace with this place. That I can drive through town with my head held high.

I park in front of Beth's childhood home where her parents still live. The shades are drawn, and I can't tell if anyone's home.

My phone chimes with a text. I lift my phone from my purse, seeing it's from my sister, Kate. How did it go? I type a quick reply. It went good. I'll call you on my way home.

I drop my phone back into my bag and survey Beth's old house. Beth had a point—after Courtney died, I did hold people at arm's length, even my own family. Since returning home from our nightmare trip, I've made an effort to keep in better touch with my sister. Now, we hardly let a day go by without at least texting.

My gaze settles on the red front door. Beth's house has hardly changed in twenty years. I want to knock on the door and embrace Beth's grieving parents in a hug. But I'm not sure they want to see me.

Beth's confession of killing Courtney made the national news after I told detectives everything that had happened on our trip, including my clubbing Beth with the binoculars in the ocean to get away from her after shooting her with the flare gun.

I pull onto the street, looking back at the familiar home in my rearview mirror. My heart goes out to them, what they must be going through, along with Gigi's parents. Although, finding out that Beth was a murderer must've felt like losing their daughter twice.

I brake at the stop sign at the end of the street and wonder if they're clinging to the hope Beth is still alive, despite learning she was a killer. A dark-haired woman walks beside my car on the sidewalk.

I draw in a sharp breath at the sight of her dark wavy hair. Sitting frozen behind the wheel, I study the woman from behind as she rounds the corner, pulling a bulldog on a leash. Goose bumps prickle my arms. *Beth?*

Behind me, a car honks. The dark-haired woman startles at the sound, whipping around. I heave a sigh, collapsing against the back of my seat. It's not Beth. I see now that, aside from her hair, the woman doesn't look anything like her. She appears to be close to fifty and is heavier and a few inches shorter than Beth.

The car behind me honks again, and I turn left, away from the woman I thought was my late best friend. I fix my gaze on the Olympic Mountains in the distance, with my hometown at their feet, as I speed away from the street Beth grew up on. It wasn't the first time since our deadly sailing trip that I'd thought I'd seen Beth. And I'm sure it won't be the last.

While there's a part of me that will always miss her, there's a part of Beth that will always haunt me.

Acknowledgments

Huge thanks to the amazing team at Thomas & Mercer for all your hard work in getting this book out into the world. To my editors, Jessica Tribble Wells and Kevin Smith, you are a dream to work with.

Jessica, thank you for your invaluable editorial insight and early guidance. Kevin, thank you for helping me sharpen this story.

To my agent, Jill Marsal, thank you for believing in me. As always, I'm so grateful for your expert advice.

Special thanks to Leslie Lutz for helping work through my early drafts and untangling every tangle.

Traci Finlay, thanks so much for your feedback on my early draft.

To Captain Nojan Moshiri, thank you for instructing me in my first-ever sailing lesson while I wrote this story and for consulting on the sailing elements in this book.

To the Columbia Basin Sailing Club, thank you for taking me under your wing and letting me join you on the water for your sailing races. I loved every minute.

Detective Rolf Norton, thank you once again for taking the time to answer my procedural questions.

Jack Lawson and Keira Henson, thanks for all the work you do behind the scenes.

To my parents, thank you for reading my draft of this story and for your never-ending support.

Elise and Anders, thank you for always cheering me on. You are my world.

Last but not least, a massive thank-you to all of my wonderful readers and to the bloggers and bookstagrammers in the reading community. Words cannot express my gratitude for your support.

About the Author

Photo © 2021 Brittney Kluse Photography

Audrey J. Cole is a *USA Today* bestselling thriller author whose work has been translated into multiple languages. Before she began writing full time, Cole worked as a neonatal intensive care nurse for eleven years. She resides in the Pacific Northwest with her two children.

Sign up for the author's mailing list at www.audreyjcole.com to receive free bonus content, promotions, and updates on new releases.